Praise for *The Gh*

"Wrapped in the form of pseudohistorical, multilayered investigative journalism full of footnotes from a skewed world that resembles our own, columnist Disabato's first novel is a paean to the modern urban landscape . . . The net effect is simultaneously breathlessly exhilarating and beautifully haunted." —*Publishers Weekly* (starred)

"Thrilling . . . A layered, well-executed story within an inventive story. Artistic ambition, cultural critique, and a revolutionary philosophy drive the mysteries underlying this complex, charismatic novel." —*Kirkus Reviews*

"A brilliant, daring and masterful novel about obsession, fame, and the complex mysteries of human existence. It's a whodunit with footnotes and glitter, and it's impossible to put down. Catie Disabato is a marvel." —EDAN LEPUCKI, *New York Times* bestselling author of *California*

"A giddy mash-up of pop culture, genre tropes, conspiracy theories, and dystopian fantasy. Imagine Thomas Pynchon possessed by the spirit of a teenaged girl who is binge-watching TMZ while shrooming out of her mind, and you get some idea of the layered, phantasmagoric effect of this wonderfully trippy book. Catie Disabato is a true original, and a young writer to watch." —DAN CHAON, author of *Await Your Reply*

"Catie Disabato's prose is as clean as a whistle and as sharp as a tack, and her imagination is wondrous. A smart and exciting debut that plays by its own rules."
— IVY POCHODA, author of *Visitation Street*

"Spectacularly original. Meta, ingenious, and totally fun."
— KATE DURBIN, author of *El Entertainment*

"As close as we'll ever get to Borges filtering Lady Gaga, Calvino analyzing Miley Cyrus, or Cortázar obsessing over FKA Twigs, the supremely talented Disabato gives us a synth-wave pop illuminati fantasy that will make your ears ring."
— MAXWELL NEELY-COHEN, author of *Echo of the Boom*

THE GHOST NETWORK

CATIE DISABATO

MELVILLE HOUSE
BROOKLYN • LONDON

THE GHOST NETWORK

Copyright © 2015 by Catherine Disabato

First Melville House printing: May 2015

Melville House Publishing   8 Blackstock Mews

145 Plymouth Street   &   Islington

Brooklyn, NY 11201   London N4 2BT

mhpbooks.com / facebook.com/mhpbooks / @melvillehouse

Library of Congress Cataloging-in-Publication Data

Disabato, Catie.

   The ghost network : a novel / Catie Disabato.

      pages   cm

   ISBN 978-1-61219-434-9 (paperback)

   ISBN 978-1-61219-435-6 (ebook)

   1. Lesbians—Fiction. 2. Women private investigators—Fiction.

   3. Lesbians—Fiction. I. Title.

PS3604.I75G46 2015

813'.6—dc23

                                        2014046529

Design by Adly Elewa

Printed in the United States of America

10 9 8 7 6 5 4 3 2

For Nancy and Ted

THE GHOST NETWORK

A NOTE FROM THE EDITOR

I inherited from Cyrus Archer a polished draft of this manuscript, but not a complete one. Cyrus's research was extensive and the majority of the plotting in the book is based on firsthand accounts of events. Unfortunately, Cyrus did not get a chance to fill in his footnotes, and in a few places, he didn't relay the source of a story or a quote. I have tried to fill in the gaps in attribution as best I can, using Cyrus's notes and in a few cases re-interviewing some of his interviewees. Any additions or adjustments from me are noted in the text or via footnotes. For visual distinction, my footnotes will be in italics.

CATIE DISABATO

THE
GHOST NETWORK

THE DISAPPEARANCE AND
SEARCH FOR MOLLY METROPOLIS

CYRUS K. ARCHER

EDITED AND WITH AN EPILOGUE
BY CATIE DISABATO

Prologue

April 25, 2010

It was the morning after a record-setting rainstorm. Chicago's mild, dry spring had given way to lighting and thunder. The soil soaked up six inches of rainfall; drowning worms emerged to cover the sidewalks with their squishy bodies and promptly froze to death in the cold spring air. Overworked eaves on rows of townhouses creaked and moaned in the strong morning winds, and streams of water rushed through the gutters. The winds had torn thick branches off the trees, which crushed the hoods of SUVs parked on the lakeside streets and cracked the pavement, causing hundreds of dollars in damages. The water in Lake Michigan was choppy and cold, below freezing; the surface of the lake was covered in fog.

Early that day, once the storm had broken, a baker named Rebecca Parker decided to take an unusual route along the lake on her walk home. Parker worked at Anthony's Deli on Wabash Street, baking bread from 3 a.m. to 7 a.m. On her way home, she usually avoided Lake Shore Drive, with its extra chill from the wind moving over the lake. Instead, she preferred to walk on Rush Street or take public transit, riding the city's elevated train line, the L. But riding the rickety train in high winds frightened Parker, and the fallen tree branches that covered the sidewalks on Rush Street made for difficult walking, so she zipped her North Face down coat to her throat and walked towards Lake Shore Drive. At East Delaware Place, she crossed the highway and started walking on the Lakeshore Trail—the biking and walking path right along the lake—so she could avoid any sidewalk debris.

The Lakeshore Trail was otherwise deserted. Parker walked briskly through the fog. Just as she was about to turn off the Trail and return to the gridded streets west of Lake Michigan, Parker noticed a dark shape floating a few hundred feet off shore: two bodies clinging to a piece of wood, one completely still and one kicking feebly. The fog thickened and Parker hesitated, questioning whether she had seen anything at all. She waited half a minute for the fog to clear and for the makeshift raft to come into full view again before dialing 911. Both bodies now lay still on the slab of wood, bobbing through the sharp waves. Parker gave the operator her approximate address and blurted, "Both people on the raft look dead now."

About five minutes later, two Chicago Police Department officers arrived on bikes and signaled a police boat with portable high beams. Parker was crying. She thought that by waiting before dialing 911, she had "as good as killed" the people on the raft.

About five minutes after that, the police boat appeared. It puttered slowly around the shallow water before the officers aboard found what they were looking for. The maritime police fished two bodies out of the freezing lake: twenty-three-year-old Regina Nix, called "Gina," and twenty-seven-year-old Nicolas Berliner, called "Nick." They were hypothermic, unconscious, and concussed, but alive. They were immediately put into an ambulance and driven to Cook County Hospital.

Berliner regained consciousness in the ambulance and was admitted briefly to the Intensive Care Unit. Nix was taken into surgery immediately upon arriving at the hospital. Two fingers on her left hand, which had been partially severed and reattached approximately one week prior, couldn't withstand the trauma of hypothermia and had to be amputated.

While the doctors worked on Nix, Berliner gave a statement to the police. He didn't remember how he had ended up floating in Lake Michigan. The last thing he recalled was spending a good portion of the previous evening with Nix and her girlfriend at their favorite bar, Rainbo.

The officers on the scene left the hospital and returned to the police station on South Racine, where they found a theft report filed by Randy Hecht. He had reported his boat stolen around 5 a.m. An officer called Hecht and spoke to him briefly:

"That's a shame about the kids almost drowning and such," Hecht said. "I filed my report right after it happened. I saw those three kids fly off and I called you right away. Did you find the boat okay?"

To which the stunned police officer replied, "*Three* kids?"

The third person on the raft was Nix's girlfriend, Caitlin "Cait" Taer (rhymes with "air"). No one has seen her or heard from her since the police pulled Nix and Berliner from the lake. She disappeared. Her body was not found in Lake Michigan; it didn't wash ashore anywhere else.

Nix spoke to the officers as she recovered from her surgery. Doped on morphine, she claimed memory loss, like Berliner. Her doctors told the officers Nix's memory loss was most likely from both head trauma and excessive inebriation. Neither Nix nor Berliner remembered if Taer was on the boat with them when it broke apart, and they couldn't remember how it broke apart in the first place. None of Taer's clothes were taken from her home; none of her meager savings were removed from her Bank of America account.

Investigators packed the facts into a neat conclusion: after a night of heavy drinking, Berliner, Nix, and Taer stole the boat for a joyride. Because none of them had any experience driving a boat, they steered themselves too far from shore, and then an early morning fog rolled in. Lost, they drifted until rough waves pushed the boat into a rock on the shoreline, then pulled them back into deep water on a breaking boat. All three passengers hit their heads during the collision, and while Nix and Berliner managed to cling to consciousness and a piece of the boat, Taer lost consciousness and drowned. Or perhaps, after the fog rolled in, they passed out in the boat and when the boat collided with a submerged rock, Nix and Berliner were revived by the suddenness of their head trauma and floated, while Taer drowned. Or perhaps, after the collision with the submerged rock, the rough current pulled parts of the broken boat in two directions. While Nix kicked Berliner to shore, Taer floated toward Canada until she became hypothermic, lost consciousness, and sank.

When I spoke with Officers Holt and Burns, they presented these three theories as only a few of many. While the conditions of their stories changed, the conclusion never did: a drunk girl drowned.

Nix and Berliner were charged with the theft of the boat. After a brief negotiation between Berliner's lawyer and the state prosecutor, Berliner and Nix agreed to perform one hundred hours of community service each to atone for the theft of the property. The felony was then expunged from their records. They were granted this leniency despite Berliner's prior legal troubles and his close ties with an incarcerated domestic terrorist named Marie-Hélène Kraus.

Three months later, on July 14, 2010, in response to a petition from her immediate family, the state declared Taer legally dead, and the *Chicago Tribune* published a short news story/obituary:

Possible drowning victim Caitlyn [*sic*] Taer, 24, was declared dead yesterday. Taer had disappeared after a boating accident on Lake Michigan in late April. Maritime police were unable to recover a body but investigators concluded that she died in the incident. The District Attorney's office has no current plans to pursue manslaughter or wrongful death charges on behalf of the deceased. Taer is survived by her parents, Natasha Tenanbaum and Andrew Taer. Taer's friend Regina Nix remembers her as a "passionate person, who never doubted herself." Private services will be held.

A coffin filled with keepsakes, sandbags, and her favorite records was buried in place of a body.

Compared to Chicago's other disappearance that year, Taer's was small potatoes. Taer was actually a footnote* in the larger disappearance of Miranda Young, better known by her stage name, Molly Metropolis.

Four months before Taer's disastrous boat trip, Molly Metropolis disappeared in Chicago during her Apocalypse Ball tour. She performed to a sold-out crowd on January 8 and was gone before sound check on January 9. As of this writing, she hasn't yet publicly reemerged. Her disappearance and Taer's are inextricably linked.

Why begin to write a book about an unfortunate girl who probably drowned and a gone-but-not-forgotten pop star?†

Social associations helped jump-start the process of writing this book; if my partner at the time, David Woodyard, hadn't written an article about Molly Metropolis and Taer, my reciprocal interest wouldn't have developed. At the time of Taer's disappearance,

---

* The sentiment is semi-lifted from a piece by *New Yorker* journalist David Woodyard, who actually used the word *addendum* in his article concerning Taer. Woodyard has asked the author to clarify that point.

† *My assumption is that Cyrus K. Archer meant to expand on this question, perhaps even try to answer it, but I think it works better if I let it stand. It's the central question of the book, after all. A question even I am trying to answer. —Catie Disabato*

Woodyard wrote for *The New Yorker*, often focusing on topics at the intersection of popular culture and politics. He noticed that both of the people pulled out of Lake Michigan on the morning of Taer's disappearance were connected to Molly Metropolis. Nix, the eight-fingered hypothermic, was Molly Metropolis's former assistant; Berliner had been friends with the pop star since before her rise to fame in 2008. Woodyard conceived of a piece about cultural obsession with mystery stories and disappearing women, critiquing the morbid curiosity in the tenor of the national response to Molly Metropolis's disappearance, as well as the anemic Chicago-area broadcast news coverage of Taer's story. *The New Yorker* wanted to publish the article the same week as the U.S. release of a new novel by Haruki Murakami, whose work frequently features disappearing women. Though in the original concept for his piece, Woodyard planned to use Taer's disappearance as a persistent metaphor for the dangers of "mystery-mongering," Woodyard's final article mentioned Taer only briefly:

In Chicago, over 200 missing persons reports are filed every year. Any number of these disappearances are runaways or murders quickly solved. Very few missing persons are actual disappearances. In Chicago, we are surprised to have two so far this year. The pop star Molly Metropolis disappeared halfway through her concert tour. Then a girl named Caitlin Taer, who was friends with Molly Metropolis's former personal assistant, vanished a few months later. No one outside of Chicago talks about Taer's disappearance because no one knew her name before she disappeared, but they still talk about Molly.

There, Woodyard's investigation into Taer's disappearance stopped. If he had pushed harder, he might've been the one writing this book.
During Woodyard's relatively brief period writing about Taer

and Molly Metropolis's cases, he noticed that in Nix's statement to the police, she mentioned Taer had kept journals with detailed notes on her day-to-day life for more than a year before the incident in Lake Michigan. Intrigued, Woodyard attempted to acquire Taer's journals; he sent requests to the investigating police officers and Taer's immediate family. Unfortunately, he didn't receive the journals before his deadline.

A few weeks after Woodyard's article ran, a small but heavy Fed-Ex box arrived at our door with a polite note from Taer's mother apologizing for the delay. Inside, we found the journals, neatly stacked. Woodyard no longer had any interest in Taer's journals but he had always been lazy about getting to the post office, so instead of sending them back immediately, he left the box in the corner of the living room, where they briefly became an unfortunate fixture of our decorating scheme. One evening, succumbing to a mild curiosity, I picked up a journal began to read.

The first entry was dated almost a year before Molly Metropolis (sometimes "Molly," "Metro," or "Molly Metro," to her dearest friends and her closest fans) disappeared. The prose was neither stirring nor poised:

> I'm totally disgusted with this carpet, and basically my whole life. I know I'm using the carpet as a metaphor for my whole life, but I can't help it. It's so gross. I can't afford a steam cleaner. Maybe I'll save up. Charles [Taer's landlord] won't do it, but he's a fucktard. Listening to "New Vogue Riche," and it's cheering me up. I could use a dance partner.

Taer's love for "New Vogue Riche," a track from Molly Metropolis's first album *Cause Célèbrety* (pronounced Cause Celebrity) was nothing compared to her deep affection for Molly's debut single, "Don't Stop (N'Arrête Pas)." The verse that introduced Molly Metro to the world and captured Taer's imagination is as follows: *I can't work*

13

during the daytime / Save my en-er-gy for night lights / The dark city is the place for more / Work, work, work the floor.

Along with rave reviews of Molly's songs, Taer filled her journals with actual notes, grocery lists, and snippets of half-baked ideas or half-remembered conversations, alongside more traditional diary writing. I flipped through the pages, mostly bored and barely noticing when the text changed from Taer's usual disjointed lists to actual accounts of her day-to-day. I did pause, however, over a single phrase near the middle of the journal, written twice the size of her regular handwriting and underlined several times:

I found the fucking secret headquarters and now we're going to find Molly.

I stopped flipping through the pages, perhaps because of the whimsical nature of the phrase "secret headquarters." I found the first entries Taer wrote about Molly Metropolis's disappearance, and began reading Taer's story. It is dramatic to the point of being almost unbelievable.[*]

Taer's journals mix fiction, diary-style writings, drafts of articles, and those grocery lists—a hodge-podge of styles with no system of transition or separation, making the truth and the context of the writing difficult for an outside reader to ascertain. Though I acknowledge that Taer's journals are tangled and scattered, and that the truth and context of Taer's writing is sometimes hard to establish, there is a profound semantic difference between "difficult" and "impossible." Having thoroughly studied Taer's journals, I developed a knack for deciphering her idiolect and an ear for her style. When she was writing something that would eventually become a

---

[*] *In fact, according to Cyrus's notes, he was urged by David Woodyard to disregard everything he read in Taer's notebook. Woodyard believed Taer's story about Molly was fiction, and didn't think Cyrus should write a book about it. Woodyard's lack of support for Cyrus's project was one of the main factors in the disintegration of their relationship. —CD*

newspaper article, she'd affect an authoritative tone, which never sounded natural. These paragraphs would then appear, in edited forms, in her published criticism.

When she was writing fiction, she would try to play with words and languages, often incorporating phrases of French and Spanish (though she couldn't speak either language). Taer's fiction would often peter out as the narrative fell apart. The beginning of a story would be written with dramatic energy, many pages filled with hurried and messy handwriting. Perhaps a few days later, another few paragraphs would appear, continuing the earlier narrative thread. Then the story would wane until it vanished. She had little control over the fictional worlds she created in bursts of fevered inspiration, so if a story messily disintegrated, it was a telltale sign Taer was writing fiction rather than fact. Maybe she transferred her stories from the journals to a computer, where she regained control of her narratives, but I never found them on her internal or external hard drives.*

Although Taer's last diary entries were written with the same drama and timbre as some of her stories, she meticulously dated all of them. She didn't date her fiction. In her final diary entries, Taer abbreviated people and place names, which she never did in her fiction, and she didn't vary the sentence structure. In short, though these later entries sound fictional, Taer wrote them like she was writing facts. Woodyard has proposed that she was writing fiction in the style of nonfiction for some aesthetic purpose, but Taer never, to my knowledge, affected that style elsewhere, nor did she ever profess a preference for experimental fiction in that mode. To steal a saying from my helpful friends at the CPD, "the best indication of future action is past action."

The events written hastily at the end of Taer's journals and

---

* Graciously, Taer's mother allowed me to access all of Taer's computers and data storage devices.

explored in this text unfold in dramatic, even fictive ways. I take full responsibly for any gaps in logic and legibility, stemming from a lack of knowledge or understanding.* I hope those gaps will be few and far between.

This book is built on over one hundred interviews with everyone from key players in the unfolding drama to those whose roles were only incidental. I interviewed nearly every living person mentioned in this text, with the notable exceptions of Irene Davis, one of Molly Metropolis's dancers and Berliner's ex-girlfriend, as well as Alice Becker-Ho, widow of the French psychogeographer Guy Debord. For their willingness to explain their take on controversial events, I would like to thank two of Molly's former dancers, in the text referred to as Peaches and Ali, at their request.

Equally as important is what Taer left behind for me: audio files (which I transcribed myself) of interviews with Nix and various discussions of Molly's disappearance with Nix and Berliner—as well as the journals, which she wrote in every day during the early months of 2010.

Molly's record label, SDFC Records, provided some limited, but helpful, information on sales figures and marketing strategy and approved brief but informative interviews with recording and publicity executives who worked with Molly. HBO Films allowed me to view uncut footage from their unfinished concert special *Molly Metropolis Presents: The Apocalypse Ball*, and for that I am grateful. I appreciate the willingness of Nix and Berliner's families to speak with me, but I am especially indebted to the families of Molly Metropolis and Caitlin Taer, who agreed to be interviewed despite the difficulty of the subject matter. Molly's team, who still call themselves the General Council, were instrumental in making Molly come alive for me. In the countless interviews, profiles, YouTube videos,

---

* *I've tried to wrap up any pieces left hanging, and I apologize for the places forthcoming where I've been unable to do so. —CD*

16

Tweets, and music videos that Molly left behind, I found the pop star she wanted to be.

Once Molly and Taer's story begins to take definitive shape, it quickly fizzles into absurdity, like a map of a world with slightly distorted proportions—almost normal looking at first, but on a second viewing, a terrible deviation, a ghost of a place that never was, a land that couldn't be, a burning and terrible world beneath everything that we know to be real.

This book isn't about the disappearance of Molly Metropolis or the death/disappearance of Caitlin Taer. It's the story of Taer looking for Molly Metropolis, and whether or not she was found.

PART 1

"When I started writing songs, I didn't have a plan," Molly said. "I didn't follow any songwriting rules, I made my own boundaries. I took whatever detours felt right to me. I wasn't like, 'I'm going to write this hit and be the world's biggest pop star.' I just wanted to feel the whole history of culture resonating through me."

—"Living in Molly's Metropolis," *The New York Times Magazine*

Chapter ①

January 2010. A new decade had recently been rung in, with less pomp and circumstance than the previous decade, which had the Y2K scare, not to mention the resurgence of Prince's fantastic "1999," selling over two million new copies over the course of the year. When the world celebrated the new millennium, Molly Metropolis was only thirteen. Born to an upper-middle-class interracial family, Molly's African American mother differentiated her from her white high school classmates. She didn't have any siblings or friends to share the experience of growing up biracial in a majority white space. Characteristically, Molly let her dissimilarities from her peers be her strength. "Sometimes I felt like an alien," Molly told *The New York Times* in late 2009, "but even when I felt completely lonely, I thought, 'it's better to be unique than to be just like everyone else.'"*

A few weeks after giving that interview, as the overwhelming success of her single, "Apocalypse Dance," and its accompanying

---

* "Molly Defies the Sophomore Slump," last modified December 23, 2009; www.nytimes.com/2009/12/23/arts/music/molly-defies-sophomore-slump.html?ref=music.

thirteen-minute *Alice in Wonderland*–themed music video portended her stratospherically successful year, Molly Metropolis disappeared.

Molly was gone just as we were truly getting to know her. Five hit singles from her outrun electro–infused* and dance floor–centric debut *Cause Célèbrety*† gave Molly pop stardom and global name recognition. Her public presentation resembled Marilyn Monroe's opaqueness disguised as translucence, before Marilyn died and was de-mystified. Like an Old Hollywood starlet with a name and back-story invented by a studio bigwig, Molly "seemed to invite you in, but then you realized you've had hours of conversation with her and you don't really know anything about her."‡ The only difference was that Molly made up her name herself. During a time when pop singers like Jessica Simpson and Britney Spears cultivated down-to-earth public personalities and signed away their last shreds of privacy to MTV's reality television factory, Molly wanted her persona to be like parties at Holly Golightly's apartment: crowded and so fun you forget you never really spoke to the hostess.§

After the premiere of the "Apocalypse Dance" music video, and amidst conflicts with her record label about her delayed second album *Cause Apocalyptic*, Molly Metropolis updated her Twitter account more frequently with pictures of her dance rehearsals and

---

* "Outrun electro" is a genre of electronic music, sometimes called synthwave, based on 1980s synthesizers played in pulsating, repeating arpeggios. Outrun had a popular following before Molly adopted the style for many of her tracks, but she was the first to introduce the sound to Top 40 pop.

† In his review of the album, *Los Angeles Times* music journalist Sam Lambert called Molly's sound "dance pop for strange and unusual kids who see ghosts," referencing Winona Ryder's famous line in the 1988 movie *Beetlejuice*: "I myself am strange and unusual." Before writing his review, Lambert must've seen Molly's first music video, in which Molly's look consciously echoed Ryder's in *Beetlejuice*.

‡ From my interview with Nadia Piereson, one of Molly's backup dancers.

§ *Cyrus based this description on something Nix said to him in an e-mail, according to his notes, but I have no more clarifying details to offer. It will be important to remember Holly Golightly tried to trick people into thinking they knew her by presenting a false version of herself.* —CD

22

workout sessions. She retweeted fans and, in true Stars!-They're-Just-Like-Us fashion, she grumbled about hangovers: "11-11-09, 2:16pm @MollyMetro Stayed up late celebrating the 'Apocalypse Dance' video premiere. Too. Much. Red. Wine." She also Tweeted quotations from her favorite philosopher, Guy Debord, often un-attributed: "11-16-09, 5:33 a.m. @MollyMetro I've written much less than most people who write; I've drunk much more than most people who drink." Sometimes she altered Debord's words to meet her own needs, for example, changing, "Young people everywhere have been allowed to choose between love and a garbage disposal unit," to "11-14-09, 4:25 p.m. @MollyMetro People are told they have a choice between love and a garbage disposal unit. I say fuck love, fuck garbage, EAT POP INSTEAD." After popular celebrity gossip website *Oh No They Didn't* posted a story about record execs cutting some of her touring perks after she badmouthed them to *Rolling Stone*, she tweeted from the first page of De-bord's *Comments on the Society of the Spectacle*: "12-03-09, 10:22 a.m. @MollyMetro I obviously can speak with complete freedom. Above all, I must take care to not give too much information to just anybody."

Although most of her fans didn't identify the real writer of some of her Tweets, savvy readers could've picked up some revealing hints about Molly's inner life from her choice of quotation sources. Gawker.com wrote a short piece titled "Is Molly Metropolis a Se-cret Guy Debord Fan?" The answer, of course, was yes.

Elle put Molly on their December 2009 cover. She returned the favor by giving interviewer Eliza L. Pinkett her most revealing in-terview to that point. She told Pinkett stories from her childhood, teetering on the edge of talking about racism without fully com-mitting to a serious dialogue: "Growing up, I was very theatrical and dramatic and strange, and I had this gigantic mane of wild, re-ally thick hair. Most of my friends were white girls with thin hair, they didn't know how to help me look good. It was the nineties so everyone was trying to have that really straight Jennifer [Aniston] look." She also talked about the difficulties of dating as a superstar, "What I don't understand are the guys who don't want to be with a successful woman. It's so sexist! It's like, don't they want to be with the best version of me? The one that sells hundreds of thousands of records and gets to spend every night with thousands of my Pop Eaters? If a guy can't deal with that, then he's the one that has a problem, not me."

Molly couldn't keep Debord out of the *Elle* interview, explaining fame to Pinkett in Debordian terms: "In the past, being a pop star meant specializing in the 'seemingly lived,' superficially representing one personality type or another. Like, one pop star is the pretty virginal one, and one is the wild child, and one is the unlucky-in-love one. But I'm not superficial, I'm not a type, I'm a woman! I don't want my fans to get some simulation of life from watching me, I want them to listen to my music and feel that it describes, and improves, their own life. I want them to identify with me, but also know that I'm my own person."*

By the time the *Elle* profile was published, on the eve of her disappearance, Molly Metropolis's following had become increasingly passionate and fervent. The creativity and ferocity she devoted to what would've otherwise been standard pop songs caught the attention of "highbrow" critics and thinkers, as well as teenage pop devotees. She insisted on her and her fans' non-conformity with society, even as she sold millions of records, as music critic Tesfaye Likke wrote in his controversial article "Eulogy for Molly Metropolis— 2 Years Later": "Molly made her 'Pop Eaters' out to be more punk than the mall-punks they grew up with, more rebellious than the pseudo–Che Guevara disciples they sat next to in Econ 101, and more revolutionary than all the kids living in filth at Occupy Wall Street. She created a scene where people could claim non-

---

* *Here, Molly's riffing off of two moments from Debord's book* Society of the Spectacle: *"Being a star means specializing in the* seemingly lived," *and "The consumption celebrity superficially represents different types of personality." —CD*

conformity by listening to music made by the most popular artist in the country. And she made that paradox feel logical. Her inexplicably powerful charisma trumped better judgment. That quality is rare in a musician, and hasn't been seen since Kurt Cobain took his own life."*

When Molly Metropolis vanished during her massive Apocalypse Ball tour, she left 152 dates unperformed, costing her record company upwards of twenty-five million dollars and disappointing thousands of fans who had given her their hearts, souls, and money. At the time of her disappearance, Molly Metropolis had more than forty million Twitter followers, and fan sites by the hundreds. The abrupt end of millions of parasocial relationships became the greatest and most frequently broadcast loss. "She was a part of my actual life!!!" a typical (though with a marginally greater grasp of grammar and spelling) YouTube commenter exclaimed. "I'm going to miss her because I really really felt like she was talking to me—she answered a question from my twitter in an interview once and it was so amazing."† Molly often Tweeted her exact location, providing a link to a map with a drop-pin, making her physical person even more present in her fans' realities than all other pop culture phenoms before her.

After Molly disappeared, a few kooks came out of the woodwork to offer elaborate explanations. A popular Illuminati conspiracy theory website called The Vigilant Citizen weighed in with their particular brand of insanity. On August 12, 2009, the website had published a long article called "Molly Metropolis: An Illuminati Puppet," which claimed Molly was a mind-controlled puppet and that every time she posed for a picture with her hair over her eye (which, admittedly, happened a lot in her early press photos and the

---

* "Eulogy for Molly Metropolis," last modified January 10, 2012; www.vulture.com /2012/01/eulogy-for-molly-metropolis.html.

† ValerieVamp22, January 22, 2010 (2:32 a.m.), comment on aPOPcalypse_hereine, "I Can't Seem to Find Molly"; www.youtube.com/watch?v=CoXL44DcJeeN.

music videos for her *Cause Célèbrety* singles) she was making herself into the All-Seeing Eye. The Vigilant Citizen wrote: "Those who have passed Illuminati Symbolism 101 know that the All-Seeing Eye is probably its most recognizable symbol."

According to The Vigilant Citizen, Molly Metropolis disappeared because her "Delta" or "killer" programming had been activated and she completed her "final Illuminati operation," then vanished to hide the evidence of her actions.* With the story, The Vigilant Citizen ran an early publicity photo with Molly dressed in a black T-shirt with a deep V-neck; she holds the back of her hand up to her left eye to reveal the tattoo of an eye inside a triangle that Molly has on her palm. Needless to say, the police never investigated "Delta programming/evil Illuminati mission" as a possible explanation for her disappearance.

Leaving behind the wildest conspiracy theorists, most people argued over whether Molly Metropolis had been kidnapped, killed, or had left of her own volition. Various broadcast news reporters and Internet commentators fought out these three opposing viewpoints until they had nothing new to say.

On January 8, Molly Metropolis was scheduled to play the first of two shows at the United Center, the heart of Chicago's ice-covered Near West Side. Despite a windchill of ten degrees below freezing and system-wide delays on the L, ticket holders arrived early and in droves. Girls and boys—the most conservative dressed in leather and leotards, the most ostentatious in full costume as Molly Metropolis herself—lined up outside of Will Call, giggling and jostling each other with excitement. The dance floor was crowded by 5 p.m., with sweaty teenagers jockeying for the spots closest to the stage.

---

* "Why Did Molly Disappear?: Molly Metropolis's Final Illuminati Mission Complete," last modified February 6, 2010; vigilantcitizen.com/musicbusiness/why-did-molly-disappear.

Molly performed songs from *Cause Apocalyptic*, at the time still unreleased, as well as all the singles from *Cause Célèbrety*, to a gyrating crowd of three thousand Pop Eaters, as her dedicated fans had christened themselves, riffing off an interview Molly gave to MTV. com: "I want to live in a world where the only thing you need to drink is music and the only thing you need to eat is pop culture."

The show began with the projected image of a glowing black-and-white skyline, not specific to any city. A "chopped and screwed" version of the opening melody of "Apocalypse Dance" then played, as the projected city started to degrade and crumble. The sound of a pre-recorded intro filled the room: "My Pop Eaters. The ones who eat pop for breakfast, lunch, and dinner. You are the city kids. The ones who ran away to the city, the ones who are born there, the ones who dream of it. I'm not talking about L.A. or Chicago or even New York City. My name is Molly Metropolis"—here, the recording pauses for a burst of applause—"and I'm the city where you live. And in my city, we live every night like it's our last."

The recorded voice faded and the fallen city turned translucent to reveal Molly Metropolis in a dress of bronze metallic lace sparkling against her light brown skin, her arms reaching toward the sky in a V. The music cut out, and she belted the opening lyrics of "Apocalypse Dance" *a cappella*: "Tonight / might be your last chance / t-t-tonight / to get one last dance."

As the *Chicago Tribune*'s music critic Bran Hollis Brooks pointed out in his review of the show, when a concertgoer is used to the pop shows of artists like Britney Spears, Rihanna, and Christina Aguilera, seeing Molly Metropolis perform is an aurally surreal experience. At the time, most other pop stars lip-synced to album cuts of their hit songs while devoting their stage energy to dancing—but Molly actually sang while she performed. The airbrushed, auto-tuned album might be more conventionally beautiful, but nothing makes a concert feel more like a concert than hearing someone sing live. In the years since Molly Metropolis debuted, most new pop stars have followed her model.

As with all of his Molly Metropolis coverage, Brooks spent a good portion of his review (published before her disappearance became public knowledge) re-examining the "phenomenon of Molly Metropolis" and attempting to draw some satisfying conclusion about the nature of her appeal, though obviously flummoxed by his own appreciation of her. Like a dog staring confusedly at his own reflection, Burns wrote, "Perhaps, in a long year of job loss and economic decline, America needs an oddity to gawk at like Depression-era Americans visiting freak shows. Molly Metropolis is no Bearded Lady, but she scratches the same cultural itch."[*]

After the concert, Molly Metropolis held an after-party at the Peninsula Hotel on the Miracle Mile with a small group of dancers and friends, including Nicolas Berliner. They kept the hotel bar open until 3 a.m., two hours past the usual closing time, after which Molly retired alone to her private suite.

On January 9, Molly woke just after 9 a.m. and ordered a breakfast of fruit, yogurt, granola, orange juice, coffee, and the Peninsula's signature Truffled Popcorn. At 11 a.m., her driver took her to the concert venue for a brief rehearsal with her choreographer. That afternoon, Molly decided to visit the Museum of Contemporary Art (MCA), again with a group of dancers and friends that included Nicolas Berliner, as well as her assistant Regina Nix and several other members of her close-knit group of creative collaborators. Although the museum was less than half a mile from the hotel, Molly insisted on driving herself there in the sporty convertible she had rented for her thirty-six hour stay in Chicago. She asked Berliner to ride shotgun. According to Berliner, Molly initiated an emotional, personal conversation in the car. She told her friend that

_____

[*] *Chicago Tribune*, "Review: Molly Metropolis at the United Center," by Bran Hollis Brooks.

28

she treasured the few minutes they were able to have together, apart from the rest of the crew, and that she wished they were able to spend more time alone. She even asked after Berliner's imprisoned girlfriend, Marie-Hélène Kraus, a subject Molly often avoided. She proposed a "weekend getaway" for Berliner and herself after the tour was over.

At the MCA, Molly had the opportunity to view pieces by Jeff Koons (including "Pink Panther," "Rabbit," and "Three Ball Total Equilibrium Tank"), as well as "The Unicorn Tapestries," on loan from The Metropolitan Museum of Art in New York. She also signed autographs for fans and art lovers. While they walked through the galleries of the MCA, Molly convinced her bodyguards that she would be fine driving from the museum to the venue by herself. She craved "space to think." Apparently Metro, as all her bodyguards called her, left her security team behind as often as she could, whenever she felt safe, especially in cities like Chicago where the paparazzi was considerably less present than in New York and Los Angeles. Molly left the museum alone at about 2:15 p.m. That was the last anyone saw of her.

By 3:15 p.m., Molly's tour manager, Florence Tse, began to get worried. Molly had a phone interview scheduled for 3:20 p.m. and they couldn't find her. By 5:30 p.m., when Molly was late for her call time at the venue, her staff and colleagues were on high alert. Despite her flashy, indulgent persona, Molly was a punctual person, and when she didn't show up on time, she called ahead. According to Tse, Molly "never arrived for anything more than five minutes after she said she would be there."

Tse called Molly's cell phone multiple times. Several of her dancers called or sent text messages; no one received a reply. Nix was also M.I.A. and didn't pick up her cell phone or Molly's. An hour and a half before Molly's set was scheduled to begin, the doors opened and the audience quickly filled the theater. Minutes before the Scissor Sisters' opening set was scheduled to start, Nix arrived at the venue, breathless from exertion, emotionally overwhelmed, and in possession of Molly's cell phone. Nix had conducted an exhaustive search of the hotel grounds and nearby boutiques, working herself into an anxious fit before hurrying to the theater. Nix had left both her phone and Molly's on silent, and in her rush to find Molly she had forgotten to check her missed calls and messages.*

Smelling disaster, Tse instructed the theater manager, Lilia Greene, to speak to the audience before the second opening act, the singer-songwriter Lissie. Greene informed the well-dressed throng that Molly Metropolis was suffering from food poisoning and the price of the tickets (minus processing fees and shipping costs, if applicable) would be refunded. Tse called SDFC. The head of their in-house pubic relations team, Kelly Applebaum, immediately issued a press release. Quoting the release, *The Hollywood Reporter* called Molly's absence "a sudden illness," and published Tweets from fans angrily leaving the venue. Someone logged into Molly Metropolis's official Twitter account using the iPhone Twitter application and wrote: "To all my amazing Chicago monsters. I would give anything in the world to be with you right now and not cold & alone."†

---

* *Cyrus K. Archer didn't have a chance to fill in the missing links in this account of the day Molly Metropolis disappeared. Molly gave Nix her phone just before the museum trip earlier that day. Molly often left her phone with Nix when she didn't feel like dealing with incoming calls or messages, so Molly getting rid of her phone didn't seem unusual to Nix. According to Molly's dancers and friends, Molly was an unreliable phone user and often forgot to return calls and texts, which was part of the reason that they weren't particularly worried when she didn't return messages on the day she disappeared. According to Nix, she discovered Molly was missing when she went to Molly's hotel room to "give her the heads up it was time to go to sound check," but found the hotel room empty, and Molly nowhere to be found. Then Nix began her small-scale search. —CD*

† Nix believes it "must've been Kelly [Applebaum]," who tweeted this. Applebaum believes it "must've been Gina [Nix]." Any number of the dancers and PR support staff knew or had access to Molly's Twitter password, and her account had been previously hacked at least once. Despite vehement denials, Nix is the most likely suspect because she was in possession of Molly's phone at the time. The final suspect is, of course, Molly Metropolis herself. The police used the fact that no one would

30

A quiet search party—consisting of dancers, security personnel, Berliner, and Nix—scoured the dark and icy city. Applebaum's staff monitored news sources and gossip sites for any Molly Metropolis sightings. They didn't find anything, no trace of Molly Metropolis in Chicago and no whisper of her whereabouts on the Internet. They wouldn't find her rental car for two more weeks, abandoned in a region on the border between Michigan and Indiana called Michiana, in the driveway of a rarely used lake house. All of her clothes, costumes, and personal possessions were left behind at the venue and the hotel; not a single shoe or pair of underwear was missing.

Molly Metropolis didn't appear the following morning. Applebaum informed Molly's family and called the police. Normally, the CPD waits forty-eight hours to file a missing persons report, but Molly Metropolis's fame made it unlikely that she could move idly around the city without being spotted, so police Sergeant Jordan Pierce decided to waive the usual time limit. Pierce and a team of detectives interviewed each member of Molly's touring crew. Nix gave the longest interview; Berliner gave the shortest.

The next day, SDFC executives and Applebaum officially canceled Molly's January 12 show in Detroit. In their official statement to the press, Applebaum and SDFC claimed Molly Metropolis still suffered from food poisoning–related complications, namely "dehydration and exhaustion." They closed the release with, "Molly Metropolis apologizes to fans in Chicago and Detroit and will appear at scheduled Atlantic City and New York City performances."

Applebaum did all she could to hide the truth, but the Gossip Media smelled a rat. Gossip websites *The Superficial* and *TMZ* speculated that Molly was suffering from complications from drug use

---

step forward to claim authorship of the Tweet as possible evidence that Molly had chosen to disappear willingly.

or anorexia. Perez Hilton, on his influential gossip blog Perez-Hilton.com, posted an entry titled, "Where Have All the Mollies Gone?" accompanied by a concert photo from a previous tour date, with a Photoshopped dribble of a white substance spilling out of Molly's nose, meant to allude to cocaine use (a common characteristic of Hilton's altered images). Perez thought the food poisoning story was "too convenient," the kind of things celebs' reps always say.

On January 14, a freezing and overcast Monday in Chicago, the chief of the CPD, Jody Peter "J.P." Weis, and Applebaum, speaking on behalf of SDFC Records, called a 9:30 a.m. joint press conference. They announced that Molly Metropolis had been missing since January 9 and they detailed the actions taken to find her. The video of the press conference was uploaded to YouTube where it has been viewed approximately 250 million times, as of this writing.

Elsewhere in Chicago on January 14, Caitlin Taer was nursing three separate obsessions: becoming a professional music critic, the Molly Metropolis song "Apocalypse Dance," and the prices of hardwood flooring—none of which helped to improve her unsatisfactory post-collegiate life and, despite growing up near the city, her hatred of Chicago winters.

Short and curvaceous, with curly dirty blonde hair and a small smattering of freckles, Taer was also a trendy dresser, who spent most of the summer in long jean shorts and thin backless T-shirts. When winter set in, she wore skinny jeans and giant, thick sweaters. She also wore a black down winter coat that covered her from chin to ankle.

Born and raised in a southern suburb of Chicago called Flossmoor, Taer spent her childhood dreaming of living in Chicago, according to her journals. At age eight, she compulsively played and sang along with a cassette tape of Frank Sinatra's "My Kind of Town (Chicago)," given to her by her father, and covered her walls with black-and-white poster prints of the city's impressive skyline at night with the word "Chicago" in a white cursive along the bottom—the kind of images purchased by tourists.

On warm weekends in the spring, her mother would take her shopping on Michigan Avenue. They woke up early and walked to the train station on sidewalks bracketed by dewy grass. They traveled to the city on the Metra Electric Line, from the train station in downtown Flossmoor to the Randolph Street Station in the middle of downtown Chicago, at the shopping district along Michigan Avenue known as the Miracle Mile.

Because the train took her to Chicago, Taer also developed a passion for Metra Electric. She didn't want to play with the electric train sets her parents bought her to try to feed her obsession, but they had to watch her closely because she would occasionally run away to the train, sometimes just to sit by the tracks and watch it go, sometimes to try to climb aboard.

Once when she was ten, she made it all the way into the city by smartly sticking near a woman with three other kids; the conductors assumed she was with the family. When the train reached Randolph Street, its final stop, young Taer followed a familiar path from the platform to the underground station's exit, emerging onto the intersection of Randolph Street and Michigan, directly into the bustle of the Loop, full of hope. Unfortunately, she didn't know where to go next. The rush hour crowds were thick, and commuters, in their hurry, jostled her. A homeless man started shouting. Very quickly, Taer realized that she shouldn't be in the city alone. She began crying and screaming loudly until a security guard from the train station noticed her. After the security guard calmed her down enough to figure out where Taer came from, a young conductor escorted her home. He let her play with his Game Boy and bought her Skittles, which her mother would never let her eat. Taer's love of the city remained untarnished. The story of her solo visit to Chicago quickly became family lore.*

In 2000, Taer began her freshman year at Homewood-Flossmoor High School. Physically, she had matured earlier than most of her female classmates and attracted attention, mostly mocking, from the boys. She wore baggy shirts to hide her breasts ("They seemed to grow, like, every second that year," Taer recalled in one of her journals) and defensively shouted "asshole" at every boy she caught looking down her shirt. The taunts didn't stop until her senior year, when such teasing suddenly seemed immature.

Gina Nix attended the same high school. The girls knew each other marginally. They didn't run in the same circles, but Taer's best friend played on the same field hockey team as Nix, and sometimes they hung out at sports parties. Nix didn't care much about the typical social hierarchies, but Taer was hung up on them.

"At these parties," Nix told me during our first interview, in my Chicago sublet's sunny kitchen, "I would just be, like, leaning on the wall having a beer, relaxed, and Cait would be very tense. I didn't know her well enough to understand that was just her default mode. She was very intense, very intense. Very intense eyes. And she thought because I played field hockey and she was on the newspaper, which I guess was nerdy, that I should be some kind of bitch to her, which I never was. At that stage in my life, I couldn't handle people that were so keyed up and I think she didn't trust people who appeared to be okay with everything. She said she didn't like 'chill people,' I remember that. She told me that at a party once and I thought she

---

* When I interviewed Taer's family members, several of them told me slightly different versions of this story. I choose to include the version told to me by Taer's paternal grandmother, Louisa Collins Taer.

34

was insulting me. Later, she told me that I made her nervous because she thought I was cool."*

During those high school years, Taer and Nix were quietly going through twin crises of sexuality. Both in the early stages of coming to terms with being a lesbian, they receded from the conversation whenever anyone said the word "gay" and barely dated anyone. Nix used her devotion to sports as an excuse; Taer pretended to have an unending crush on a boy who didn't like her back. Nix explored lesbian porn links on her brother's computer. Taer fantasized about a friend from gym class who took off her shirt in the locker room to show off the quarter-sized hickeys her boyfriend had left on her breasts. Besides the newspaper for Taer and field hockey for Nix, high school bored them both.

Taer went to Oberlin College† in Ohio. Nix went to the University of Chicago (U of C), where she met Molly (still going by her given name, Miranda) in a nineteenth-century fiction class. Nix and Taer didn't stay in touch. If Facebook hadn't been invented their first year of college, they might never have thought of each other again. Instead, they "Friended" each other sometime during their college years and remained marginally aware of each other's love lives and music tastes.

Nix and Taer graduated college in May of 2008. Molly Metropolis hired Nix as her new assistant, while Taer moved back to Chicago to pursue a career in music journalism. As of January 14, when the CPD announced Molly's disappearance, Taer still wasn't progressing in her occupation of choice. Very occasionally, she wrote for the popular music news and criticism website Pitchfork.com

---

* *In my conversations with Nix, she added: "Let's be real—Cait probably wanted to fuck me, and was having emotional problems about it. Maybe I was having emotional problems about wanting to fuck her." —CD*

† *Cyrus taught English and creative writing at Oberlin College while Caitlin Taer matriculated there. She didn't take any of Cyrus's classes, but they almost certainly crossed paths. Archer taught in the same departments Taer studied in. —CD*

and the *Chicago Tribune* music blog *Sound Effects*, for which she was barely paid. Taer never wrote professionally about Molly, but wrote about her frequently on her personal Tumblr blog, caitmusic .tumblr.com. She posted the audio of "Apocalypse Dance" with the following caption:

THIS. THIS FOREVER.
I'm so deeply in love with this song, it's a little bit sick. There are just a few perfect pop songs in this world—"Like a Prayer," "PYT," "Toxic," etc.—and this has joined the ranks of Prince, of Justin Timberlake, of Madonna. This is the Molly song people will play forever.

Because her work with the *Chicago Tribune* and *Pitchfork* wasn't translating into more paid opportunities with other outlets, Taer worked as a barback and sometimes bartender at a bar called Rainbo, in a neighborhood known as the Ukrainian Village. (Deceptively named, Rainbo is a dive with a reputation for being a favorite of local musicians, not a gay bar.) Sometimes, she sold clothes to resale store Buffalo Exchange for grocery money. Taer lived in Humboldt Park, a grungy but cheap and gentrifying area near the more expensive and yuppie-filled Wicker Park neighborhood. Her apartment was on the top floor of an unkempt walk-up on the corner of North Monticello and West Thomas Street, with no architectural distinctions to speak of and at least two warped window frames that let in cold air.

She spent each day's otherwise empty hours obsessing about her carpet. Taer hated her apartment's carpeting with an intense fervor most people generally reserve for sentient beings. She paid for a steam cleaning, a huge expense in relation to her income, but while her roommate's dust-related allergy attacks stopped for a few months, the cleaning didn't improve the color or texture of the dingy gray-white carpet.

Taer petitioned her landlord for a flooring upgrade; she preferred Brazilian Cherry Wood, but would be satisfied with anything,
really, so long as it wasn't carpeting. Her landlord refused. Taer
wanted to move, but didn't want to break her lease or deal with a
subletter. She pouted, instead, to her diary: "It's like I'm trapped in
hell." Her frustration didn't subside until Molly's disappearance
distracted her.

On January 14, scrolling through her Facebook page's News
Feed, Taer clicked on a link one of her friends posted to the You-
Tube video of Weis and Applebaum's press conference.* She watched
the full thirty-minute press conference, lying in bed, scribbling dis-
mayed thoughts into her journal. When Weis mentioned that Taer's
old acquaintance Regina Nix was the last person to see Molly Metropolis, Taer got out of bed. She quickly read through articles from
the *Trib*, CNN, and *Oh No They Didn't*, looking for quotes from
Nix. She called her editor at the *Chicago Tribune*, David Hurwitz, and
asked if they had spoken to Nix. He hadn't, but one of his journalists
had been trying to contact her for a longer, more thoroughly researched piece on the hours before Molly Metropolis disappeared.
If Taer got an interview with Nix, she could get a contributing
credit on the piece. She called in sick to her shift at Rainbo, put on
a heavy sweater and her quilted coat, and caught the Metra Electric
Train Line from the Millennium Station (a renamed and refurbished
Randolph Street Station) to Flossmoor. Taer was hoping Nix was
hiding out at her parents' house.

Taer wrote in her journal while riding on the Metra, her handwriting shaky due to the train's constant motion:

> I know it's not really a journalistic hunch like in the movies,
> but I'm pretty sure Gina went home. I was thinking about

---

* *To put together Taer's discovery of Molly Metropolis's disappearance, Cyrus drew both from
Taer's Tumblr posts and her notebook. —CD*

that party at Rachel's senior year when everyone just knew Gina was having sex with Christopher Brooks, of all fucking people, in the bedroom. A few of us went around the yard and looked through the windows, which was terrible of us. She didn't leave her mom's house for the rest of the summer. That's where she goes to hide.

If she didn't find Nix at home, Taer planned to ask Nix's mother to help find her.

After arriving in Flossmoor, Taer walked to her own house, ate lunch with her mother, and asked to borrow the family car. She drove through Flossmoor's small downtown to a neighborhood called Heather Hill and tentatively knocked on Nix's door. Nix's mother, Diane, answered and led Taer to the small living room at the back of the house. Nix was lying on the couch, wrapped in a blanket, listening to Philip Glass with her eyes closed. Diane left them alone.

Nix unwrapped herself and stood up. She was tall, and thinner than she had been in high school; her athletic body had given way to a more sinewy look. She had thick, slightly wavy brown hair, which she wore past her shoulders, with long bangs swept over her forehead and pinned back. Her nose came to a sharp point.

Nix initially refused to let Taer interview her, denying Taer access the same way she would eventually, temporarily, deny me. Taer convinced Nix to change her mind with self-effacing honesty. Taer told Nix the interview was her first real chance to impress her editors. She explained she was working at a bar and hated her life. She explained her frustrations with her carpet. Nix laughed at her a little bit, but it worked. She agreed to give Taer a few quotes, if SDFC would let her. Nix called Applebaum, who agreed to let Nix give the interview, and coached Nix on what she could and couldn't say.

Taer turned on her iPhone's voice recorder and Nix talked for three minutes about visiting the MCA and Molly insisting on leaving without her bodyguards. Their conversation was as follows:*

"Does she usually go to museums or do other tourist things while on tour?" Taer asked.

"No, she doesn't usually do this kind of cultural tourism; not in the U.S., at least. When she goes out of the country, there is more of that kind of thing," Nix said.

"I guess what I'm asking is, was it unusual behavior for her to go to the museum?"

"Yes. Sort of. I don't want to say 'yes' because she is always doing unusual things. Was this unusual behavior? Yes. Was unusual behavior a matter of course? Yes. I'm not just talking about the crazy outfits and the weird videos. She doesn't act like a usual person. Even though she never acts *normal*, you get used to her, and you can predict how she's going to act or respond to something. This wasn't predictable behavior. Molly is just as crazy as everyone thinks she is, but at the same time, she is the most level-headed, clear-thinking, sharp person I've ever met. No one is like her. And she is nice to everyone. Can I tell you something off the record? And you won't print it?"

"Yeah, sure. Like, legally, I'm not going to be allowed to print something you say is 'off the record.' My editor will listen to this recording. The fact-checker, I mean, they'll listen to it."

"Okay. Well, off the record: I'm pretty sure [Molly] had some deep dark secrets she was keeping. I wouldn't be surprised if there was this huge part of Molly and her life that no one knew about, that she somehow kept hidden, and she just decided to go do that instead. Or it consumed her, without her being able to stop it."

Nix told Applebaum she had given Taer this strange, almost rambling, conspiracy theory–esque quote, and Applebaum asked her to

---

* As with this conversation, all further dialogue is taken from Caitlin's various audio recordings, captured by her iPhone's built-in voice recorder and saved to her computer.

put it on the record, for reasons Nix still doesn't understand.* Taer and her editors included the quote in the *Tribune* article. It was the starting gun for a thousand more conspiracy theories, opinion pieces, blog posts, and status updates. It became one of the most enduring sentiments of the early days of Molly Metropolis's disappearance.

It also makes Nix seem unbalanced and spastic; she's not. Nix has a steady temperament. She's more inclined to recede than to babble. Molly's disappearance brought out an extreme in her.

As Taer turned off the voice recorder and awkwardly started to leave, Nix burst into tears. She cried into the corner of her blanket, apologizing and trying to stop. When she couldn't, she hid her face and asked Taer to leave. Instead, Taer grabbed Nix's upper arm and squeezed it. Nix hated when people said "don't cry" to try to comfort a crier, and she expected that out of Taer. According to Nix, Taer subverted expectations and said, "You keep on fucking crying for as long as you need to. I'm just going to hold onto your arm like this."

They sat together for a long time. Nix cried, and Taer held her arm. Taer wrote that she was attracted to people who expressed their deep emotions honestly and even more attracted if the person wasn't usually effusive; it made Taer feel special. She latched on to Nix that afternoon.

Nix captured Taer's attention, but Molly Metropolis captured her imagination. Taer wanted to know everything about Molly's possible secret life. Her pursuit of Molly Metropolis began that night, perhaps even in those quiet moments while Nix wept and she held her arm. Taer's Molly Metropolis idolatry was already the

---

* *Although they spoke to Cyrus, neither Kelly Applebaum nor anyone on the SDFC public relations team returned repeated calls and e-mails for comment on this decision or any other part of the book. My best guess as to Applebaum's motivations here is that the SDFC team assumed a conspiracy theory controversy would help sell* Cause Célèbrety *and eventually* Cause Apocalyptic. *—CD*

embodiment of pop star fixation, but with the added hook of a mystery, it developed into a full-blown obsession. Over the next few weeks, she investigated Molly's secret activities and the deeper mystery of her disappearance. As Taer sunk into her obsession, she too became progressively more secretive, until she also disappeared on a rainy weekend in Chicago.

Chapter ②

Inside her blanket fort on her mom's couch, Nix snuggled her laptop and watched her quote about Molly's possible secret life go viral. She liked seeing her name pop up thousands of times. She felt like she was doing something while the rest of the world stagnated around her. However, she hated that she liked trading on Molly's name. She called Taer and asked her not to use their interview again. Taer agreed, and asked Nix to come visit her.

Nix wanted to see Taer but refused to go into the city where Molly Metropolis's touring staff waited impatiently for marching orders. Their anxiety made Nix anxious, so she texted with them to keep updated on the gossip and goings-on, but didn't participate in their stilted social gatherings. At Nix's insistence, Taer returned to Flossmoor to walk down the snow-caked dirt paths of the park that bordered their junior high school, where Nix used to get high with other field hockey players during the off season. Taer and Nix had a lot to catch up on. They found, as they shared stories about terrible roommates and awkward sexual awakenings, that they had grown more similar since high school. They had both come out during college, and they bonded over their high school friends' similarly shocked reactions.

When they got cold, they stopped at the Flossmoor Station Restaurant and Brewery, a refurbished train station with hearty portions of bland Midwestern cuisine and windows that rattled each time a Metra train pulled into the working station next door. The girls took off their mittens and, clutching pints of the excellent house Hefeweizen, moved on to more intimate conversation. Taer told dirty little stories about parties that developed into groups of students making out and having sex during Oberlin's cold, dark Winter Term. Nix talked about fake I.D.s, Chicago clubs, and mounds of cocaine.

Eventually, Taer turned the conversation to Nix's relationship with Molly Metropolis and the fallout from her disappearance. Taer recorded the discussion,* even though Nix asked for their chat to be off the record. Taer assured Nix that she wouldn't give the *Tribune* her quotes "but if they ask me to get something specific from you, and I already have it, I can just ask you about it. Plus, there are laws to protect anonymous sources, if you want to become an anonymous source."

"I think they would guess my identity," Nix replied, a little angrily. "But fine. And you have to buy my drinks, then."

Taer was using the *Tribune* as a scapegoat during that conversation. Her editors at the paper never solicited her for more quotes, and she knew she wouldn't be asked for them. Taer recorded the interview for her own purposes. Regarding this recording, she

---

* This recording is a harbinger of a fixation Taer developed with her recording device. She zealously recorded most of her conversations about Molly, spurred on early in her investigation by something Molly wrote in her own notebook: "Never work, always document!"—the phrase itself was a cheeky bastardization of a Situationist assertion "Never work!" Molly strove to make the act of living her life its own art. The documentation of her actions was compulsory, so art could be made without work.

wrote, "I'd better keep track," though she avoided explicitly spelling out her motivations for doing so.

As they ate potato skins and drank a second beer, Taer and Nix intensely debated whether or not Molly Metropolis had disappeared as a publicity stunt. Taer thought Miranda Young might be trying to kill off Molly Metropolis, to make way for a new character or to return as herself: "So, 'Molly Metropolis' disappeared, and that's part of the canon of the story of Molly Metropolis that Miranda Young is writing—like, the end of a narrative, a cliffhanger, sort of an end. Then she comes back as like, the Thin Black Duchess or something. 'Molly Metropolis Is Alive and Well and Living Only in Theory.'"

Letting the David Bowie reference go by without comment, Nix disagreed. "She wouldn't do that to her family and they don't know where she is."

"Maybe they're in on it."

"No, they are really freaking out and I've met them—they're not like Molly."

"I mean, you're the one that knows her, obviously, but are you telling me she wouldn't pull some Brian Slade–style shit?"*

"She would but I don't think she did, and if it was a game she wouldn't wait so long to come back," Nix said. "Besides, 'Molly Metropolis' isn't some Ziggy Stardust thing. She's not so split personality about it. Calling herself Molly is like me calling myself Gina. It's really just a nickname."

"Really?"

"Really. It's so much less fucked up than you think it is."

"Okay."

"You want it to be fucked up," Nix said.

"No," Taer replied, defensively. "I don't care what it is. I just want to know about it."

---

* "Brian Slade" refers to Todd Haynes's 1999 film *Velvet Goldmine*, about a David Bowie pastiche character who faked his own death onstage.

This conversation, and similar ones that followed, were no more meaningful than a speculative blog post; Taer's investigation into Molly Metropolis's disappearance truly began several days later, on January 24, when Nix asked Taer if she wanted to visit Molly's last hotel suite.

By the end of January, SDFC was ready to give up the ghost. They had already let go of most of the touring staff, but continued to pay for Molly's hotel room at the Peninsula because Applebaum had been using it as a PR office and media war room. Applebaum stayed in Chicago for ten days waiting for Molly Metropolis to re-emerge, but ten days was her limit. She needed to return to Los Angeles. Applebaum called Nix, asked her to clean out Molly's hotel room, and offered her an entry-level position on one of SDFC's publicity teams. Nix declined the offer because she wanted to stay in Chicago, but agreed to clean the hotel room so Applebaum would keep her on the payroll until the end of the month. Nix had signed several non-disclosure agreements assuring SDFC she wouldn't reveal details of Molly's private life to outsiders. Nix says she shouldn't have invited Taer to join her, but at that moment she didn't care.

The Peninsula Hotel is only half a block off the Miracle Mile, a short walking distance from the Millennium Station and the nearby Millennium Park. Nix rode the Metra Electric Line from Flossmoor to the Millennium Station at Randolph Street, while Taer waited for a Green Line L train in the cold, shivering in her jeans, wood-heeled boots, and coat. Taer transferred from the Green to a Red Line train to downtown Chicago.

They met in the lobby of the hotel. With their cheap coats and messy hair, they did not blend with the Peninsula's upscale clientele,* but they walked confidently through the carpeted halls of the top floor, linking arms at the elbows and flirtatiously bantering, while a

---

* Molly Metropolis wasn't the only celebrity who stayed there. Brad Pitt and Angelina Jolie famously favored the Peninsula whenever they stayed in Chicago with their brood.

concierge led them to Molly Metropolis's penthouse. When they walked into the suite, giddily tripping over a pair of ankle boots, they saw that all the rooms had been ransacked and Molly's belongings were scattered across the floor. Taer and Nix assumed the mess was the result of a police investigation, but they were wrong.

The CPD had combed through the suite and confiscated anything that could be evidence of some kind of wrongdoing or could hint at a reason why Molly would willfully disappear, but they had done so neatly and without haste, according to both the officers' written reports of the investigation and my interviews with the same officers after the fact. They had taken Molly's laptop, her cameras, and several articles of clothing, but they hadn't been concerned with finding "clues" among Molly's shoes and clothes because Molly's hotel suite wasn't officially a "crime scene." In fact, at the time, the CPD believed that Molly had probably vanished willingly, either as part of a publicity stunt like Taer had suggested or as a way to escape the pressures of public life.*

Nix started sorting through the clothes, folding and packing them neatly. Taer couldn't fold the shirts well, and Nix quickly became frustrated with her messiness. She sent Taer away from the neat piles, tasking her with collecting all the far-flung items. Taer began gleefully exploring the hotel room mess. She sidestepped a pile of lingerie and peeked into a closet, looking for Molly's stage costumes. She didn't find them; they had been stored at the venue and shipped back to SDFC's offices in New York. The costumes Molly officially owned would eventually be turned over to her family, who in turn donated them to the Costume Institute at the Metropolitan Museum in New York City, where they were featured in a

---

* This is a theory that her family and friends contested to the police as strongly as Nix contested it to Taer. In September 2009, on an unreleased date, Molly Metropolis's mother, Melissa Young, underwent open heart surgery. Molly stayed with her family at the hospital for a week, and was attentive all through the tour. Molly's family believed that she never would've disappeared purposefully while her mother was still recovering.

special exhibit which debuted at the 2012 Met Ball. Her best outfits and accessories—her LED glasses from the "Light Brite" video, the black leotard with metallic sleeves she wore in the "New Vogue Riche" music video, all of her insane Johan Van Duncan Haute Couture shoes—are now enshrined and on display.

With permission from Nix, Taer took off her shirt and put on one of Molly's. The shirt fit poorly, so she tried on another. Nix joined in. They tried on tight black jeans, Marc Jacobs black blazers, vintage leather ankle boots, Jeffery Campbell wedges, studded black leather vests and coats, T-shirts by Mary-Kate and Ashley Olsen's clothing line The Row, tights with holes up the back of the thigh, Chanel pantsuits and see-through shirts made of vintage lace. They took pictures with Nix's phone. Nothing fit; Nix's hips were too wide, her feet were too big, and her torso was too long. Taer's breasts were too large to fit into Molly's shirts and the pants were too small. When they finished trying something on, they folded it and packed it into one of their cardboard boxes, which Nix would eventually ship to Molly's family.

They packed for hours, drawing out the process by ordering a boozy lunch from room service. Eventually, and only half seriously, Taer started looking for hiding places. She searched for secret drawers in the desk and checked to make sure the mattress, sofa cushions, and pillows were plush, not re-stuffed with "money, drugs, or other secret things." Then she went around the room, moving each painting to see whether a safe was hidden behind one of them. Some of the art on the wall belonged to the hotel; some of it belonged to Molly and traveled with her to each stop on her tour. Molly had a map of the original Chicago L system, a screen print of an island, and a screen print of a map of changes to the Chicago L system that had been proposed by city planner Daniel Savoy in 1962, but rejected by the Chicago Public Transport Subcommittee.*

---

* The Transit Subcommittee chose plans designed by Savoy's rival, Ronald Mansfield,

Taer didn't find anything until she reached the screen print above Molly's bed: the island, printed in a shocking pink ink, with several dozen tiny drawings of ships surrounding the coastline. The screen print was signed by "Antoine Monson." Unlike the maps of the L, obvious depictions of Taer's own city, which seemed normal to her only because she didn't think about them hard enough, the screen print of the island seemed unusual. Taer asked Nix about it, but Nix only knew Molly liked it, not why she did. She suspected Molly was drawn to the shipwrecks, represented by those tiny ships dotting the shoreline. Shipwrecks meant error, disaster, and horror; those were the kind of monstrosities that captivated Molly. She clung to frightening things. Nix knew that, but she didn't know anything about the screen print; she didn't even know the island's name.

Molly Metropolis's family graciously allowed me to borrow the screen print during the writing of this book, to facilitate my research. (It also served as a kind of motivational poster for me—like the kitten hanging from the tree with the caption "Hang in there!"—when completing this project seemed like an impossibly daunting task.) Because of the Young family's generosity, I was able to research the island in Molly's hot pink map.

The island on the screen print is called Sable from the French *île de Sable*, or "Sand Island," though the island's foundation, while sand-covered, is actually made of solid rock and below that, reef. The island is a narrow sliver of land, 27 miles long but never more than 1.2 miles wide, located in the Atlantic Ocean 109 miles off the southeast coast of Nova Scotia. Discovered by Portuguese explorer Joao Alvares Fagundes, the island was originally named Fagunda.

After thoroughly traversing the waters adjacent to what would become Nova Scotia, Fagundes returned to Portugal and published

but those plans weren't implemented either because the Commercial Transport Committee eventually chose to divert the L restoration funds to building another Metra line, the Metra Electric South Shore Line that Taer and Nix used to travel between the city and Flossmoor.

a map of the coastal area, including the island he called Fagunda. He also published a detailed land map of Fagunda itself. Nearly fifty years later, after Fagundes's death, an inconsequential trading ship that happened to be carrying a somewhat well regarded cartographer, Lázaro Teixeira, reported that Fagunda wasn't where Fagundes's map claimed it should be. Teixeira drew up a new map of the area that excluded Fagunda and spread the story that Fagundes created a false island in order to give something his own name. Several other cartographers and shipmen on the trading vessel corroborated Teixeira's story.

It was a testament to Fagundes's lasting popularity in Portugal and Spain that the royal families and academics of each country assumed that Fagundes hadn't lied but instead that his island had been "lost," washed away by a storm or sunk into the sea. They called it a "phantom" island and attributed it with ghost-like qualities, such as the ability to appear and disappear. More than one shipman, dying from wounds or delirious from illness, claimed to see "Fagunda, the Island of Dead Seaman" beckoning him from beyond the grave.

A century later, Fagunda is still the poster child for cartographic misconceptions of the early exploratory age. However, Fagundes's island wasn't a cartographic misconception; the island actually existed—it was just so narrow, and the cartographic equipment of the time so crude, that it was difficult to find. The island's extreme thinness makes it difficult for even military-grade radar detection devices to pick it up.

At some point in the late nineteenth century, another sailor found the island, took some measurements of it, and reasserted its validity, but no one publically documented it until the Nova Scotian government commissioned a map of the coastline in 1902, and renamed Fagunda as Sable Island.

Currently, the island officially sits within the Halifax Regional Municipality in Nova Scotia, but as part the 1972 Canada Shipping Agreement between Canada and Nova Scotia, the Canadian Coast

Guard is responsible for the island's safety and security. No one can visit without written permission of Canadian Coast Guard College (CCGC). Approximately five people permanently inhabit the island; they all live and work at the Sable Island Station, an environmental research complex owned by the University of Toronto. The island's true inhabitants are the wildlife, most prominently several thousand snub-nosed blue seals and over 300 feral horses.

Because the low, thin island is so difficult to see, it's caused a large number of shipwrecks over the centuries, often illustrated on maps of the island, like Molly Metropolis's screen print where the shipwrecks are represented with tiny drawings of colonial-era ships. With approximately 350 shipwrecks on its shores between 1583 and 1999, Sable earned the nickname "The Graveyard of the Atlantic."

The final shipwreck to date, in 1998, was also the only wreck of a private yacht, called the *Merrimac*. The yacht possibly belonged to an American family. The CCGC investigated the crash but determined that the causes were "non-criminal." The records of the investigation, like all records of non-criminal investigations that occurred before the police digitized their files, were trashed ten years after the investigation closed, in 2009, before Molly disappeared. The Canadian aquatic force sent two or three copies of the report to the FBI summarizing the investigation, indicating that they believed the victims were American. Although the FBI was more than willing to provide me with the files under the Freedom of Information Act, they couldn't find them. Probably misfiled, the records won't be recovered for years, when the FBI finishes digitizing many decades' worth of physical, low-priority files. As a result, few verifiable details of the wreck survive.

Relying on rumor to guide me towards truth, I discovered that an American family was causing some trouble about Sable a year before the shipwreck. Charles and Margot Pullman, a wealthy couple, both successful architects and cousins to the Daley family on Margot's side, had a ten-year-old daughter, Elizabeth—a spoiled and precocious child. Elizabeth read about Sable in an *Encyclopedia Britannica* and developed a strong desire to own one of the island's feral horses. Charles and Margot, to reward Elizabeth's inquisitive bookishness, began pursuing legal means to acquire a Sable Island horse for their daughter.

When the Canadian government denied their requests, the Pullmans allegedly threw an epic public tantrum and planned to illegally abduct a horse. They reportedly bribed a young member of the CCGC to allow them unfettered access to the island on an appointed night. Later that year, the *Merrimac* washed up on the Northeastern shore of Sable, the area of the island that has collected the highest number of shipwrecks. The CCGC aquatic force pulled four bodies out of the water, three adults and one child. The remains were DNA tested but the results are unavailable somehow the reports were never sent to any other U.S. authority other than the FBI, or the bodies were never identified even through testing, or the identities of the dead were never otherwise reported by some other bureaucratic folly. The recovered pieces of the *Merrimac* had been fitted with animal containment devices a few days before the crash. One week later, the Pullman family and their stable manager, Anthony Perkins, were reported missing. When the family didn't reappear and were presumed dead, their substantial financial holdings, reportedly in the hundreds of millions, were transferred to an urban renewal charity, the Becker-Ho Foundation, in accordance to Charles and Margot's last will and testament.

The Pullmans didn't own a yacht but certainly had the means to buy, rent, or borrow one quickly. In 1999, only three of all the yachts registered in Canada, the United States, and Nova Scotia were called *Merrimac*. Two of them are still in use today. A Chicago resident named Bruce Adler, a wealthy bachelor in his fifties, owned the third *Merrimac*. Adler registered the *Merrimac* with the Chicago Yacht Association and reported that he docked the yacht at the Inner Jackson Harbor until 2001, when he broke the ship down to scrap wood.

However, the Inner Jackson Harbor's longtime Harbor manager, Nancy Gould, remembers that that sailboat, not a yacht, was always tied to Adler's dock.

Did the Pullman family borrow Adler's yacht, sail it to Sable with the intent of stealing a horse, and accidentally crash on the shore of the island? If so, what would Alder have to gain by concealing this fact? And why would a twenty-three-year-old pop star have a screen-printed version of a map of the island on her wall? Where would a map like that even come from?

I can only answer the final question. Molly Metropolis commissioned the screen print on her wall, but it was copied almost exactly from a map called "Sable Island: Known Wrecks Since 1583," drawn by John Fauller and now part of the collection at the Nova Scotia Museum of Natural History.

For whatever reason, Molly must've considered her screen print version of that map one of her most important wall hangings. Besides the place of prominence she gave it above her bed, she also used it as a hiding place. When Taer moved the print, a notebook, which had been wedged between the wooden box frame and the wall, fell onto the bed. Nix recognized it immediately. It was Molly Metropolis's personal diary.

Chapter ③

After packing the rest of Molly Metropolis's belongings into boxes and ferrying them to the hotel's mailroom, Nix and Taer left the Peninsula, taking Molly's notebook with them. When I spoke with Nix, she told me they stole the notebook out of "simple curiosity." However, in an interview with Berliner, when I asked him if he could provide an outside perspective on Nix's comment, Berliner said: "Their curiosity wasn't simple."

Nix and Taer didn't examine the notebook's contents until they got back to Taer's apartment and Taer's roommate had gone out for the evening, leaving dirty dishes in the sink. For half an hour, they thumbed through the pages together, reading passages out loud and examining Molly's sketches of outfits and accessories. After this brief examination, Nix decided not to delve any deeper into Molly; she felt done with the notebook. Reading it felt like a betrayal, or like "grave-robbing your grandmother," as Nix told me.

Taer had the opposite reaction. She wanted to read every word and look for clues in the sketches of costumes and half-finished song lyrics. Although Taer and Nix found the notebook together, and Nix arguably had more claim to it as Molly's ex-assistant, Taer treated the notebook like it was her property. Unfortunately, she had it with her when she vanished into Lake Michigan. The final written words of a figure about to become an icon sank to the bottom of a lake. Only ghostly secondhand information about Molly Metropolis's notebook survives.*

Although I would've preferred to examine Molly's notebook firsthand, I enjoyed Taer's tour of the contents via her own writing. Taer's personality enticed me from the first moment I picked up her diary. She lacked self-awareness, but occasionally had a sharp critical eye. Just after "Apocalypse Dance" was released, she wrote:

> Metro started out as a stand-in for the listener, someone as obsessed with fame as the listener (me? us?) is. With "Cause Apocalyptic," she appears to be going in a different direction. Fame is inside her (infected her?) and she can no longer be a stand-in for me, or a version of me, but that sense—of her having once been me—lingers . . .

Taer liked the idea of being an obsessive as much as she liked obsessing:

> So I can do a deep criticism here, on the lyric level, about love and revenge being the same thing, because they are both about obsessive attention, but then it gets all twisted because of course I'm obsessing. Like, would my time really be more valuable if I was just listening to *Boxer* or *Doolittle* for the

---

* *If Taer had left Molly's notebook behind that night instead of her own, perhaps Cyrus would have been writing a book only about what Molly did. Instead, Cyrus read what Taer wrote and spent time inside her head rather than Molly's. According to Cyrus's notes, by the end of his first day with Taer's notebook, he decided to do some research of his own. He barely mentioned his interest to his partner, believing Woodyard would disapprove (he discovered, later, that he was right). He waited until their summer together was over before making his first research trip to Chicago, riding the same L lines Taer did, heading south of the Loop to visit the National Archives and delve deep into the fraught history of the trains Cyrus and I—and Taer—rode. —CD*

billionth time?* Would my time be more "legitimate?" Is the level of fame important in determining the quality of the obsession? Is the type of fame important?

Most of Taer's notes on Molly's notebook are somewhat muddled, even big direct quotes—except one note, dated a few days before she disappeared, written with sloppy and hurried handwriting: "It was all in her notebook, in some form or another, it was all in there!"

Nix remembers some of what Molly wrote, but she never examined it as closely as Taer. Berliner was with Molly when she wrote some of the entries, so he can make good guesses at what was inside. Combined with Taer's notes, this allowed me to partially reconstruct the contents.

According to all my sources, Molly Metropolis had written in the notebook during the nine months prior to her disappearance. Scattered throughout the notebook were sketches, lyrics, and plans pertaining to her music career, but a significant number of pages were given over to Molly's other pursuits. She had divided the notebook, roughly, into thirds. The first third was written in April, May, and parts of June 2008. Molly spent the majority of this first portion discussing the work of Antoinette Monson, a fifteenth-century cartographer, who Molly describes as a "cartographer of the potential." Because Taer gave Molly's hot pink screen print of Sable Island only the most cursory of examinations, she didn't immediately realize that this "cartographer of the potential," has a nearly identical name to the one signed on the screen print: Antoine Monson.

Molly wrote the second third of the notebook in late June and early July. In this section, Metro wrote a number of song lyrics and concept notes about her third album, which she had tentatively

---

* *Boxer* is an album by the indie rock band The National, released in 2007. *Doolittle* is an album by the band The Pixies, released in 1989. They are both highly regarded albums, and two of Taer's all-time favorites.

titled *Cause Oceanic*, and which, of course, was never recorded. Taer didn't quote from this section at all in her journal, Nix had to describe it to me. Nix doesn't remember any of the final lyrics Molly wrote, much to my chagrin as a converted fan of Molly Metropolis's music.

The most significant portion of Metro's notebook was the final third, which she wrote from July to December. In those pages, Molly described an ambitious project called The Ghost Network, which had to do with the Chicago L system. Molly planned to design a gigantic map which would catalogue every single L train line ever built in Chicago and combine them with every single L train line *not* built—that is, every train line proposed but never incorporated into the system.

Molly Metropolis wrote, and Taer quoted: "What is a public transit system consisting of elevated trains? It's not just a transport for bodies. It's a system to transport systems (digestive, nervous, etc.), a series of tracks that transport ideas. It's not the accessories of a city, lying on top of the skin, but the veins and arteries within the body."

Calling Chicago's public train system an elevated train line is a lie—many of the train tracks aren't elevated—though it hasn't always been so. In 1898, when the Chicago Transit Authority approved the plan for the train line in conjunction with Democratic mayor Carter Harrison, Jr., they planned a completely elevated train system and envisioned a glistening, futuristic track with trains whizzing between the tops of Chicago's towers. The *Chicago Tribune* referred to the upcoming train system as the "Alley Elevated" or the "Alley L." By the time the inaugural train took its twenty-mile-per-hour journey around the short, looping track,* the two most prominent Chi-

---

* The train carried two passengers during its first trip: Mayor Harrison Jr., a proponent of government-owned transit versus privately owned transit, and his wife, Edith Ogden Harrison, a literary celebrity at the time (though her novels are barely read now).

cago newspapers were using "the L" to refer to the train and the nickname became part of the urban nomenclature.

The owners of the *Trib* and the *Evening Journal* (which later became the *Chicago Sun Times*), Mayor Harrison Jr. and prominent Republican politician Conrad Kelsey, put aside their long-standing rivalry to mutually use the L to wage a propaganda war against New York and its mayor William L. Strong. Prominent regional historian Albert Whitfeld asserts that both Harrison Jr. and Kelsey prompted their reporters to trump up or instigate some kind of competitive feeling between New York City's underground subway and Chicago's new elevated train line. From the September 17, 1899, issue of the *Tribune*:

Indeed, New York City's train system runs below their streets, shaking automobiles and pedestrians alike when a train passes below, and forcing the families and professional men who use the train lines to crowd into dark tunnels. In contrast, Chicago's glorious Elevated Train Line will hang above the city like some silver necklace on the neck of a comely heiress, rising above our shining city like a jewel.*

In the decades that followed Chicago's first train ride, private companies started building and running elevated train lines, and the city let the corporate world take on the burden of building public transit.

In 1939, as countries in Europe began fighting among themselves for the second time in a century, a savvy but generally disliked businessman named Samuel Insull owned two-thirds of the train lines,

---

She liked hats with huge feathers and threw lavish, controversial séance parties, which the *Chicago Evening Journal* parodied in a political comic that depicted Edith Ogden as Chicago's Marie Antoinette.

* The original article from which that quote was taken was lost in a fire, but the quote survived in an article the *New York Post* ran several months later.

cars, and stations. Insull treated Chicago utilities like a game of Monopoly, and because he controlled much of the L plus the Edison Electric Company and half of the Port of Chicago, Insull was winning.

Mayor Harrison Jr. dreamed of a publicly owned transit system. He wanted the city to buy all the existing train lines, then build new ones underground to serve as bomb shelters. Should the Blitzkrieg terrorizing London ever come to the United States, the ruling body of Chicago wanted a safe space to hide and convene a war council. To both gain control of the L and build his safe underground shelters, Harrison Jr. waged a publicity war against Insull. The *Trib* called him an Anglophile and a homosexual. Several of Insull's male lovers, who may or may not have been well-paid actors, gave interviews with both of the city's major newspapers, describing not only their "lewd lifestyle," but also Insull's plans to defraud major stakeholders in his company. Insull's CFO implicated Insull in criminal activities, and Chicago detectives arrested Insull on charges of profiteering, racketeering, electioneering, and bribery. The state seized his business holdings, including all of his L lines. The city held him without bail and he died in prison before his trial began, succumbing to stab wounds accidentally inflicted as a bystander to a yard fight.

Harrison Jr. hired the architect-designer H.W. Benthom in 1943 to develop a plan to replace the entire elevated system with subways, each fortified. Benthom's designs were a work of architectural beauty, a system that resembled a great river and its tributaries, with the Loop as a whirlpool at the center. A year later, the city completed construction on the first underground station at State Street. The disused station's closely spaced support columns are still visible today through train windows when the Blue Line travels between Chicago and Damen.

By the time Benthom finished drawing his plans for the rest of the subway stations, Hitler had been put down and America had

already bombed Hiroshima. The war was over. The appeal of underground shelters got lost among the plans for victory parades.

Plans for Benthom's L underground systems are archived in the
Chicago Public Records, along with every other rejected proposal.
The Public Records contain every blueprint of every proposed addition, whether the addition was adopted or the proposed stations
and lines were built. Since the first steam locomotive pulled its
wooden coaches out of the Congress Street Terminal in 1892, the
hundreds of proposals that were never adopted have grown into an
overlapping maze of alternate L train lines and stations, an "alternate
universe transit system," as the science fiction blog *io9* put it.* The
train lines that were never constructed are the bastards and doppel-
gangers of the L that covers the city today.

For reasons I failed to comprehend during my first research trip
to Chicago, Molly Metropolis was fascinated enough with the L to
dedicate years of her life to designing a map that layered each potential, but never constructed, alternative or expansion to the L on
top of a map of all the functioning L lines. She also included train
lines and stations that had once been part of the system but had
gone out of use. She created the map on a computer and also painted
it onto the wall of a secret office she kept in Chicago. This giant,
unwieldy map is the project she called The Ghost Network.

Molly's Ghost Network is a strange piece; it catalogues not only
a hypothetical transit system, but also one that would be nearly impossible to build and ridiculous to implement. The Ghost Network
has, for example, dual train lines riding side by side for their entire
route, save one or two stops; it has places where both elevated and
underground trains run the exact same route. The Ghost Network
exists in a world without decisions, where every proposal is adopted,
where construction isn't based on the realities of the city.

---

* "Chicago's Never-Built Train System Looks Like a Giant Octopus," *io9*, last
modified January 12, 2011; io9.com/Chicagos-never-built-train-system-looks-like-
a-giant-1280648619.

While The Ghost Network was the most interesting discovery Taer made while reading Molly Metropolis's notebook, it wasn't the most immediately useful. Before Taer could begin to put The Ghost Network in its proper context, she had to first act on the simplest note, scrawled on the inside cover: Nicolas Berliner's name, phone number, and e-mail address.

When Taer showed the number to Nix, Nix immediately recognized Berliner's name. She knew he was a paid member of the Governing Council (as Molly called her creative team, often shorted to the GC), but Molly had never told Nix exactly what Berliner's job was. For a little while, Taer and Nix thought Molly and Berliner might've been lovers.

Once Taer saw Berliner's number, it got into her head like an earworm. She couldn't forget that she had "secret access" to someone deep in Molly's inner circle; she couldn't help thinking of Berliner's number as the light illuminating a path. Nix, on the other hand, remembered a very strange exchange between Berliner and Molly.

Berliner's number was on all of Molly's phones and he was a permanent fixture on her "Approved Callers" list. If he called and insisted that the call was important, Molly would interrupt anything except a live performance. For example, during the production of her last music video, for "Apocalypse Dance," Molly twice halted production for half an hour to accept frantic phone calls from Berliner.* According to Nix, after the second "Apocalypse Dance" call, Molly came back to the set pale and shaking. Nix brought her some water and as the dancers took their places, Molly whispered to Nix something along the lines of, "If you ever need to speak to Nick

---

* To apologize for making their day longer, Molly bought lunch for the entire crew. According to Nix, she also told the assembled cast and crew (that included a dancer named Irene Davis), "I am so sorry. I promise I wouldn't waste your time like this if it wasn't a matter of extreme importance. Not life or death, but with similar stakes."

directly, I would like you to remember that things with him aren't safe."

"Do you want me to take him off the call list?" Nix asked.

"No, no, of course not. Nick himself is a good person. He is very special to me. But there are certain . . . I don't want you mixed up in certain elements of his life. His girlfriend, Marie-Hélène, is in prison, you know. She killed someone. She says it was an accident. The police thought Nick was involved but they couldn't prove it—I'm not saying he was but there is really no way of knowing what someone has done."

Nix asked Taer not to call Berliner and Taer obliged, for a while, probably because sometime just before or just after finding the notebook, Taer and Nix's relationship had become sexual. A week after the hotel room excavation, hidden among a transcription of the lyrics of Molly Metropolis's song "I'll Find You," Taer recounts, almost dispassionately, "Gina and I had sex again this morning." She didn't note when their first encounter took place.*

Sex in general, like Molly's notebook, is often hidden, lost, undocumented, and unread, especially sex between two young queer women. The real goings-on between two people are basically unknowable.† It doesn't matter that we don't understand the nature of Taer and Nix's relationship. It's only important that we know it did happen, because in deference to the girl she was having a sexual relationship with, Taer delayed calling Berliner. But she didn't wait very long.

---

* *In my interview with Nix, she maintained that she didn't remember when, exactly, the sexual element of her relationship with Taer began. "But that's how Caitlin is," Nix said. "Once you start fucking her it's like you've always been fucking her. At least, that's how she treats you. You've always been fucking her and you will always be fucking her." When I asked her what she meant, Nix said: "Oh, you know, she annexes you. She claims you as a territory. You know what I mean." Nope, I do not. —CD*

† Unknowable, even if Nix had been more forthcoming with me about the details of her romantic relationship with Taer.

Chapter ④

On January 24, two weeks after Molly disappeared, three days after Taer and Nix found Molly Metropolis's notebook, and three days before Taer finally broke down and called Berliner, Nix asked Taer if she could move into her living room temporarily. Taer and her roommate needed help with the rent, so despite the possible romantic complications, Taer agreed. Nix told her mother she was going to stay with a friend in the city, packed some winter clothes in a large suitcase, and proceeded to make camp on Taer's couch. Occasionally, Nix slept with Taer in her bed, but more often she retreated to the living room after their nighttime trysts. Nix and Taer both enjoyed sleeping alone, and the couch reminded her of narrow tour bus bunks and unfamiliar hotel beds. After months of living on tour with Molly Metropolis, Nix had come to enjoy living like a nomad—just as Molly had enjoyed it.

Though the on-the-road lifestyle suited them both, Nix and Molly grew up with completely different temperaments. Where Molly was bombastic, Nix was reticent. Nix had spent much of her childhood quietly watching Bulls and White Sox games with her father. Victor Nix taught his daughter to value healthy competition, good sportsmanship, and even tempers. His favorite athletes were calm, collected, and professional; he loved Scottie Pippen and hated Dennis Rodman for everything except his rebounding record. Nix easily adopted her father's favorite characteristics. Prone to moodiness as a child, she learned to carefully control and conceal her emotions from both of her parents, pursuing her passions without ever acting passionately.

Molly, even in college, was the absolute opposite. She was a dramatic personality, a theater nerd who expressed herself aggressively. Molly befriended Nix not because they were opposites but because they were both performing. Nix performed the lack of emotion. Molly performed the excess.

Under Molly's influence, Nix loosened up. "I changed after college, when I started working for Molly, I know that," Nix said. "I enjoyed myself more. It helped that I didn't have anything to live up to, not a team or a GPA, nothing like that. I started painting my nails a lot even though I kept them short."

Nix worked for Molly during the majority of the pop star's short career. Her job went from a twenty-hour-per-week, minimum impact position to an eighty-hour-per-week, intense scramble to keep up with Molly's rising profile. When Molly's first tour, the Célèbrety Ball, was in full swing, Nix worked about twelve hours a day, every day, with only non-performance days off. The non-performance days were few and far between. Nix was unfazed by the increased hours. Her compensation had swelled accordingly, and with the record label covering most of her expenses while on tour, she managed to save a nice amount of money, a financial cushion that made her father proud. Furthermore, although a professional distance always existed between them, Nix became one of Molly's friends and confidants.

Nix was unaware of the extent to which Molly hid things from her, because Molly always made it seem like Nix knew all her secrets. They gossiped about the dancers; while she was getting her hair done, Molly told Nix detail-laden stories about her tumultuous romance with her first producer, Davin Karl; in the evenings, they drank wine together and talked about the purpose of art, sometimes just the two of them.

When Molly disappeared, Nix slipped into a depression. Still unwilling to exhibit deep emotions in front of her parents, and without an apartment of her own to run to, Nix escaped to Taer's. From the moment she moved in, she did nothing to hide the depths of her melancholy. She slept for twelve hours a day, and stayed up half the night. She sometimes paced the short, carpeted hallways in Taer's apartment, picking at the chipping white paint on the walls. She pulled Taer's books off her IKEA shelves, read ten pages, then left them on the coffee table. She sat on the couch for hours, scrolling through Tumblr, absorbing nothing but a constant wash of bright colors. In the middle of a conversation, she would stop talking mid-sentence, stand up, and walk away. Bundled in sweatpants and a flannel button-down pajama top, swaddled in a gray fleece blanket with a pattern of yellow ducks, she spent the night staring at the ceiling.

For the first week and a half after Nix moved in, Taer tried to help. She bought Nix presents, like a chocolate bar or a used DVD of *Love and Basketball*. She cooked Nix meals and brought home bags of bar pretzels from Rainbo. She tried very hard to be good to Nix, becoming more like a girlfriend every day, but according to Nix, Taer got irritated easily over the small annoyances of sharing space with another person. Taer snipped at Nix over leaving towels on the ground or crumbs on the kitchen counter, then got angry because Nix's apologies seemed forced. They would both snap back and forth, raising the stakes with each rejoinder, until the little bitch sessions turned into proper fights.

When they fought, Taer screamed at Nix, opened the door, and demanded that Nix move out, take the train back to Flossmoor. Nix would try to talk Taer down or, if she was feeling particularly frustrated, she would ice Taer out, refusing to speak to or acknowledge her.

These fights ended when Taer apologized, cranked up the heater, and crawled under Nix's blanket. "Even though she got mad fast she'd forget about it even faster," Nix said. "Cait doesn't hold grudges. Like, fifteen minutes later we could be talking about music or watching Netflix like she'd never been pissed."

While Berliner certainly experienced fewer of Taer's mood swings, he was more blunt in his discussions of Taer's relationship with Nix. He said, "Nix always said, all Taer needed to forget she was upset was a back rub and a blow job."

While Nix wallowed in depression, Taer descended into her own crushing obsession with Molly Metropolis and her notebook, a fixation that demanded more of her focus every day and sometimes took precedence over Nix's emotional well-being. Even though Taer could see that Nix was falling apart, she prodded her for details about Molly's day-to-day life, her hobbies, her proclivities, anything that could give Taer a clearer picture of what might've happened to Molly. Nix gritted her teeth and obliged. She also tolerated Taer's compulsive listening and re-listening to Molly Metropolis's posthumous album.

The day after Nix moved into Taer's apartment, SDFC released Molly's last album, *Cause Apocalyptic*. The album debuted at number one, while all eight songs battled over the top spot on iTunes' digital singles chart. SDFC sent a complimentary copy of the CD to Nix, who gave it to Taer. Taer played *Cause Apocalyptic* dozens of times while she read Molly's notebook.

Taer's reading and research brought her to a series of dead ends, which brought her again to Berliner's phone number, her only remaining unwalked avenue. Unable to contain herself, Taer decided to call Berliner without telling Nix—her first betrayal. Taer also stole Nix's cell phone to make the call, assuming Berliner might recognize Nix's number and pick up the phone. Berliner did answer and after an awkward introduction, Taer told Berliner she had Molly Metropolis's notebook.

Berliner refused to discuss the notebook over the phone. He instead asked Taer to meet him at a soul food restaurant in the Loop called Redfish—"neutral territory." As Taer agreed, Nix walked into Taer's bedroom, still dressed in her pajamas at 4 p.m., and overheard the end of the conversation. Taer said goodbye to Berliner staring directly into Nix's eyes, guilty but unwavering. After Taer hung up, Nix snatched the phone out of her hands, checked the number and, recognizing it as Berliner's, asked, according to Taer's notes, "What the fuck have you done?"

Nix and Taer had another screaming match. Nix fought with the moral high ground; she had been dismissed and deceived, her desires had been ignored, and so on. Taer cut deep and low; she dismissed Nix's depression as self-indulgence, and questioned her devotion to Molly, shouting something like: "Why is it that I, who never fucking met her once, give a shit about where she is, and all you can do is sit on your ass all day?"

Eventually, they calmed down. Taer cried a little. Nix swept up shards of a glass Taer had thrown on the floor in anger. Taer apologized for calling Berliner behind Nix's back and for saying terrible things. Nix didn't apologize for anything, but told Taer the reason she was reluctant to call Berliner: Molly's strange insistence that Nix not trust him, and the several strange encounters Nix'd had with him. When he visited Molly on tour or on the set of the "Never Work, Only Party" music video, he either ignored Nix completely or spoke animatedly about his time working in a vintage map store as if Nix had asked him questions about it. Berliner had been sleeping with one of the dancers, Irene Davis, and the whole tour crew gossiped about his weird sexual proclivities, some kind of architectural fetish Nix never really understood. "I guess he likes to rub his dick against sconces or something," Nix told Taer. Taer thought that was so funny, she posted it on her Facebook page.*

Nix didn't want to give Molly's notebook to Berliner, and thought he might be capable of overpowering them and taking it out of Taer's purse. Taer suggested they rent a safety deposit box to stash the notebook in, and despite the theatricality of the idea, Nix agreed. Before going to Redfish, they took the L to the Chicago First National Bank and Trust. They locked up the notebook, then took the train downtown.

Berliner never met them at Redfish. Taer and Nix ate fried green tomatoes, chicken gumbo, and jalapeño cornbread as they glanced around the dark restaurant, mostly empty except for a few over-worked businessmen and tired assistants picking up carry-out for the office. They sat for two hours, quickly working their way through several beers, watching the door. Taer tried calling Berliner, but he didn't answer his phone.†

Eventually they gave up, paid the bill, and walked slowly from the restaurant to the Randolph and Lake entrance to the Brown Line. They walked through the Financial District, which had emp-tied out at 5 p.m. and echoed like a ghost town at night. Around them, the city's tallest skyscrapers gleamed; hundreds of stories of empty offices hovered over their heads. The dark street was covered with snow, pounded so hard into the pavement that it cracked like glass under their boots.

On the empty Brown Line, the trains seemed unusually rickety as they whipped around the sharply curved corner of the Loop. Taer

---

* Caitlin Taer's Facebook page, accessed June 28, 2012; www.facebook.com/caitlin .taer/posts/9302341872395726138572.

† *To fill in a gap in Cyrus's story: Berliner later told Nix one of the reasons he stood them up was because his girlfriend, Kraus, didn't think it was a good idea at the time. I get the sense Kraus changes her mind a lot, and has kind of poor instincts. —CD*

and Nix held hands and Taer attempted to curb the dark mood by insisting that Berliner was probably delayed, without his phone, in an area with no reception, or running out of battery power. Nix said nothing. The train went along its course, shaking. They transferred to the Blue Line and rode it back to Taer's apartment.

Nix asked to stay in Taer's bed and Taer agreed with a little half hug against Nix's shoulder. They planned to drink some more and watch television—probably *Law and Order: SVU*, a mutual favorite—but their plans evaporated when they returned home.

Inside the apartment, they found a terrible mess. The cushions on Taer's couch had been slashed; her refrigerator and freezer doors were open and some of the contents had been pulled out. Her pots and pans were on the floor. In her bedroom, Taer's dresser drawers had been pulled out of their frames and upended. Her mattress had been cut open, her bed frame was dismantled. The suitcase Nix had been living out of was turned over and her clothes had been picked through. There was a hole in Taer's bedroom wall.

Nix accused Berliner; to her thinking, he was the only possible culprit. It did seem likely she was right, as Berliner hadn't shown up to dinner and knew they would be out of the house at that time. Nix thought the whole dinner was a ruse. Taer called the police. A pair of CPD uniformed cops arrived half an hour later and took down a report. Although Taer mentioned Berliner, they told Nix and Taer evidence was too scarce and no one would have time to investigate the burglary.

Taer and Nix slowly cleaned the apartment. They swept up the broken glass, put the pots and pans back in their cabinets, and threw away any food on the floor, but—exhausted—they left the mess in Taer's bedroom. They fell asleep on a torn mattress with the empty dresser drawers on the floor around them, like a kind of vegetation. They slept pressed together on one side of the mattress until Taer woke up suddenly. She heard, from somewhere inside the apartment, a loud thud.

Waking Nix, who relayed the story to me later, Taer slid out of the bed and grabbed a dictionary off her bookshelf to use as a blunt weapon. She crept into her living room and saw the silhouette of an intruder picking through the remains of her couch cushions. As the silhouette turned, Taer swung the dictionary at his or her head as hard as she could. Her hit landed, but Taer dropped the dictionary because of the pain and shock in her arms. The intruder also dropped the items he or she was carrying, before slamming Taer into a wall and sprinting out of the apartment. Dazed, and bleeding from the side of her head, Taer groped for the light switch. With the lights on, she turned her attention to the items that the intruder had left behind.

Nix stumbled into the living room and found Taer examining her spoils of war: a pocket-size sketchpad and gun. The gun was a .22 caliber, single action, Smith & Wesson pistol with a thumb safety, wooden grip, adjustable target sights, and a blue steel finish.[*] Nix picked up the pistol, made sure the safety was on, and unloaded it, while Taer thumbed through the sketchpad. Each page of the pad was filled with a hand-drawn street map, and on the inside of the front cover, someone had written Molly Metropolis's personal cell phone number.

Under the harsh florescent bathroom lights, Nix put Neosporin on Taer's scalp. Both wide awake and jittery, Nix opened a beer and Taer opened the sketchpad. Taer hoped for text more illuminating than Molly Metropolis's had been. The sketchpad disappointed her, however. Berliner never wrote. He drew, and he only drew maps. On each page, Berliner had drawn a crude street map and dated it. Occasionally the maps were labeled with street names, or landmarks.

---

[*] Thanks to Berliner allowing me to briefly examine his sketchpad and for relaying the weapon's details, as I didn't have access to the firearm.

Berliner also drew a series of symbols on each map, though he didn't provide a key for what the symbols meant.

Finding the sketchpad indecipherable, Nix and Taer's conversation devolved into perhaps their most significant argument. They had been fighting so often because, as Nix puts it, "sometimes you get into a mode where you're fighting all the time and the only times that feel honest and passionate are the times you're fighting." The gigantic blowup, which Taer recounted in her journal and Nix explained to me in detail, ended their pattern of argument and reconciliation that characterized the earliest part of their relationship.

The meat of the fight was about Nix and Taer's personal safety. Though Nix's mother and her family were devoted hunters, Nix, like her father, hated guns; the appearance of one was enough to put her off entirely. She wanted to destroy Berliner and Molly Metro's notebooks, flush the pages down the toilet, and never think about them again. She tried to do so. In response, Taer grabbed Berliner's sketchpad from the vanity and ran out of the bathroom. Nix pursued her. They tussled over the sketchpad; Taer tripped over a cabinet drawer and fell hard, smashing her head on the wall and floor, and tearing open the skin on her elbow.

Taer's fresh injuries chastised Nix. She brought out the Neosporin again and apologized profusely. According to Taer: "I wouldn't have cared if I broke my wrist, she was so guilty about hurting me, it fixed everything. She's going to help me look for Molly!" Nix agreed to let Taer call Berliner again in recompense for making her fall. Again, they called from Nix's phone, but discovered the number had been disconnected.

Nix told me the story of the break-in sitting at my kitchen table, while the sounds of the street blew in through open windows. Nix smoked, a habit she had picked up from Berliner after the Lake Michigan incident. Left-handed, her smoking emphasized her missing fingers. I think she always took off her prosthetic fingers before coming to see me.

"After we called Nick and found out his phone was disconnected, we were just tired. We went back to bed, and I was rubbing her back—she liked that—and telling her all about Molly. She liked that, too. Molly had this thing, where she'd buy a lot of books on a subject, and sit on the floor, and surround herself with the books, and read little bits from all of them. When she was trying to learn about something. We didn't usually have time for her to do that, so it didn't actually happen all that often. She hadn't had time for it for months, by the end of it. But early on—before 'New Vogue Riche' came out, especially—she had a few days where she could just, you know, 'learn stuff' on the floor, with all these books. I was telling Taer about that, and she asked me what kind of things Molly liked to learn about. The only one that I could remember was the Situationists. She loved reading about the Situationists. Do you know about them?"

I did, but I asked Nix to explain.

"They were this political group in the 1960s, sort of led by Guy Debord, and they were interested in the city and culture. Anyway, I was telling Cait about this and as I was talking to her, I realized: every time I'd seen Molly do her book thing, I mean, every single time, she was researching the Situationists. There wasn't some other topic. There wasn't even a plethora of topics. I hadn't noticed before because I had my own work to do, but I'd gone for months thinking Molly was a dilettante, but she actually had this razor-sharp focus. She might've even tried to make me think she was treating things lightly, so I wouldn't start to wonder why she was so interested in the Situationists, I don't know.

"So, obviously, Cait was into figuring out what was going on with the Situationists. She didn't have anything else to do. And that was one way Cait and Molly were alike. Razor-sharp focus, I mean. Tunnel vision. Like that Justin Timberlake song." Nix sang a few bars: "*I've got tunnel vision / for you.*" Her singing voice leaves something to be desired.

The morning after the break-in, Taer woke Nix up early. She bought Nix a cup of coffee and they took the Blue Line to the giant Harold Washington Library Center in the Loop. Taer checked out a dozen books on the Situationists; she and Nix carried them home in two heavy backpacks. Taer wanted to read all the books Molly had read.

Back at her apartment, Taer sat on the floor of her bedroom, spread the books out all around her. Nix took a picture, told Taer she looked very Metro-esque, then napped. Taer started devouring the Situationists texts.

Chapter ⑤

In July 1957, in the middle of a warm but dry summer, activist and aestheticist Guy Debord "summoned,"* eight compatriots to a small town in northern Italy called Cosio d'Arroscia. Attendee Ralph Rumney took some candid black-and-white photographs of the group on the city's streets. In Cosio d'Arroscia, all the buildings are made out of stone, all the doorways are narrow, and the shadows cling to the structures like skin.† The city looks so much like a rocky labyrinth that anyone would think the eight women and men chose

---

* "Summoned" comes from Situationist Ralph Rumney's account of the trip.

† *Cyrus's description of Cosio d'Arroscia is partially based on his examination of Rumney's pictures, and partially based on his own visit to the small city in the summer of 2011. At the time, Cyrus was in a long-distance relationship with his partner, Woodyard. The two had spent every summer together in New York, and their summers were an important cornerstone in their relationship. Cyrus chose to spend two and half weeks in Italy finishing his book during the summer of 2011. That constituted the first time Cyrus had chosen his work over his relationship, which Woodyard considered a betrayal. Cyrus considered the trip a test. He later regretted gambling with his relationship. If he had known what would happen, he would've conducted himself differently, and you wouldn't be reading this book. —CD*

Cosio d'Arroscia because the design of the city fell in line with the group's ideas about architecture, but the draw of the location was at least partially free room and board. They stayed at a hotel run by one of their aunts. The meals were provided; the wine was cheap.

The eight were all members of one or another of several prominent avant-garde groups active at the time: the Letterist International, the International Movement for an Imaginist Bauhaus, and the London Psychogeographical Association. The goal of their trip was to combine the three groups into a single entity and after a week of drinking, writing, talking, and wandering the streets, they christened their newly formed avant-garde group the Situationist International (SI). For several years, the SI pursued an aesthetics-based approached to social change, but by 1968 the Situationists had transitioned into a completely political group; their early creative concerns had been shed like an ill-fitting coat. The Situationists' role in the political unrest that gripped French students and factory workers in May of 1968 has been well documented, but is not of interest here. It is with the SI's early years that Molly Metropolis concerned herself.

The group's beginnings were inauspicious, but their aims weren't modest. Debord and the Situationists wanted to tear cities down and rebuild them; they wanted to remake the world. As with so many of us, the Situationists didn't achieve their lofty goals.

Cosio D'Arroscia barely remembers the Situationists. The bar where Debord and the others drank still stands and is still owned by the same family, who commemorate their Situationist heritage with a little plaque outside the bathroom. That plaque constitutes the entirety of the town's acknowledgement of the origins of the SI. In the 1980s, the city had gained control of the old hotel the Situationists stayed in and converted it to a nursing home for the town's rapidly aging population. There are no other Situationists sites to visit.* Ultimately, the bar and hotel don't matter; only the streets matter.†

In the early days of the SI, Debord focused on aesthetic social practices. In late 1950s and early 1960s, in the hours between midnight and sunrise, the Situationists roamed the streets of Paris. They drank wine as they walked, in pairs or in groups of six or seven, getting drunk and talking about architecture. The SI's drunken nighttime walks through the streets of Paris were not a pastime, but "playful-constructive behavior."‡ They put a high value on playfulness and took their walking very seriously.

The walking groups could contain any of the core members of the Situationists: Asger Jorn, who funded much of the Situationists' activities even after being expelled from the group for being an artist; Ivan Chtcheglov, a wild, charismatic, beautiful, and precocious twenty-three-year-old who was known for his explosive personality, and was at one point committed to a mental hospital by his wife (where he received shock therapy); Jacqueline de Jong, a poised and sharp student of fashion and drama, who was born somewhere in the Netherlands but fled the country as a child with her parents just before the Nazi occupation; Elena Verrone and Verrone's husband Piero Simondo, whose aunt owned the Cosio D'Arroscia hotel; Constant Nieuwenhuys, who always referred to himself only as

---

* *During his trip, Cyrus took a photo of the plaque in the pub, it says, in French of course: "Guy Debord and the Situationists drank here during the founding of the Situationist International." Cyrus also visited the nursing home that had once been the SI's hotel, and reports that it smelled like old bandages and rotting seaweed. —CD*

† I walked the same streets as Debord and the others. Walking with them, separated only by time, was much like writing this book. Any place the Situationists had walked, so had Molly, then Taer, then me. I followed them—away from Woodyard, but toward the end of this book. [*This footnote was the last thing Cryus wrote when putting together this book. —CD*]

‡ Simon Sadler, *The Situationist City* (Cambridge: MIT Press, 1998), 77.

75

Constant (like Cher or Madonna) and was the immensely gifted artist and architect of the Situationist city New Babylon; Michèle Bernstein, Debord's wife and the Situationists' most gifted writer, who authored some of the Situationists' most important and coherent statements of purpose; and of course, Debord himself.

Debord was tall, wore round glasses, and was more charismatic than physically attractive. He had a loud voice. He liked to drink and argue passionately, preferably at the same time. A French news broadcaster once asked Bernstein to describe Debord's best attribute and she deadpanned, "He wears a suit very well." Debord's clothing was often rumpled, stained, and torn.

A decade younger than most of the Situationists' other prominent members (not including Chtcheglov, who wrote some of the movement's most influential early pieces, then missed many of the group's pivotal moments while institutionalized), Debord asserted his influence on the Situationists through the force of his personality. As a leader, he was both aggressive and enigmatic. He was also charming, well-read, and gentle when he needed to be, but he was ambitious and never backed down from a fight. He devoted himself singularly to the group from the first days of its existence and expected everyone else to have the same level of commitment. Though some historians have argued that Constant or Jorn or even young, crazy Chtcheglov really steered the Situationists during their early years, most people consider Debord the leader of the avant-garde both logistically and ideologically. Through sheer force of will, creating a cult of personality around himself and his writing (each essay carefully edited by Bernstein), he conquered history. When most people think of the Situationists, they think of Debord. It was Debord who wanted to tear down the cities and build new ones.

Understanding the Situationists' desire to remake the city begins with World War II, specifically with the bombings carried out all over Europe by both the Allies and the Luftwaffe. After the war, huge swathes of European cities had to be rebuilt from rubble. An architectural design movement called "modernism" or "functionalism," which favored function and rationality over all else, dominated the rebuilding process. As functionalism took over, art and spontaneity were leeched out of city planning. Even in cities like Paris that didn't sustain much wartime damage, urban planners developed and implemented new architectural techniques for moving people around like products on a belt in a factory.

One of the first Situationist writings, "Formulary for the New Urbanism," written by Chtcheglov and heavily based on Debord's ideas,* described this "disease" of functionalism and the Situationists' cure: *unitary urbanism.* Unitary urbanism is the Situationist social theory that art and the movements of everyday urban life shouldn't be separated into isolated sectors, but continually mixed together as a way of life. By collapsing the boundaries between art and life, work and leisure, public and private, the Situationists wanted to recast the city as a space of fun and play.

In his fantastic analysis of the Situationists' early years *The Situationist City*, Simon Sadler discusses the Situationists' desire to "collectively rethink the city." To fully escape and undo functionalism,

---

* "Formulary for a New Urbanism" was actually first written and published in 1953, four years before the Situationist International formed, when Chtcheglov and Debord were both members of a predecessor to the Situationist International called the Letterist International. Chtcheglov was only nineteen at the time of writing, and he published the piece under his pseudonym Gilles Ivain as part of a continued effort to devalue the relevance of a single author of an idea. Although the piece received high praise when it was first published, the 1958 reprinting of the essay in the first issue Situationist journal *Internationale Situationniste* is what gave the essay a lasting influence and historical relevance. Think of Blondie's 1978 hit "Hanging on the Telephone." Many people didn't know that song is a cover, originally written by Jack Lee and recorded in 1976 for his power pop band The Nerves. The quality of the original recording—and it really is very good—is overshadowed by the overwhelming response to the cover. Without the success of the Blondie version, it's possible that The Nerves, and their fantastic, perpetually relevant song of universal yearning, would've been forgotten by all but music obsessives.

Debord and the SI imagined building a brand new city in the Situationist image, which would eventually span the whole globe. The Situationists weren't trying to do something simple; they wanted to change the whole world in a massive way. "They were at war with the whole world, but lightheartedly."* As an answer to their hunger for a new way to live, in the mid- to late 1950s Constant began developing the plans for this world-changing city, which Debord named New Babylon.

Constant was born in Amsterdam in 1920. His father was a corporate manager and his mother was a music lover. Constant took up the violin at age ten and continued to play until his death. Debord met Constant through Jorn, the Situationist whose art-world success funded most of the SI's exploits.

In 1957, when the SI formed, Constant was in the midst of his second marriage (of an eventual four). He had a receding hairline, a sharp wit, and by all accounts smiled often. Debord and Constant's friendship bloomed over long stretches of drinking and talking at late night cafés when they were in the same city, and over the exchange of letters when they were apart. They both dedicated themselves passionately to their various artistic and political projects, and for a time they got along very well because of that shared enthusiasm.

Riffing off Debord's ideas, Constant's New Babylon was the only large-scale project to fully incorporate all the Situationist ideas about aesthetics. Constant believed architecture should be playful, and respond to desire rather than urban efficiency. In New Babylon, no one was treated like a statistic on a Traffic & Congestion report. Instead, New Babylon was *"une autre ville pour autre vie"*—another city for another life.

Constant designed models of sections of New Babylon; he de-

---

* McKenzie Wark, *50 Years of Recuperation of the Situationist International* (New York: Princeton Architectural Press, 2008), 7.

picted New Babylon in paintings and sketches. He also collaborated with Debord to create collage art, the most famous of which is called "The Situationist City," which served as an aesthetic guideline for New Babylon. Constant also wrote frequently about New Babylon for *Internationale Situationniste.*

These collected renderings showed New Babylon as a giant playground, a city whose shape was constantly shifting because inhabitants would build and rebuild constantly, using lightweight building materials, like future plastics or fiberglass. The continual building of the city would be like a huge game, with all New Babylonians in a state of perpetual play and leisure. Work, commerce, and culture as we know it would dissolve. The continual game of world building would dominate life.

For New Babylon's actual physical spaces, Constant designed transitory buildings, which would shift and change based on the whims and desires of the inhabitants: a "restless architecture." All the residents of New Babylon would engage in an endless drift, their lives defined by an equally endless chain of encounters, both between themselves and other drifters, and themselves and the architecture of the city around them.

Mark Wigley gives the best description of the city in an essay for *Architectural Design* magazine:

New Babylon is to be a covered city, suspended high above the ground on huge columns. All automobile traffic is isolated on the ground plane, beneath which trains and fully automated factories are buried. Enormous multilevel structures . . . are strung together in a chain that spreads across the landscape. This "endless expanse" of interior space is artificially lit and air-conditioned. Its inhabitants are given access to powerful, ambience-creating resources to construct their own space whenever and wherever they desire. The qualities of each space can be adjusted. Light, acoustics, colour, ventilation, texture, temperature and moisture are infinitely variable. Moveable floors, partitions, ramps, ladders, bridges and stairs are used to construct "veritable labyrinths of the most heterogeneous forms" in which desires continuously interact. Sensuous space may rise from action but also generate it: "New Babylonians play a game of their own designing, against a backdrop they have designed themselves."*

Constant intended New Babylon to carefully interact with the structure of the cities and non-urban areas it was suspended above. He and Debord planned to integrate the first vestiges of New Babylon architecture with some existing place—they didn't mention exactly where, or even vaguely where—and then spread it outwards. In the *Internationale Situationniste,* a writer in an unattributed essay floated the idea of building a base camp, possibly on the Alle des Cygnes, a long, narrow uninhabited island on the Seine. The island connects two bridges, the Pont de Bir-Hakein and Pont de Grenelle. Using the bridges, the Situationists could venture into the actual city, drifting, creating situations, and slowly converting the areas around the Alle des Cygnes until they became part of New Babylon—and so on, until Europe, Asia, and Africa disappeared into New Babylon. Then New Babylon could venture into Alaska, via Russia (perhaps sailing there on some kind of New Babylonian fleet, though the author or authors of the unsigned article weren't specific on that count).† Debord and Constant were adamant that New Babylon wouldn't sequester itself from the rest of the world, but rather integrate itself continuously. He didn't want to create an isolated utopia, which he called "holiday resorts." He didn't want to be

---

* Mark Wigley, "The Great Urbanism Game," in *Architectural Design* 41, No. 3 (2001): 9.

† Although the author of the piece was never identified, more likely than not Bernstein wrote it, or else she had a strong editing hand in it.

known as that kind of failure. "New Babylon is a *whole world* at play"* [*italics mine*].

However, New Babylon was also doomed from the beginning, because Constant gestured only vaguely toward the practical matter of building the city. He never explained, in practical real-world terms, what the "ambience-creating recourses" would be. He never described the specific mechanisms that would power and control the city. He only vaguely referred to a co-operative system of repair and public safety. The "how" didn't matter to Constant or to Debord at the time, only the ideas.

The SI also suffered early on from logistical complications: too many strong personalities living in cities and countries too far flung. Conceptually, they could never rally together behind one clear model or goal. Jorn was too preoccupied with his successful career as an artist; Chtcheglov went insane and, besides that, had all the fickleness of youth. Constant wanted to eradicate all artistic work from the moment, while at the same time diving head first into New Babylon, which some members thought of as an art project.

Debord spent an inordinate amount of time policing the minutia of language about the Situationists. From the first issue of the *Internationale Situationniste*: "There is no such thing as situationism." In a letter to Simondo, Debord delivered a threat about the misuse of language: "In my *Report*, I only used the word 'situationism,' once— in quotes—to denounce it in advance as one of the stupidities that our adversaries will naturally use in opposition to us. To my knowledge, this term has never been used elsewhere (neither in writing, nor verbally), by any of us. You are the first to pose its existence in your last letter. Happily, it was to oppose it!"† I shudder to think

---

* Guy Debord, *Correspondence: The Foundation of the Situationist International (June 1957–August 1960)*, trans. Stuart Kendall and John McHale (Los Angeles: Semiotext(e), 2009), 12.

† *Correspondence*, 42.

of Debord's response if Simondo hadn't been so explicit in his opposition.

The SI had filled their ranks with artists, then when those artists focused on art, they were accused of undermining the basis of unitary urbanism. Constant criticized Debord for not guiding the artists with a firmer hand, and the two men began to squabble. Debord expelled several artist members of the SI, including Debord's close friend Giuseppe "Pinot" Gallizo, who had the audacity to achieve art-world success while referring to himself as a Situationist. As soon as the gallery owners started calling Pinot's work "Situationist art," an oxymoron according to Debord, Pinot was out.

The expulsions didn't satisfy Constant. When Debord began to voice doubts that New Babylon could ever be made and decided to shift the New Babylon project to more metaphorical grounds, Constant quit the SI. Debord and Constant broke up badly, over letters. Their correspondence became passive-aggressive, then aggressive, then it stopped all together. Debord went on with the Situationist International; Constant continued to work on his plans for New Babylon long after they lost their vitality. Without the SI's appetite for utopia to give New Babylon life, the city started feeling more like Atlantis than NYC.

In the late 1960s, Constant wearily allowed the New Babylon project to wind down. In an interview with architectural journalist Rem Koolhaas for Dutch weekly *Haagse Post,* Constant said, with just a hint of despair: "I am very much aware of the fact that New Babylon cannot be realized now."* After Constant left, Debord shepherded the SI away from play and toward politics. By 1964, Debord was "embarrassed by 'the fantasies left over from the old artist milieu.' "†

The SI fell apart in the dawn of the '70s. In the early days of the

---

* "The City of the Future," in *Haagse Post* 102, No. 12 (1966): 126.
† *The Situationist City,* 12.

SI, Debord had written to Pinot, "Not being declared, the [Situationist International] cannot be officially dissolved."* It could, though, stop functioning—and it did. Debord stopped writing. Various Neo-Situationist sects persisted until the early 1980s, but Debord stayed silent. He aged bitterly; he considered his life's work a failure. In 1984, Debord was a suspect in the murder of his friend, publisher and patron Gérard Lebovici. The Police Nationale never brought Debord up on charges, but the ensuing scandal pushed Debord even further away from public life. He and Bernstein divorced and he married someone who had never been a Situationist, a poet named Alice Becker-Ho. When old friends would visit, they were met only by Becker-Ho; Debord refused to leave his room to meet with them.†

In 1987, Paris's museum of contemporary art, the Centre George Pompidou, in conjunction with the London-based Institute of Contemporary Arts, organized an exhibition about "situationism." They invited Debord to speak at the French opening in 1988, but he refused, utterly insulted. He wrote the curators of the exhibit a letter brimming with vitriol, concluding, "If you think you like the situationists, you are fucking wrong. There is nothing more antisituationist than putting false situationist 'art' in a museum. You are cunts, and I hope your buildings fall apart."‡ Following the exhibitions,

---

* *Correspondence*, 145.

† *While Cyrus was writing about Debord's decline, his relationship with Woodyard ended. Apparently, when Woodyard came to visit campus, during a small gathering of faculty, Cyrus spilled a glass of red wine on Woodyard's signed copy of* The Collected Stories of Lydia Davis, *then called Lydia Davis "fake profound." According to my ex-roommate Rachel (who overheard an adjunct professor mention it to her boyfriend while Rachel was waiting for the adjunct's office hours to begin), Woodyard thought Cyrus had spilled the wine intentionally and then Cyrus passive-aggressively brought up the fact that Woodyard hadn't yet published a book. When I spoke to Cyrus weeks later, he told me he and Woodyard broke up on that trip, while Woodyard was still on campus. —CD*

‡ Thanks to Woodyard for help with the translation, and for the Centre George Pompidou for providing a copy of the letter.

interest in the Situationists increased exponentially, and has never really waned.

On December 1, 1994, Debord shot himself through the heart. Disturbingly, his death was followed by the "copycat" suicides of two of his friends, his publisher Gérard Voitey on December 3 and the writer Roger Stéphane on December 4.

For a few years, "situationism" was quiet. Then, in the late 1990s, a secretive political activist group emerged out of Chicago, calling themselves the "New Situationists." They spouted a bastardized and modernized version of Debord and the Situationists' basic critique of the Spectacle and consumerist culture. They functioned in absolute secrecy and pursued invisibility until, like the original Situationists, the New Situationists were brought down by their own politics. In late 2001, in response to the "fascist government response to the 9/11 attacks," "blatant presidential war-mongering," and "disgusting attempts of corporations to capitalize on a national tragedy," the New Situationists planned a series of bombings at various Chicago L stations. The bombings were planned for the middle of the night, when the stations were closed; the New Situationists meant to take no lives, but destroy transportation only. Eleven members of the New Situationists set off bombs in various L stations throughout the city; Berliner's girlfriend Marie-Hélène Kraus was one of the bombers. In her station, a drunk and passed out security guard slept through the fire alarm Kraus set off to make sure the subway stations were completely empty, and he died.

Remarkably, despite the legal proceedings and media frenzy that followed the bombings, only three of the members of the New Situationists were ever publically identified: Kraus, Berliner, and a man named David Wilson. None of them could be persuaded, legally or otherwise, to divulge the names of the other members. Berliner, Wilson, and Kraus were all arrested; the Chicago DA's office handled the criminal prosecution, while the FBI came in to look for the other members of the New Situationists.

Wilson served eighteen months in jail for refusing to answer questions at a Grand Jury trial at which he had been subpoenaed to testify. Because he was still seventeen years old at the time of sentencing, Berliner served five months in a juvenile detention facility for the same reason. Kraus was charged with manslaughter and the destruction of public property. Charges of conspiracy to commit a terrorist activity originally brought against Kraus were dropped due to the court's inability to produce any conspirators. Berliner and Wilson both had alibis proving they weren't involved in the bombings, which held up in court.

The media story on the New Situationists focused on the group's "cult of silence"*; many people were upset that the FBI found no way to force Kraus and her two fellow terrorists to name their co-conspirators. Berliner, Kraus, and Wilson pled ignorance; they insisted that the New Situationists always maintained absolutely secrecy, hiding their real names and identities even from each other, except David Wilson, who, as the New Situationist "Public Relations Liaison," made his name known, but was kept out of any "real" New Situationist business, whatever that was. He also claimed not to know the names of any other New Situationists, though they all knew his.

During Kraus's trial, the District Attorney of Chicago asked her questions about the identity of the other New Situationists. In response, Kraus paraphrased Debord: "New Situationism cannot exist because there is no dogmatic doctrine that is called 'Situationism.' There is only the possibility of the creation of Situationists that follow a certain pattern." When she said the word "Situationism," Kraus used air quotes.

Following a well-argued motion from the highly regarded attorney hired by Kraus's father, Kraus's trial remained closed to the public. The judge on the case gave Wilson, Berliner, and Kraus's

---

* As CNN called it. —CD

family permission to attend. Wilson showed up about half the time, whenever something interesting was bound to happen. Berliner came every day and watched every second of the proceedings.

The trial didn't go well for the prosecution. The defense proved that the bombs had been built by an amateur, not a professional, which helped refute the conspiracy charges. They showed that New Situationists had never threatened or carried out any acts of violence or terrorism before, and didn't seem to be planning any others. Only one subway station suffered serious damage; the staircase was completely destroyed, the ceiling caved in, and the tracks ripped out of their hinges in a few places. The defense also presented ample evidence that neither Kraus nor her nebulous New Situationist colleagues intended to kill anyone.

Kraus was found guilty on one count of murder in the second degree and one count of criminally malicious property damage. She was found not guilty on six other property damage counts, for the subway stations the other New Situationists had bombed, for which she wasn't present. The presiding judge sentenced her to life in prison, with the first possibility of parole after twenty-five years.

After the trial and sentencing were complete and the media firestorm died down, the FBI decided the New Situationists no longer constituted a real threat against America and left Chicago. The government had more important terrorists to chase, ones that weren't white, blond, suburban girls. While most of the general public moved on, a few people remained obsessed with discovering the identities of the other New Situationists: some true crime nerds, people interested in the minutiae of Chicago politics, and a teenager from New York named Miranda Young.[*]

The fourteen-year-old proto–Molly Metropolis lived in the North Loop and matriculated at the Chicago Lab Schools, one of

[*] *This particular piece of information about Molly's teenage obsession comes from Berliner. Cyrus stitched together the story of her upbringing using information from Molly's magazine profiles and interviews with her family and former teachers. —CD*

the best high schools in the state. According to Molly Metropolis lore, at this time in her life Molly was working as a waitress at a now-closed Italian restaurant in Lincoln Park, using a fake I.D. to get into dance clubs North of the Loop, singing Fiona Apple–esque pop songs while accompanying herself on a small keyboard, starring in a school production of *Bye Bye Birdie* (which her theater teacher agreed to gender-swap just so Molly could play "Connie" Birdie), and consuming intoxicating quantities of *Sex and the City*. Molly never told people like James Laksy, author of her first major profile in *The New York Times Magazine*, that along with all the musical theater and underage tattoos, Molly fantasized about becoming a member of the New Situationists.

Molly didn't condone the June subway bombings. In surviving AIM chats with her best friend Audrey Benton, Molly disavowed the New Situationists' violent tactics; her lofty goal was to take over the New Situationists and steer them toward more productive ends. However, Molly's fascination with the Weather Underground of her time was nothing compared to the full-on obsession she developed when she started reading about the original Situationists and Debord.

According to Berliner, *détournement* is the first Situationist idea that Molly Metropolis latched onto, like a gateway drug into a deeper, darker world. *Détournement* is "both the *appropriation* and the *correction* of culture as common property" [*italics mine*]. *Détournement* isn't unlike today's remix and meme cultures, which take pieces of culture, like pop songs or photos of famous actors and actresses, and shove them next to or on top of other pieces of culture or cultural references, to create something new. Sometimes these newly created objects fall into the comedic realm, like the popular Tumblr blog *Feminist Ryan Gosling*, which took an already existing Ryan Gosling "Hey Girl" meme (photoshopping various Ryan Gosling–esque sentiments onto pictures of Gosling, preceded by "Hey girl," as if Gosling was speaking these things directly to his legions of female

87

fans) and added academic feminist rhetoric. Other times, these new cultural items are created with a political purpose. Elisa Kreisinger, a self-described "pop-culture pirate," creates remix videos of popular TV shows, re-cutting scenes from *Mad Men* and *Sex and the City* to reform the narratives, creating new feminist and queer stories out of the source materials.

Musicians like Greg Gillis, who creates remix music under the name Girl Talk, and writers like David Shields in his book *Reality Hunger,* are modern *détourneurs.* Molly practiced *détournement* every time she drew a gold circle on her forehead, explicitly referencing David Bowie's Ziggy Stardust phase, or stole vocal tricks from Britney Spears, copying the iconic "oh baby, baby" that opened Britney's first very single ". . . Baby One More Time" for the bridge of her *Cause Célèbrety* album cut "Rewind, Repeat."

The Situationists began practicing *détournement* by *détourning* literature, political theory, visual art, and film. Usually they practiced *détournement* for political reasons, but occasionally they wielded the practice for personal causes. Once, when Debord and the SI were low on funds, Debord asked Bernstein to write a commercial novel with the intention of making a bit of money to fund further Situationist endeavors. She called her two novels of semi-autobiographical fiction "*détournements* of literature, life and love." (They're also delightful little reads, though somewhat maligned by both the author and her husband.)

The Situationists took *détournement* very seriously. They practiced what they preached, freely offering up the contents of their published writing in the *Internationale Situationniste* for anyone to use and/or alter, without consent or acknowledgement. *Détournement* wasn't plagiarism, stealing an idea to pass it off as one's own. Nor was it quotation, which acknowledged a boundary between various elements an artist or writer wanted to fuse together. *Détournement* was like welding: two pieces of steel melted, reformed into one singular object, then cooled to solidify the bonds, rendering the prior separation between the previously disparate pieces not just invisible, but also irrelevant.

Détournement was also a political act against corrupt culture, which they called "The Spectacle." To *détourn* maps and novels was to raid culture, like politically motivated vandalism, like graffiti. In Debord's most famous text, *The Society of the Spectacle*, he described a world and culture corrupted by capitalism, sponsored by business and bureaucracy, creating complacency in the masses rather than creativity. The Spectacle removes authenticity from creation, Debord wrote, and needs to be destroyed. *Détournement* was the best weapon against it.

Reading *The Society of the Spectacle* and Debord's various writings about *détournement,* Molly took special note of something Debord wrote just before he began to shift the Situationists away from aesthetics and toward politics: "To reach this superior cultural creation—what we call the Situationist game—we now think it is necessary to be an active force in the actual sphere of this era's culture (and not on the fringes of it, as we cheerfully were ...)"* When Debord talked about being an "active force in the actual sphere" of culture, he meant the Situationists should become a political action group. When Molly read it, she thought about becoming a pop star.

Molly recognized the Situationists' somewhat hypocritical relationship with mass culture. On one hand, they distained and disparaged the Spectacle, and considered celebrity the human incarnation of it. In *Society of the Spectacle*, Debord wrote:

> The celebrity, the spectacular representation of a living human being, embodies this banality by embodying the image of a possible role. Being a star means specializing in the seemingly lived ...The agent of the spectacle placed on stage as a star is the opposite of the individual, the enemy of the

---

* *Correspondence*, 164.

individual in himself as well as in others . . . The admirable people in whom the system personifies itself are well known for not being what they are.*

On the other hand, the Situationists felt the need to stay abreast of popular culture so they could *détourn* it. As Odile Passot puts it in the Afterword to Semiotext(e)'s translation of Bernstein's first novel *All the King's Horses,* "the Situationists themselves were avid spectators, especially of certain films." In the early years of the SI, when they still talked about building cities, Debord, Bernstein, and Constant discussed using mass-cultural tropes to create Situationist desires in the public. They also discussed the problematic hierarchy between "high" and "low" culture, ultimately disavowing the idea of highbrow versus lowbrow, which indirectly endorses the pop culture in general.†

Molly Metro considered the Situationists' two-faced relationship with pop culture an important part of their ultimate aesthetic failure. She concluded that their semi-disavowal of mass culture was what relegated them to the fringes forever. To truly shift the desires of the public, you had to be a global figure that didn't have to face term limits. As a budding singer-songwriter, Molly concluded that in order to create a Situationist world, one would first have to become a pop star, a one-woman "active force." This is part of what makes her disappearance so baffling. If her ultimate goal, as she wrote several times in the notebook Taer perused and copied from, was to finish the work Debord and Constant never completed by

---

* Guy Debord, *Society of the Spectacle* (Detroit: Black & Red, 1983), section 60.

† Molly's early artistic output, especially the images of herself she and others produced in the months before and after *Cause Célèbrety* was released, also concerned itself with the problematic distinction between highbrow and lowbrow. One of my favorite images of Molly Metropolis is an animated gif of her wearing a white V-neck T-shirt with words projected onto her stomach, one after another, forming the phrase OPERA IS LOWBROW, EAT POP INSTEAD. Molly looks very young in the gif; it was built from a video she shot in late 2007 or early 2008.

remaking the world in a Situationist image, why did she disappear at the height of her powers?

To begin realizing her Situationist goals, Molly Metropolis first had to make herself into a star. She began working with a producer named Davin Karl, who had written and produced songs for Britney Spears and Kelly Rowland. Karl suggested she change her persona from a Fiona Apple disciple to a dance-pop artist. Molly dove into the challenge, relying heavily on *détournement*. To build an identity authentic in its artifice, she developed part-Britney coquettishness, combined with what Molly called a "dirty Outrun Electro synthesizers" aesthetic, combined with Freddie Mercury, combined with Holly Golightly. Although somewhat influenced by R&B, Molly worked hard to distance herself from the genre by heavily borrowing from disco instead, knowing many people at the record companies would rather lump her in with the black women who sing R&B than add her to the sable of white girls who sing pop.

Molly created a new self with a new image, the way she hoped the world would remake itself into one huge Situationist city. At the time, Molly was still adolescent, a teenager, and still discovering her identity; like so many of us during our teenage years, her personality was still in flux. Molly Metropolis was what Miranda Young wanted to be, so she became it.

As she began remaking herself into Molly Metropolis, she read about Debord's friend Pinot. As a "Situationist Artist," Pinot produced something called industrial paintings, which the Situationists endorsed before Pinot's expulsion from the SI. Industrial paintings weren't made using machines, but were created to feel repetitive and mechanic, to undermine the idea of the "unique gesture." It was an extension of *détournement* and undermining of the authorship by refusing to use bylines in *Internationale Situationniste*. Molly decided the musical version of industrial painting was the pop song. She didn't just allude to her influences; she invoked them bodily. She *détourned*. As Molly wrote in an e-mail to Berliner on October 26, 2009, "I consider the first year of my career as a sort of long term *détournement* experiment and what I learned is that at some point the *détourned* thing becomes un-*détourned* and just is. No doubt this is the point, and I've succeeded." Though immodest, Molly Metropolis was right; she had succeeded. As media studies scholar Kate Durbin, founder of the academic journal *Molly Skyscraper*, puts it, during the era of her debut album *Cause Célèbrety*, "Molly literalized and embodied the spectacle."*

In making herself into Molly Metropolis, she became much better at *détournement* than Debord or the other Situationists had been. At the time of her disappearance, Molly had already had more of an impact on the culture of the globe than the Situationists ever had, or ever would achieve.

---

* Kate Durbin, "From *Célèbrety* to *Apocalypse*: Molly Metropolis and the Evolution of Identity," *Molly Skyscraper*, December 29, 2009; mollyjournal.blogspot.com/2009/12 /from-celebrety-to-apocalypse.html.

Chapter ⑥

After Molly's disappearance, the fifty dancers, musicians, roadies, assistants, and "Governing Council" members that made up Molly's tour machine drifted around Chicago for a few weeks. SDFC put them up in a Holiday Inn while everyone waited for news. In late January, when hope that Molly would reemerge was still alive, but the financial burden of supporting her tour became too frustrating for SDFC to stomach, the record company dismissed the crew. Berliner's dancer ex-girlfriend, Irene Davis, took the Amtrak to Romulus, where her parents had retired. She planned on staying for a few days, but while she was visiting her mother slipped, fell down a flight of stairs, and broke her neck. Davis remained in Michigan after the funeral.

Meanwhile, Taer read about the Situationists for days before she got bored and tired of research. She liked absorbing the same knowledge as Molly Metropolis, but knowing what Molly knew wouldn't help her find Berliner. She pestered Nix for suggestions on how to proceed. Nix proposed that they speak to Davis, because she had dated Berliner for six months. Nix called Davis. Though she refused to talk over the phone or to leave Romulus, Davis agreed to chat with them if they came to her.

Taer and Nix rode north on a freezing Metra train. Taer wrote in her shaky train handwriting: "Gina wants me to stop, but it would feel like I was abandoning [Molly]. I know it's presumptuous to think that she'd want me to be looking for her, or that I have a responsibility to find her, but I feel like I'm in too deep. Even though I'm not really in anything. I mean, I could drop it, but then I would never stop thinking about her."

They checked into a room at the Ramada Romulus and arrived at Davis's parents' small house later that evening. Davis met them at the door wearing a pair of black leggings, a huge knit sweater, and her legwarmers, a staple of any dancer's wardrobe. She wore a circular piece of purple quartz around her neck on a long silver chain, a gift her mother had given her for her sixteenth birthday, and which she had worn almost every day since. Her hair hung loose and tangled around her face, and her eyes were bloodshot. She looked tired and bloated. Davis didn't have the willowy, long-limbed body of a dancer. She was shorter than most and somewhat voluptuous, especially in comparison to the rail-thin bodies dancers usually maintain. Nevertheless, Davis was still incredibly graceful. Each of her movements seemed deliberate to Taer, from the way she poured her fifth glass of wine to the absentminded scratch of an itch on her arm. Taer thought Davis's face was plain, but found her sexual anyway, despite, or perhaps as a result of, the dancer's deep grief over her mother.

The mood in the house was grim and the architecture unforgiving. Berliner later described the house as having "that kind of built-in-the-seventies-under-communist-rule vibe, you know, like, with a bleakness to it, a house that just attacks you with its ugliness." Davis invited Taer and Nix to sit at the glass table in the sparsely decorated kitchen and opened an expensive bottle of wine her father had been saving for a special occasion. Taer turned on her iPhone voice recorder and Davis asked, "So what did Nick do to you? I'm assuming he didn't fuck either of you."

Taer told an abbreviated version of the break-in story, to which Davis replied, "Yeah, I wouldn't put it past him."

Then she coughed out the smoke from one of her mother's Virginia Slims and asked: "So do you want to hear his life story?"

"Yeah," Taer said.

"I know him a little," Nix said.

"Did he tell you about all that weird stuff from his childhood?" Davis asked.

"No," Nix said. "I just met him around the music video sets, or when the tour came to Chicago, you know."

"His life . . ." Davis trailed off.

"Do you need—" Taer began to say, but Davis cut her off.

"I guess I'm inconsequential in a lot of ways," Davis said. "That isn't to say what I've been doing with my life isn't important, but what does it mean to the greater world? Especially now that Molly fucked off—you know what I mean, Gina. You get used to your life meaning something because you're doing something for someone whose life means something. I felt that way when I was dating Nick, too.

"So, yeah, I'm convinced that Nick's life is important because he had this really cinematic childhood. Like, his life fits perfectly with a movie story, youthful rebellion, betrayal, sexual deviance, whatever. The rest of our lives have to be altered in some really significant way to make it into a movie—not Nick."*

•

---

* From a feminist perspective, Taer writes she was bothered by Davis's characterization of her life finding meaning only externally, through her boyfriend.

Nicolas Berliner was born in 1983 in the college town Champaign-Urbana, Illinois.* In 1984, his father, Ronald, left his position as an adjunct professor of Natural History at the University of Illinois for a tenure-track position at the University of Chicago. Ronald moved his family into the city and settled in a spacious, three-level back-house in Lincoln Park.

Berliner entered his teenage years as a gentle, well-mannered child. He preferred reading books to playing sports (although he eventually grew out of his bookishness enough to build the kind of stamina necessary to keep up with Molly Metropolis). He argued but never lost his temper. He liked broccoli without butter or cheese. His parents took hundreds of photos of him and catalogued them, extensively, in photo albums. They took him to museums and bought him new books every weekend for his "personal library," the bookcase in his basement bedroom.

On June 28, 1998, when Berliner was fifteen years old, his father died suddenly in a four-car pile up on I-94. Perhaps it's reductive to attribute all of Berliner's subsequent actions to the impact of his father's death on his psyche; that kind of semi-psychoanalytic over-simplification is a terrible way of assessing the labyrinth of a person's emotional life. On the other hand, when Berliner's father died, his whole life changed.

Berliner's mother, Dana, previously a stay-at-home mom, found a job at a small advertising firm. His maternal grandmother, Helen Raulson, moved into the backhouse to watch Berliner in the afternoons after school and to help out around the house. An observant Roman Catholic, Raulson quickly became active in the local Catholic congregation; Dana, who had mostly ignored her religious upbringing since she met her secular husband in her early twenties, returned to the church.

---

* *The story of Berliner's life is culled from Taer's recording of her and Nix's conversation with Davis, as well as from interviews Cyrus conducted with Berliner and his family.* —CD

While his mother found God, Berliner began taking aimless walks through the neighborhood. At first, he walked down the same blocks over and over again; then he branched out and walked deeper and deeper into the city. He let himself get lost, then tried to find his way out of the maze of unfamiliar streets into a part of the city he knew. The maze got smaller and smaller as he learned more and more streets. If you know a place, he realized, it's no longer a trap.

Berliner walked for several hours a day. He reacted to loss by trying to turn his slippery memories into something solid. Too mature for his own good, Berliner worried he was young enough that he'd forget his father. He forced himself to go over the happy memories and the dark ones, and all the while he walked and walked and walked.

The first summer after Berliner's father died, Berliner and Raulson lived symbiotically. Raulson initially encouraged his walking, thinking of it as an appropriately stoic and masculine form of mourning. She hated television and video games and loved that Berliner found his entertainment in physical activity. She enrolled Berliner in a summer baseball league and encouraged him to try out for his school's team. Her own son had played for half a decade on the Chicago Cubs' farm team before a knee injury took him out of the game; she still hoped to find a baseballer in the family. Berliner took to the game well enough, easily made St. Ignatius High School's varsity team as a third baseman and sometimes outfielder.

Despite his success with the baseball team, Berliner's school record took a turn for the worse. He skipped classes and refused to tell his mother and grandmother where he was going. His relationship with both his mother and grandmother deteriorated as the school year continued. They occasionally spied him walking with a young woman in her twenties, whom they believed he had started dating. They were terrified the relationship had become sexual. Over the course of the next year, Raulson and Dana worked themselves into a frothy moral panic, which boiled over when Raulson happened to see Berliner in a neighborhood park, laying on a blanket under an architectural archway, making out with the young woman who had long red fingernails. Raulson interrupted them, forced Berliner to empty his pockets, and dragged him home in horror when she saw he was carrying a condom.

Raulson contacted an extremist, deviant order of nuns based in Southern Italy, outside of a small town called Ripacandida. The nuns specialized in cures for homosexuality and off-site exorcisms, a kind of "we'll pray it out of you from afar" program. The matron of the convent was named Sister Ernestina Greco. She diagnosed Berliner with a "second soul," an infestation of the "Wandering Devil." Berliner's walking, Sister Ernestina insisted, was an early symptom of profound religious doubt that would soon overtake every aspect of his life. If it was allowed to stay inside him, he would never be able to settle in one city, town, or country; he would spend thousands of dollars on new material items because his preferences for color and design would change quickly; he would be a fickle lover, and if he ever married, he would leave his spouse without producing any children.

Sister Ernestina reassured Dana and Raulson they were not responsible for Berliner's infection. The death of a parent, especially a father, leaves the body of a male child very susceptible to demonic infestation. The Sister offered to cut her rate of 60 million lira (approximately $30,000) in half because she was moved by the boy's story. Raulson and Dana decided to employ Sister Ernestina and her convent's long-distance exorcism services.

On October 7, 1999, Dana and Raulson added a very small dose of a drug the sisters had provided to the pop Berliner drank with dinner.* He passed out and woke up tied to his bed. His grandmother and mother were sitting on folding chairs against the opposite wall of his bedroom. Raulson phoned the sisters and put

---

* Probably Rohypnol.

them on speakerphone; they began the exorcism ceremony, speaking in Latin and Italian. The only phrase they spoke in English was, "Out, demon!" presumably switching languages so Berliner, Raulson, and Dana could understand them. Drugged and held captive, Berliner shouted back.

The ritual took seven hours to complete, from around 11 p.m. to 6 a.m. By the end, Raulson and Dana were dizzy with sleep deprivation. Raulson especially was physically overwhelmed, and could barely stand. Berliner, however, seemed invigorated. His eyes were clear and wide, his breath was even. His body shined with a layer of cooling sweat. He felt like a marathon runner on the last mile of the race; the adrenaline had taken over his body completely, so he felt no pain.

Sister Ernestina, her voice hoarse from exertion, instructed Dana to untie Berliner. She asked Berliner if he felt different. He responded that he did. "He will still feel the urge to walk, at first," she said, "but the desire will leave him. Remnants of the bad spirit. It can't live inside a person without having some—harmless, I assure you—lingering effects. But a year from now, your son will have no desire to walk, and he will look back on all the walking he did and wonder, 'What was it that made me enjoy walking so much?' The devil is out of him. The devil is out of him."

According to Sister Ernestina and Berliner's mother, he was cured. Berliner has a different interpretation of the events: "The nuns and I fought all night, and they thought they won but they didn't. I won."

With his mother and grandmother's fears allayed, Berliner was free to return to his twenty-five-year-old girlfriend, Marie-Hélène Kraus, and their friends, the New Situationists.

Kraus was born in the U.S. but had been conceived in France, so her mother chose to give her a French name. Her parents were both children of Russian Jewish immigrants, but Kraus didn't identify with her ancestral Jewishness or Russianness. She felt, spiritually, more in common with some semi-fake notion of "the French." In kindergarten, she spent half the year speaking in an exaggerated French accent and convinced the other students she was European. When she got tired of the accent, she told her classmates that she had finally learned to "speak like an American." Her best friend believed she was French until their sophomore year of high school. When she was sixteen, she was hit by a car while roller blading and broke her back. She spent a year in a body cast, during which time she memorized the number of casualties of each battle of the Civil War and read a lot of novels.

In high school, Kraus took great pains to style herself like an old Hollywood movie star, specifically Lauren Bacall, whom she identified with because they both had low voices and small breasts. Kraus smoked cigarettes constantly to emphasize the scratchiness of her voice, and even though she was very tall, she always wore heels to emphasize her height. She was a fashionable dresser with an encyclopedic knowledge of current American politics and popular culture. Perhaps because she spent so much time creating a fantasy around her persona, Kraus had a hard time connecting with people. Although she had many boyfriends during high school and college, she felt that Berliner was the first person to "love her honestly."

Berliner and Kraus met in a coffee shop in Wicker Park shortly after he began walking. At the time, Kraus worked as the Chief Officer in Charge of Recruitment for the recently formed New Situationists. In contradiction to her intentionally ironic title, Kraus's job was to dismiss or divert anyone who seemed captivated by the New Situationists, whether the interest was academic, political, or personal. Her job was difficult; she not only had to convince people to give up their curiosity, she had to convince them that there was nothing to be curious about. "The New Situationists can't exist," she often reminded Berliner. "That was how Debord would've wanted it."*

Well-suited to her position with the New Situationists, Kraus gave a first impression of cold indifference; she rarely developed sentimental attachments. With David Wilson, she was the exception to the New Situationists' program of extreme secrecy. While the two of them would have some level of visibility among the members and to the outside world, every other member remained hidden as much as possible. Later, after the New Situationists made themselves known through their act of domestic terrorism, the State Prosecutors and the public conflated the New Situationists' historic secretiveness with long-term plans for the bombing. However, Kraus always insisted the Chicago Subway Bombings were a flight of fancy, planned in a few months, maximum; the secrecy grew out of an adherence to Situationist principles, plus a flair for theater.

"We were not above some *Eyes Wide Shut*-esque displays. Not the orgy part, but the masks, the passwords, the secrecy. We were feeling very dramatic at the time. We wore animal masks like in some movie," Kraus told Anna Kirkpatrick during a 2009 exclusive video interview for Kirkpatrick's political commentary show on MSNBC. During the same interview, Kirkpatrick asked, "Most of a decade has passed since the New Situationists disbanded. Can you tell us what they were exactly?" Kraus responded, "Anna, what makes you think the New Situationists have disbanded?"†

---

* Actually, that idea is a slight bastardization of Debord's ideas, but the 1990s weren't like the 1960s and certain aspects of Situationist ideas had to be altered to fit a new group of people who were acutely aware they were on the cusp of a new millennium. David Wilson's toast at the New Situationists' New Years Party in 1999 was: "Not just a new year, not just a new decade, not just a new century, a New Situation!" Kraus was the party's DJ; she played Prince.

† The episode aired on September 7, 2009. The entire interview is a fascinating watch—Kraus appears to be half-joking, half-serious at all times. Kirkpatrick can keep up, and she continues to push Kraus to say something substantive about the New Situationists, while fully aware Kraus is using her as the unwilling partner in a piece of Live News Theater.

At the coffee shop where Kraus and Berliner met, the first location of the high-end organic coffee retailer Intelligentsia, Berliner sometimes flirted with a young vegan barista named Anna. He often talked to Anna about his devotion and compulsion to walk. Anna also knew Kraus, a regular at the café, and had seen her reading a book about Debord and psychogeography. When Berliner and Kraus happened to stop in at the same time, Anna suggested Berliner ask Kraus for book recommendations. They spoke for a little while and left separately, but Berliner had already developed a bit of a teenage crush. Berliner walked to the coffee shop when he knew Kraus would be there, acting surprised to see her, and asking her if he could sit down at her table. After a few weeks of this, Berliner dropped the ruse and planned his run-ins with Kraus; they met several times a week to discuss urban planning philosophies and music.

Kraus didn't like Berliner at first, but she never liked anybody at first. She slowly warmed to him, then surprised herself by thinking about the strange teenager when he wasn't around. She broke up with her boyfriend of a year, a non–New Situationist, and a month later realized she'd broken up with him for Berliner. On a Saturday afternoon in August, she invited Berliner back to her mod apartment in the Ukrainian Village, and took his virginity on her maple platform bed.

Kraus was pleased that Berliner didn't say anything too sentimental after their first time having sex; she was also pleased that he fell asleep with his head on her chest while she smoked a cigarette, drank wine, and thought about him. After a thirty minute post-coital nap, Kraus woke Berliner. She slowly and thoroughly explained that she had what previous lovers had called an "architectural fetish," which she became aware of during a therapy session when she was sixteen. Under hypnosis, she had remembered her twelve-year-old self, masturbating against certain kinds of doorways because the molding was more beautiful. Kraus told Berliner that while she was pleased with devirginizing him, the two of them couldn't continue a sexual relationship if he didn't feel comfortable indulging in her preferred sexual practices. Kraus needn't have worried. Kraus's descriptions of her preferences were arousing to Berliner. He happily became her sexual protégé.

They began a secret affair. They talked extensively about their personal histories and the historical architecture of Chicago. Kraus introduced Berliner to Debord and the Situationists and he learned quickly. Even while avoiding Dana and Raulson, the lovers found a way to see each other every day. Sometimes, after Berliner's mother and grandmother had gone to sleep, Kraus snuck into Berliner's basement and spent the night in his bed. She attended most of his baseball games, pretending to be the cousin of one of Berliner's teammates, an outfielder whose parents never came to games. She sat in the bleachers, wearing black high-waist jeans, a white button-down shirt, and one of many colored scarves, heckling like she was at Comiskey Park. She drank beer from the bottle or whiskey from a flask and smoked clove cigarettes until the mothers asked her to stop.

The New Situationists were mostly supportive of Kraus's relationship. Some of them had known her for many years and were amused that she'd finally become enamored of someone. They weren't happy, though, when Kraus asked to bring Berliner into the group. Up to this point, Kraus had done a thorough job squashing any scrutiny of the NS and its members. Because of Kraus's efforts, the group was invisible to the outside world and their identities were secret from her and from each other. Asking to bring Berliner in, the antithesis of her job, surprised the other New Situationists despite the depth of her feelings. But because the New Situationist higher-ups respected Kraus, they agreed to see Berliner. They all met in an empty office in a building in the middle of the Loop. Each member of the New Situationists who interviewed Berliner wore a full-face animal mask and used voice-modulating devices when they spoke. They quizzed Berliner about his school and political beliefs, but the thing that really struck them was Berliner's story about his grandmother's attempted exorcism. It convinced a few reluctant members that he was interesting enough to join. At the same time, Kraus staged a test of romantic fidelity, hiring an actress she knew to try seduce Berliner. He didn't stray.

In early November 1999, Berliner was accepted into the New Situationists as a "junior" member and Kraus's assistant, specializing in Negative Recruitment. They threw a party for him at the group's headquarters; all the members attended in masks. Some wore wigs, long gloves, or cowls to hide the color of their hair or skin. Kraus wore a purple mask in the shape of a unicorn head and an elaborate horned headdress. Berliner's mask was red. The loud and lavish party lasted all night. Kraus pulled Berliner into her personal rooms for a quick tryst, then they rejoined the party to dance and drink champagne.

At the party, Kraus introduced Berliner to David Wilson. Unconcerned about protecting his identity, and lacking Kraus and Berliner's flair for the theatrical, he didn't wear a mask. Physically, Wilson was an unimpressive man: short, slightly hunched from years of sitting in front of a computer, and graying early. He was nearsighted but had a face-shape that rejected nearly every style of glasses. Round glasses were too small, rectangular glasses were too long, and the square-ish Wayfarers that had recently come back into style made him look like he was trying too hard. He wore a pair of tortoise-shell Wayfarers anyway. He took a picture with masked Kraus and Berliner. Although the picture from the party doesn't show it, the three of them oddly look like they could be related: big eyes, dark hair, pale skin, and big smiles with large teeth. Lay pictures of Wilson, Kraus, and Berliner side to side and it will look like you're assembling a family photo album.

During these early days, the New Situationists focused on entertainment and aesthetics. Like the Situationists before them, they wanted to inject playfulness and fun into their droll, serious lives.

Berliner immediately began participating in the New Situationists' aesthetic activities as they attempted to interact with Chicago psychogeographically, in the style of Debord and the SI.

Because of their secrecy and their (possibly?) relatively small numbers, the New Situationists didn't spark any musical or visual art movements, even on a local level. They either didn't make much art or it burned in the fire that eventually destroyed their headquarters. They published a few pamphlets or zines without the words "Situationist" or "New Situationist" on them, with unsigned articles in a style both borrowed from the Situationists and helpful in protecting their identities. Some of the articles were reverent histories of Chicago architectural topics; some were personal essays about the L or a particular building in Chicago. They also wrote scathing diatribes against traffic and urban congestion, which they blamed for most of society's ills. The contemporary urban architect's tactics, they argued, hemmed people into capitalism-directed movements through an urban area, with pedestrians and drivers diverted to the routes that would pass the most billboards. This was essentially undiluted Situationist rhetoric. The unsigned, photocopied zines didn't attract any attention, but were for a short time available for purchase at a local independent bookstore called Quimby's.

Following the path the Situationists had paved, the New Situationists began focusing on politics rather than aesthetics after a few years of existence. In 2000, without revealing their identities, they helped organize and secretly fund a number of far-left political causes and candidates, mostly focusing on social issues, the politics of intellectual property, and creative freedom as it related to the Internet. However, after the events of September 11, 2001, their politics took a radical turn.

They planned what they believed would be a "low-risk, zero-casualty" act of domestic terrorism, to prove that "domestic terrorism was as much of a threat as foreign terrorism and that terrorism itself wasn't an act of war between nations, but could be a zero-casualty act of social change within a nation."* They decided to detonate bombs in eleven L stations across the city. The crippling of the L, which they called the "arms and hands of Chicago," was intended to mimic the wound New York City received when the Twin Towers fell, to literally stop the city's movements. In a declaration of intention sent to the *Chicago Tribune* the night of the bombings, the New Situationists insisted, "We revel in the beauty of this city and her infrastructure, and the destruction of this infrastructure, which we hold so dear, shows how absolutely necessary we believe this demonstration to be."†

According to Kraus's testimony, "sometime in May" she and ten other members of the New Situationists were separately informed their involvement was suspected. By the time her compatriots looped in Kraus, every detail had already been planned for 3:15 a.m. on Monday, June 18. The New Situationist leaders had chosen stations that would be closed at that time.

Sometime after 10 p.m. on June 17, Kraus and the ten other New Situationist bombers met with leaders in the New Situationist headquarters. During this meeting and for the rest of the long night, they all wore ski masks with holes for the eyes and mouth. Kraus's ski mask was dark pink, which looked black enough in the dark. She hadn't lost her Situationist instinct that play was as important as politics.

At the headquarters, Kraus received a backpack full of plastic explosives. No one told her where they sourced them. She was told that an "advance team" had been deployed to disable the alarm systems and unlock the doors. She was instructed to enter a particular door at her assigned station, drop her backpack and set the bomb to

---

* From the confessional note they sent to the *Chicago Tribune* the night of the subway bombings, signed "The New Situationists (25 concerned parties)." Because of the New Situationists' pattern of secrecy and promoting confusion about the group, it is likely that twenty-five doesn't reflect the group's actual numbers.

† From "The New Situationists (25 concerned parties)."

detonate, then pull the fire alarm to clear out any security guards or stray homeless. According to Kraus, she was told that there wouldn't be any security guards or homeless people; she was told pulling the fire alarm was just a precaution. The bombers planned to reconvene at the headquarters by no later than 4 a.m.

They believed their plan was simple and in its simplicity, doable.

Kraus's evening began according to plan. She walked to her station, dropped her bag, and pulled the fire alarm—but then Kraus noticed a security guard passed out at her desk, unmoving despite the noise. Kraus spent several moments trying to wake her, only running at the last moment. Kraus managed to escape the bomb's blast radius, but only barely. The force of the explosion knocked her to the pavement; she landed on her chin, breaking her front two teeth. The police found her bloody and wailing. They arrested her on the spot. Safe in their headquarters, the rest of the New Situationists escaped notice as police tried to contain the mass chaos.

When questioned that evening, Kraus told the arresting officers, senior detectives, and the District Attorney that she would give them everything she knew, then claimed to know very little. Kept in an interrogation room for twelve hours, her jaw swollen and aching, she repeated the same facts over and over again: she didn't know the names or faces of any New Situationists, except David Wilson and Nicolas Berliner; Berliner and Wilson didn't participate in planning the bombing and were completely unaware of the plans; she didn't participate in planning the bombing but did what her superiors told her; she didn't know the names of her superiors; she didn't know the faces of her superiors; she didn't know what they wanted; she didn't know where they were. She ate three peanut butter and jelly sandwiches, drank three cans of Diet Coke, and took four bathroom breaks. She waited until the eighth hour of her interrogation to ask to speak to an attorney.

The *Chicago Tribune* sent the manifesto they received to the CPD and published it alongside the report of the bombings. The CPD arrested Wilson and Berliner. Wilson lawyered up immediately and refused to say anything except "I didn't have anything to do with that." Panicking, Berliner talked a lot, but the more he said the more it became clear to the detectives and the DA that he had no information. Berliner's mother and grandmother provided an alibi, as did the classmate who had stayed up with him past 4 a.m., playing *Halo 2* over the Internet. Wilson had spent the night at his girlfriend's apartment, which had a doorman and security cameras. The detectives wanted to charge both Berliner and Wilson anyway, but the DA decided to focus on Kraus.

The Grand Jury proceeding that anticipated Kraus's criminal trial was something of a surprise in the hubbub it caused. The DA, the defense attorneys, the judge, and the court reporters all expected Wilson to refuse to speak, and to serve some jail time as a result. No one expected Berliner to do the same, but sometime between his arrest and the Grand Jury, Berliner got with the New Situationist program. He sat stone-faced and unspeaking in the witness stand. The judge called a recess; Berliner's attorney took him into a small conference room in the building, and Dana and Raulson both begged Berliner to talk. He refused to speak even to them. The judge cut him some slack, due to his age and because she considered him a victim of sexual assault (statutory rape). Berliner spent the next five months in a juvenile detention facility; he was released the day he turned eighteen.

Kraus pleaded not guilty to her one count each of involuntary manslaughter and property destruction, against her lawyer's wishes. The jury found her guilty on both counts. The judge sentenced her to life in prison, without the possibility of parole for twenty-five years. In her ten years of incarceration so far, she's agreed only to two interviews, the aforementioned one with Anna Kirkpatrick, during which she expressed remorse for the life she took but excitement that the city took the opportunity to "better the property" she had damaged by building an improved new station. The second interview, actually a series of interviews, was with me, toward the end of the assembling of this book. She spoke to me because Berliner negotiated the meeting.

When I asked her if she felt remorse for killing a security guard, she snapped, "Yes, obviously. I'm not a murderer."

"But, you admit to killing someone?"

"If you don't mean to kill someone, you aren't a murderer, not in your heart. My violence accidentally caused a person's death. That's unfortunate, I have nightmares, I've cried, but I'm not a murderer."

She also told me the article about her in *Vanity Fair*, written by Nancy Jo Sales, and the movie based on that article, directed by Sofia Coppola, are both "complete bullshit." However, she did like that she was played by Jennifer Lawrence in the movie, even though Lawrence looks nothing like Kraus.

During our conversations, Kraus barely spoke about the New Situationists. Although I now know more about the New Situationists than anyone outside the membership ever has, except Molly Metropolis, the organization remains a mystery to me. Berliner says he still doesn't know the names of the New Situationists' leaders. He wouldn't give me the names of any of the members, or even describe them using pseudonyms. He insisted that he could only speak about people who were already "out in the open," and he told me that I was lucky the person he was the most "emotionally involved" with was already identified, otherwise he wouldn't have been able to talk about the New Situationists at all. If someone other than Kraus had been arrested, this book couldn't exist.

Everything Berliner did admit, the details of his induction party for example, he ran by his "higher-up" before he told me. "So, the New Situationists still exist?" I asked him.

"Yes and no," Berliner said vaguely, as was typical in the conversations we had about the group: "There were a few projects in motion when the group disbanded, I didn't even know about them

109

during the real days, or until the whole thing with Cait, but a skeleton crew, myself included, has to keep them going now. They're not the kinds of things we'd want to stop in the middle."

"Can you tell me about any of these projects?"

"Not really."

"You can't tell me anything at all? Do they take place in Chicago?"

"I really can't say."

"Is someone keeping you from talking? Threatening you in some way?"

"No. When I said 'can't' before, I meant 'won't.'"

"Are they paying you anything to keep quiet?" I asked.

"They are paying me to work, and I keep quiet because I want to."

"How much are they paying you?"

"I won't say."

Berliner delivered all these refusals to speak with a schoolboy smirk, smoking cigarettes and looking very pleased with himself.

"So, no new projects, no new members?" I asked.

"No new projects," he said, "But as for members, I might say Taer was a member. Before she died. And, after everything happened, we asked Nix if she wanted to join so we could look after her. We offered her a job."

"When you say we," I asked, "do you mean to imply that you have become a decision-making member of the New Situationists?"

"I really won't say," he said.

When I asked Nix about her membership in the group, she said, "I didn't need their help, but I did need a job and the money's good."

"Are you still working for them?" I asked.

"I am and I'm not," she said.

"Talking to me right now, is that working for them?"

"They're not paying me for this, if that's what you mean."

110

"I'm wondering if the New Situationists condone you and Nick speaking to me," I said.

"They aren't in charge of who we talk to. I mean, they aren't in charge of who I talk to, they aren't in charge of who Nick talks to anymore. They aren't like that anymore. We're just kind of . . . keeping some projects going. We're kind of a skeleton crew."

"Did they tell you to say that? Nick used the same phrase, 'skeleton crew.'"

"That doesn't come from them, Nick and I talk all the time. He said it to me once, I think."

"And you don't know who any of them are?" I asked.

"No, and I don't care. Like I said, the money's good. And legal. I had my lawyer make sure. Basically the New Situationists don't exist anymore. Berliner says everyone really fell apart after Kraus was arrested. Don't believe him when he implies that they're still some big thing. He just wants them to be. He can't give anything up."

Taking into account my interviews with Berliner and Kraus, and the hostile tone of the letter I received from David Wilson when he rejected my request for an interview, I believe the New Situationists are masters of smoke and mirrors, and not much else. A group of young people got together, wanted to change the world, and latched onto the pseudo-academic ramblings of another man who'd wanted to change the world and failed. People consider them important and powerful only because of the firm devotion of all members to keep quiet, despite the personal consequences Kraus suffered. They have the appeal of a secret society. Berliner, an isolated teenager, was particularly susceptible to the charms of hidden knowledge. They taught him to make screen prints and how to draw maps, and then put him to work creating new secret cartographies. But if someone from the New Situationists decided to talk, I think the New Situationists would turn out to be less powerful than most people think they are. The silence and secrecy makes them special, but there is nothing behind the curtain but a few angry children and a poorly planned terrorist event.

Berliner obviously still harbors a deep sentimental attachment to both Kraus and the New Situationists. He agreed to speak with me only if I promised to include the following quote he prepared:

"The death in the L bombing was accidental and not considered a 'casualty necessary to the betterment of their cause,' as Marie-Hélène Kraus's prosecuting lawyer argued. The plan was to make a revolution without bloodshed. Marie-Hélène Kraus is a killer but she isn't a murderer. She isn't morally corrupt."

Berliner visits Kraus weekly at the Dwight Correctional Center, a maximum security prison for female violent offenders about an hour and a half outside of Chicago. He drives to the jail every Saturday, bringing with him a carton of cigarettes, nail polish, the cashmere cardigans from Nordstrom that Kraus likes best, and any magazines or books she requested the previous week. He doesn't use his car for any other purpose; he bought it just to see her. Even though he's taken other lovers, Berliner still considers himself Kraus's boyfriend. They plan to get married as soon as she makes parole. I believe one of the main reasons Berliner agreed to speak with me at all was to lobby on Kraus's behalf.

In Davis's parents' lakeside home, Davis finished recounting Berliner's early years. Taer asked if they could open a third bottle of wine. Davis told her to go ahead, and flicked a lighter over and over again, to light another cigarette. With the new bottle of wine open and poured, Taer pushed Davis to move ahead to the parts of the story with Molly Metropolis.

Davis snapped back at her, "There's some important stuff that comes before that, but I can skip it if you're going to be a such a bitch about it."

"Sorry," Taer responded. "I'm just anxious."

"Whatever," Davis said.

"Sorry," Nix echoed. "Do you want some water or something?"

"I'm fine," Davis said, "The next thing you need to know about Nick, is he has this apartment. He thought it up sometime after Kraus went to jail, but before he met Molly. It's this weird, incredible place. He had it built after he went to juvie and got out, then Kraus went to jail. He said he was really solitary and sad all the time. I started calling it his 'Blue Period,' just as a joke. He didn't like that at all."

In the years following the New Situationists' unraveling, Berliner designed an apartment for him and Kraus to share when she finished her long prison sentence.* The apartment was a fantasy from Kraus and Berliner's sex life—the perfect erotic space; they designed it together as a kind of ongoing foreplay. Berliner drew his blueprints of this perfect apartment based on his memory of their conversations. He started saving money, but with his low-paying job he knew it would be a stretch to complete the project before Kraus was paroled. Then he met Molly Metropolis and she offered to build it for him.

In 2006, when Molly and Berliner met, Molly had dozens of projects in the conceptual stages mostly relating to her music career (her albums, her General Council, The Ghost Network—none of them had names yet) and she wanted Berliner, the only accessible former member of the New Situationists, to help her with her cartography projects. Berliner initially refused. The secrets of the New Situationists needed to stay secret, Berliner told her, but Molly already knew enough about the music industry to know that for the right reasons, almost everyone would open up. Molly found out (perhaps by visiting Kraus in prison) that Berliner was trying to

---

* According to Cyrus's notes, Berliner invited Cyrus to visit the apartment in late 2011. The amount of access Berliner allowed Cyrus seems complicated, with a lot of push and pull. —CD

build an apartment, and offered to fund the project in exchange for his secrets.

So, Berliner agreed to work with Molly Metropolis. A few weeks later, Kathy J. purchased a song Molly wrote ("Love Me Sweet," an album cut on Kathy's pop debut *One of the Boys*) and she used that money to buy a warehouse space in Old Town. A month later, Berliner began aggressive renovations.

Though Berliner's design evoked the rooms and flow of an apartment, it was more like a Situationist drawing than a real living space. He didn't include any hallways in the design, just a series of rooms that opened into other rooms, like a beehive. The front room, a narrow rectangle, had mirrors and a kitchen-like space. The middle area was a labyrinth of interconnected rooms. Some of them had no windows and only one door. You had to walk through the rooms in a particular order to make it to the huge back room, which was the bedroom and living area. Berliner also designed a bed built into the wall, twice the size of a king bed. The floors were dark wood; the walls were painted eggshell white. Berliner found the exact molding that Kraus had enjoyed as a child.

Molly made only one mark on Berliner's apartment. On Berliner's original blueprint, there were two rooms labeled bathroom. Molly changed the smaller room from a bathroom to a walk-in closet. During construction, Molly checked in with the progress frequently and attentively, to make sure the contractors were following the blueprints to the letter, but Molly never visited the apartment after it was completed. Perhaps she didn't want to violate Berliner's private space or perhaps she didn't want to insert herself into his sex life.

The first time Davis visited the apartment, she thought construction had only recently been completed. The rooms still smelled like paint. In the strange front room, a silver refrigerator stood next to a seven-foot-tall mirror, which leaned precariously against a wall. Berliner had been there at least once—he had beer and water in the fridge—but the place felt unlived in. They drank a few beers sitting on the floor, against the wall across from the mirror. According to Davis, she kept looking at herself accidentally.

She asked for a tour and Berliner led her through the maze of middle rooms—"Thank god I was drunk the first time," Davis said, "or else I would've probably freaked out"—into the back bedroom. They immediately went to the bed. Experiencing a transferred reverence for the space, Davis tried to be quiet as she and Berliner copulated. From the scrubbed walls and waxed floors she thought Berliner wanted quiet awe. She kept her eyes closed and her hands to herself. According to Berliner, the sex that day was mediocre. In fact, Berliner's fantasy was the opposite of Davis's assumption. His sexual excitement didn't come from the pure space, but the violation of it—specifically Davis's (or any female visitor's) violation of it.

Once he explained what he wanted, Davis was more than happy to oblige. "He liked things like cracked tile, broken light fixtures, all kinds of stuff," Davis said. "Sometimes he'd tell me what to break. Once, while he was asleep, I cut up all the curtains with a knife, then woke him up to show him what I'd done. He really liked that."

Once, in a fit of anger and sexual excitement, she used a chair to punch a hole in the wall, then threw the chair at the bedroom window where it broke the glass, then hung in the frame for a few seconds before tumbling to the sidewalk. That night, she and Berliner had their most passionate sexual experience and most emotionally revealing post-coital conversation. They talked about music, and Davis told Berliner about her childhood in rural Ohio, where her parents kept bees.

The downside of Berliner's unusual predilection was that it required costly upkeep. Berliner had the walls repainted monthly and a cleaning crew came to wash the floors and windows every week. He had a close relationship with his contractor, who often repaired dented walls, chipped plaster, or scratched molding. When Davis realized how intensely Berliner kept up his apartment, she had to confront the fact that she probably hadn't been the first lover to visit. She was right; Berliner also occasionally brought home a librarian who worked at the Chicago city archives, but their encounters were sporadic.

In the early days of their relationship, Davis couldn't find her way around the apartment to save her life; Berliner had to walk her everywhere, to the fridge to get water, to the front door to go home in the morning, even to the bathroom. By the time their relationship was deteriorating, Davis could move from the front of the apartment to the back with her eyes closed. She had found the secret second bedroom buried in a dead-end, and she slept there when she was angry with Berliner.

Davis spoke to Taer and Nix about these patterns of their relationship disdainfully, regretfully, but like Berliner, without shame. Despite their odd sex life, Davis never felt shy about the details. For her, it didn't even feel transgressive. "In a certain sense, I never really could 'get it up' for him, you know? I mean, it just felt like normal sex in a strange place, to me. But it wasn't supposed to feel like normal sex, it was supposed to be some new merging of person and architecture in a way that was supposed to open up the world. That's how he told me I should feel about it, but I never did. Not really."

Berliner was also shameless but for a different reason; he doesn't mind, even likes, even revels in, being abnormal.

Davis talked and smoked for close to three hours with very few interruptions from Nix and Taer. They polished off two more bottles of wine in the last hour and although they were all drunk, Davis's hands remained steady and her footsteps straight and even.

When Davis finished explaining her breakup with Berliner, no one said anything for almost twenty seconds, until Taer broke the silence.

"Well," Taer lisped drunkenly, "I feel like I'm not going to be able to digest all this until tomorrow morning."

"For sure," Davis replied.

"But it's like—I still don't know what to do next."

"Maybe we should avoid him," Nix said.

"He's not dangerous," Davis said. "Just weird and sort of amoral. Just find him and talk to him."

"He broke into our apartment," Nix said.

"My apartment," Taer said.

"And he hurt Cait's forehead," Nix said.

"The break-in, that's something he would do. But he doesn't hurt people," Davis said.

"I hit his head with a dictionary," Taer said. "He hit me back in self-defense."

"Don't defend him," Nix said.

"But this argument doesn't matter because I don't know where to find him," Taer said. "Where's his apartment?"

"I can't tell you," Davis said.

"You can't or you won't?" Nix asked.

"I won't," Davis said, giving Nix a taste of the medicine Berliner would later feed me. "He won't be there anyway. He doesn't live there."

"Where does he live?"

"I don't know."

"We could go ask Marie-Hélène," Taer said.

"She won't see you," Davis said.

"Well, then, what are we supposed to do?" Nix asked.

"Look, I'll give it to you that something is going on here, with Molly's disappearance and Nick," Davis said. "But I don't know why you two in particular feel like you have to take it on."

"It's her," Nix said, meaning Taer.

"Molly," Taer said, thinking she was agreeing with Nix.

"Okay, then. My guess is that hunting down Nick is the right

117

thing for you to do," Davis said. "He knows way more than I do. He'll be able to help you out. I'm just not sure how to find him."

Taer pulled Berliner's sketchpad out of her bag. She held it out of Davis's reach. "We have this," she said.

Davis held out her hand. "Give it to me."

Taer didn't want to, but handed it over anyway. Davis flipped through the sketchpad, stopping at some pages, running her fingers along the middle binding.

"I can't decipher it fully. But I know what it is. He'd draw a map of wherever he went during the day. You see these arrows here? That's his path."

Davis flipped to the last map in the sketchpad. In the margins, she wrote a key to the map. She defined some of Berliner's personal annotations, like the arrows she had mentioned, labeled a prominent diagonal street "North Clybourn Avenue," and made a few guesses of the names of some smaller streets branching off North Clybourn. She pointed out all the maps that were a similar shape to the last map, as if Nick was revisiting the same places.

"What does this mean? This name here?" Taer asked.

"Antoine Monson?" Davis asked. "It was Nick's assumed name, I think, kind of a code name. I don't know where it came from, but some of the screen prints in Nick's apartment were signed Antoine Monson."

"Molly sometimes had me sign her into hotels as Antoinette Monson," Nix said. "I didn't think it was that weird, just some fake name to hide her."

"Huh," Taer said. "Maybe it was some way they communicated with each other."

"Whatever," Davis said. "I'm glad to be done with the stress of dealing with both of them, to be honest."

Nix and Taer left Davis cigaretteless, drunk, and wallowing in her own emotional filth. Davis gave the distinct impression that she wouldn't be seeing or speaking to them again. The way she closed the door seemed aggressively final. They went back to the Ramada Romulus; the lobby bar was still open. They installed themselves in a booth, ordered two Martinis, and gossiped about Berliner and Davis's sex life. After the bar closed, Nix and Taer went up to their room. They danced together to music from Nix's favorite band at the time, Sleigh Bells.

Very late that night, or very early the next morning, when the music had switched to Taer's favorite band, The National, they argued again about whether they should continue their search for Molly Metropolis. Nix half-heartedly suggested giving up. Taer refused. She would go on by herself if she had to. For the first time in her life, she felt important; she thought that she and Nix were looking for Molly in a place that no one else—not the police, not the record company—could see. Taer promised, sweetly, to protect Nix, but she wouldn't be able to save Nix from the danger ahead of them.

They slept and in the morning, hungover, they took the train back to Chicago and began to retrace Berliner's steps.

Chapter ⑦

Taer and Nix made the somewhat desperate decision to search for Berliner by walking around Chicago with a half-labeled map as their only guide. They spent many fruitless days trudging in the snow; they thought they had no other choice.

They would've had an easier time finding answers to all their questions if they had researched another mystery in their midst, the mystery of Antoine Monson. Monson wasn't an important person, or a famous one, or someone who became a darling to historians. As such, he isn't an easy man to know. His name occasionally comes up in newspaper articles and crime reports printed during his life, but only a small number of articles and two books have been written about him. One of them is a short, out of print, and hard to find biography, written in 1892 by a French historian and philosopher named Jacques-Jerome de Poisson (second cousin to the Madame de Pompadour, on her father's side). The name of the biography has been lost. In 1916, a student pursuing an advanced degree in French history at the University of Westminster found a single copy, broken at the binding and missing an index. He copied the book and sent it to one hundred or so friends and colleagues in the field, but no press ever officially reprinted de Poisson's text. If the book ever included an index or bibliography, it's been lost (or it resides alone in a library or archive), providing reference to nothing. Without a bibliography to give the reader a guide to his sources, it's impossible to imagine where de Poisson could've found any information on Monson at all.* The following is a summation of de Poisson's exploration of Monson's life:

Born in 1470, Monson grew up with four brothers—Freddie, Gerard, Thomas, and Raphael—two of whom died in childhood.† The details of Monson's upbringing are fuzzy at best, but he appears to have been a farmer who taught himself, without attending a university, to be a navigator, geographer, and cartographer.

De Poisson relays certain events in Monson's life with the disclaimer that the stories "may have been altered by popular fable and rumor,"‡ including the story of how Monson became an apprentice navigator on Christopher Columbus's second voyage to America by poisoning the intended assistant cartographer, Lucas Wadsworth.

That particular episode began on October 12, 1493, in a rough port on a rain-soaked Canary Island, the evening before Columbus's second fleet set sail for the New World. Wadsworth went to a pub in the port town Palos de la Frontera for a last hurrah before months of toil and exhaustion. He drank heavily and bragged loudly about his imminent voyage, especially to a baby-faced, red-cheeked boy, about twenty-two years old, who bought him drinks and begged to hear all the details of his upcoming trip. After a few hours of drinking, Wadsworth keeled over, foaming at the mouth. The baby-faced

---

* Thanks to Jade Ashley Zanotti at Bauman Rare Books in New York for helping me track down a copy of the de Poisson biography and to Professor David Whittier of the University of Chicago for an account of the book's history.

† This birth-order information might've been lifted from the biography of Monson's contemporary (and probable rival-in-absentia) Martin Bohemus. [*I'm not sure what Cyrus means here. Is there another lost biography? What does rival-in-absentia mean? —CD*]

‡ Quotations from de Poisson's untitled biography have been adjusted to reflect modern spellings.

boy told the owner of the pub that he would carry Wadsworth to the docks, where he could pass out near his ship and stumble aboard in the morning. Instead of taking him to the docks, the boy put Wadsworth in a wheelbarrow and pushed him to the local general practitioner, who immediately recognized that Wads-worth had been poisoned. The boy told the doctor that he found Wadsworth in that condition on the side of the road and picked him up; the doctor tipped the boy for his trouble.

The next morning, "Luke Wadsworth" reported for duty on Columbus's flagship vessel, the *Marigalante*. Columbus noted in his captain's log: "The assistant cartographer, while a man of twenty-two, has the face of a child. He insists he is up for the task and indeed carries his own equipment, which he has himself constructed."* While the real Wadsworth struggled to stay alive in a nearby hospital (he eventually pulled through), Monson sailed toward America under his name.

Columbus's primary cartographer, Juan de la Cosa, suffered from terrible seasickness. Constantly nauseated, he spent most of his time in his quarters with a compress on his forehead. He passed his duties off to "Wadsworth." Columbus and Monson quickly became close. Monson confessed his secret to Columbus, who took the revelation well: "Young Wadsworth actually called Monson. Will never remember to use new name."† Columbus was true to his word; in later entries in his Captain's Log, Columbus continued to call Monson "Wadsworth."

Columbus's fleet made excellent time. Seventeen ships and approximately one thousand men reached what are now known as the Caribbean Islands on November 3, 1493. While Columbus explored the islands, searching in vain for the mainland of either China or

---

* *Christopher Columbus's Second Voyage to America, In His Words*, eds. Olivia Dunn and Jamie R. Havert (New York: Farrar, Straus and Giroux, 1999), 15.

† *Christopher Columbus's Second Voyage to America, In His Words*, 54.

Japan, Monson stayed at a settlement called Isabella, working on his maps with de la Cosa, who had recovered as soon as his feet touched land. Monson, still working under the name Wadsworth, then served as a deputy to Columbus during the disastrous year and a half when Columbus was Governor of the settlements on the newly discovered islands. In April of 1497, Columbus decided to return to Spain on the *Marigalante* to beg for more supplies to help the struggling colonies. Monson accompanied him on his voyage; de la Cosa stayed behind to work on a series of maps of the islands.

On the voyage home, Columbus and Monson grew even closer. The two often dined together, discussing mapmaking, the period's equivalent of deep-sea fishing, and the relative importance of Greek philosophy. Columbus asked Monson to proofread an account of his second trip, which he submitted to various newspapers in Europe. Monson advised him to gloss over a few of the hardships of the colonies, specifically the difficulties of living without access to medical technicians. On March 26, the *Marigalante* anchored in Lisbon to pick up supplies before continuing on to Spain. Monson chose to leave the ship rather than accompany Columbus on the last leg of the journey. Records indicate the two never reunited. Monson traveled home to France on horseback, arriving just in time to see his father die.

After burying his father, Monson started publishing his maps. As Columbus's secondary cartographer, and with the primary cartographer still abroad, Monson's maps were in high demand, considered by shipmen and collectors to be the most accurate trans-Atlantic maps on the market. Monson made enough money selling maps to purchase a farm large enough to support himself, his wife, and his two living brothers. He also bought a coach and stabled four horses.

For two years, Monson lived well. Then his maps reached Spain. Columbus was appalled. Every single map (except one, the very first topographical map of Sable Island, then called Fagunda) had huge flaws; mistakes so large Columbus believed they had to have been made intentionally. Existing islands were left off the maps. Open stretches of ocean were decorated with nonexistent archipelagos. Shorelines were distorted. Columbus immediately denounced the maps and sent word to his royal patrons, the Spanish King Ferdinand and Queen Isabella, as well as King Charles VIII of France, explaining that Monson's maps were riddled with falsities—"errors," Columbus insisted, "which have no other explanation than to have been intentionally made. I have shared many meals with Monson and reviewed his drawings and notes extensively. What I saw then were accurate depictions. What he has now produced don't reflect the notes I examined. His published maps are distortions."* Monson was discredited, his work was thrown out, and for his affront to the good name of French cartography, King Charles exiled him. Monson didn't appear in court to hear his short trial, but he must've gotten word of the verdict, because he was never seen again in France. De Poisson's biography ends with Monson's disappearance. For centuries, that was the last word on Antoine Monson.

Although de Poisson's text reads like a rigorously researched account, there's a very real possibility that he was wrong. According to public record, no one named Antoine Monson was born or lived in France during the Exploratory Age. It is simple, however, to find the birth records of an *Antoinette* Monson.

In 1921, a Harvard-educated historian named Simon Charles published a response to de Poisson's work, a detailed counter-biography of Monson called *History's Most Hated Cartographer: The New Biography of Antoine/Antoinette Monson.*† Charles explains in the introduction to his book that he decided to do his own search for

---

* From a letter Columbus wrote to the Monarchs. The quotation appears in several books about Columbus, including two that Cyrus owns: The Second Voyage and Ferdinand and Christopher, both by C. W. Peters. —CD

† Simon Charles, History's Most Hated Cartographer: The New Biography of Antoine/Antoinette Monson (San Diego: Harcourt, Brace and Howe, 1921).

Monson's birth records and "discovered the secret identity of Antoine Monson—'history's most hated cartographer.'"*

According to Charles, Antoinette's upbringing differed dramatically from de Poisson's description of Antoine's simple farmer's life.
Charles wrote that Antoinette's parents died a few years after she
was born. Her uncle, a French lord named Philippe Monson, and his
wife Charlotte, the daughter of a duke, raised Antoinette alongside
their three sons. Charlotte had always wanted a daughter and favored Antoinette over her own children. Philippe, while closer with
his sons, also had a soft spot for Antoinette and agreed to buy her a
title so that she could marry their youngest son, Aimé. The marriage
was a good one for Antoinette. She and her cousin had been close
since childhood. Aimé never got along with his studious older
brothers; he preferred to play with Antoinette. The two of them
frequently ran away from their tutors to swim at a nearby lake. They
preferred card games to reading, and when they got older they made
up little word puzzles, trying to outwit each other. According to letters between Philippe and Charlotte, which Charles relied on heavily for his account of Antoinette's childhood, Aimé and Antoinette's
relationship might've remained platonic even after their marriage,
when Antoinette was sixteen and Aimé was eighteen. Charles believes Aimé was gay and Philippe was aware of his youngest son's
preferences and allowed him to marry Antoinette, despite her common birth, to spare himself the indignity of dealing with the social
ramifications of a son who refused to copulate with a wife.

Recently married, and with the new title of "Lady," Antoinette
was allowed to appear at Charles VIII's court. She became a fixture
there: her bright smile, loud laugh, and red cheeks (she probably suffered from acne rosacea) were so recognizable that when she spent
two years out of society, in bed with tuberculosis (from which she

---

* Simon never revealed his source for the quotation "history's most hated
cartographer."

eventually recovered), her absence was noted in the Queen's own diary. Antoinette's bedridden years coincide almost exactly with the dates of Columbus's second voyage.

Charles's account of Antoinette's years with Columbus mirrors de Poisson's biography, with some cross-dressing thrown in. Charles believed that Antoinette disguised herself as a boy and named herself Luke Wadsworth—he discounts the poisoning tale—because she was desperate to live like a man. Charles thought her "gender frustrations," in his words, later prompted her to create the false maps.

Despite the allowances she had in her personal life, due to her permissive guardian and the scarlet fever–induced sterility that kept her from bearing children, Antoinette was emotionally dissatisfied and craved power.* When she returned from her ocean-crossing and gender-crossing adventure, and had to put dresses on and go about as a lady again, she was so frustrated by polite society that she started producing her maps with rampant falsities as a way to get revenge on the society she resented. She tricked the explorers and map collectors, firstly to be cruel, and secondly to frustrate them as they did her.†

Charles and de Poisson's biographies were largely forgotten by academia. Only a few responses popped up over the years. As an undergraduate at the University of Paris in Sorbonne, a young

---

* The idea that Antoinette was barren began as court gossip and, in Charles's hands, became historical myth. Antoinette actually bore three children. Aimé didn't father any of them, but raised them as his own; as a private, perverse joke, Aimé and Antoinette named each of the children after their biological fathers, Antoinette's various extramarital lovers. Any record of the children's proper names was lost, but Antoinette recorded their pet names: Lo-Lo, Freddie, and Bébé.

† *The New Biography of Antoine/Antoinette Monson*, 206.

Simone de Beauvoir wrote a scathing feminist critique of Charles's theories of Antoinette's "gender frustration."

In 1989, a group of PhD students from Berkeley College's history department published a paper on Monson in the *Journal of American History*, describing the Charles and de Poisson versions of Monson's biography. They came up with a new theory, that de Poisson's Monson died when he returned to Nuremberg after Columbus's voyage and his wife, poor and starving, had to finish and publish his maps herself to survive. The falsities on the maps, in their estimation, came from her lack of knowledge, not any intentional attempt to mislead the public. They criticized Charles for not acknowledging the fact that the births of lower class farmers, like de Poisson's Monson, were sometimes not recorded by the state. Also, when men were exiled, sometimes their birth certificates, and those of their family, were burned. Either of those customs could account for Antoine's lack of documentation.

The mystery of Monson's identity might never be solved. De Poisson's lowborn man who swindled his way onto Columbus's ship is as likely to be real as Charles's cross-dressing aristocrat. "The mystery is more interesting than any answer to the mystery," the Situationist Ivan Chtcheglov wrote in his private, unpublished diary on the subject of both Monson and life in general.* Chtcheglov became interested in Monson during the five years he spent incarcerated at a mental hospital in Paris, following his attempt to blow up the Eiffel Tower because the lights shone into his apartment at night, making it difficult for him to sleep. The mental hospital's library, stocked with cast-offs from the *Université de Paris*, included a copy of Charles's *New Biography*. Chtcheglov smuggled the book out of the hospital when he was released, then tracked down a copy of de Poisson's biography through his friends at the university.

---

* Thanks to Berliner for letting me examine the diary. [*Thanks from me, too. —CD*]

Molly Metropolis found Monson through Chtcheglov, during Molly's first frantic inhalation of Situationist texts, when she read some of Chtcheglov's letters in which he indicated he kept a diary while he was committed. Determined to track it down, Molly contacted Chtcheglov's daughter, Lynnette. She agreed to sell Molly her father's diary, and Molly received a bounty in return: Chtcheglov's copies of both Monson biographies had been attached to his diary by rubber bands.

Inspired by the mystery of Monson's life, Molly Metropolis asked Berliner to sign the screen prints he made for her as either Antoine or Antoinette Monson. She also seems to have established a legal identity for Antoinette Monson. As I was researching Molly's connection to the historical mystery figure, I found Monson in Chicago, on a deed. An Antoinette Monson owned an office building, which was damaged in some kind of fire in early 2010—though when Taer began searching for Berliner, the building had not yet burned.

Marie-Hélène Kraus told Anna Kirkpatrick, "As a Situationist, walking somewhere doesn't count if you have a destination in mind." I wonder how Kraus would've weighed in on Taer and Nix's walking through Chicago; they had a destination in mind but they didn't know where the destination was. Most likely, Kraus would've approved. Their progress was slow; the conditions were terrible. Chicago has a reputation for rough winters because of the wind, which both lowers the temperature and blows the snow and freezing rain into the faces of pedestrians. Sometimes the wind is so strong that the rain falls horizontally. According to Taer's notes, she and Nix suffered through at least one day of horizontal rain. Once, to avoid getting hit by hailstones the size of quarters, they had to huddle for twenty minutes in a narrow doorway that smelled like urine. One evening it was warm enough that it rained instead of snowed, but overnight the rain froze to black ice on the sidewalks, which was hard to see and easy to slip on. The temperature made their jeans feel like sheets of ice against their legs. Taer loved to complain about the cold.

They had problems with Berliner's map, too. They realized quickly that it probably wasn't drawn to scale. Even with Davis's notes, they weren't sure which streets the maps depicted. Berliner had drawn the street that Davis had labeled North Clybourn Avenue vertically, but on a regular street map aligned to a compass, North Clybourn ran diagonally from northeast to southwest. Most of the streets that crossed North Clybourn adhered to a strict north-south, east-west grid system, so when the streets hit North Clybourn, they formed a row of triangles. Berliner's map depicted one of those triangles, a very strange one where two of the streets didn't actually meet. Taer and Nix interpreted this as Berliner having walked through most of the triangle except half a block on one street. It was either that, they assumed, or he simply drew the triangle sloppily. They tried to figure out which triangle of streets Berliner had drawn on his map. They hiked the same streets over and over again, talking about music, people in college they had slept with who had then avoided them in the dining hall, and their first big breakups. Sometimes they walked silently because they had to wrap scarves around their mouths and noses to block out the snow and wind. They slipped on ice and fell.

As February progressed, Taer became more frustrated as their search proved futile. She also gained some weight, as she always did in winter, which made her cheeks and breasts look rounder, but also upset her. Nix slept on the couch more often; they had lethargic, sometimes orgasmless, sex. Nix avoided walking around with Taer, and Taer let her recede. Taer went out alone, moving aimlessly through the snow, barely even looking at the buildings. She walked every single triangle of streets off North Clybourn but couldn't distinguish the building that would crack open and spill out secrets from all the other offices and apartments and store-fronts. She sometimes left the triangles, refusing to turn at a stoplight when she felt like continuing on straight ahead. She was stuck.

In the months before her disappearance, Molly Metropolis spent most of her time with her creative team, her General Council. The General Council included her choreographer, her personal trainer, her stylists, her dancers, and her manger/creative director Momo Waxler, among others. She was inspired by Andy Warhol's infamous Factory and tried to include that kind of collective art-making in her own life. Molly published a list of the original members of the General Council, with their nicknames, in the liner notes of *Cause Célèbrety* when it was released on September 16, 2008. It reads as follows, with my notes in parentheses and italics:

Metro. (*Molly Metropolis*)

T.T. (*Tasha Taylor — Molly's personal assistant before Nix*)

Momo. (*Momo Waxler — Creative Director*)

Peaches. (*Anna "Peaches" Fontaine — Dancer*)

Ali. (*Ruann Alison West — Dancer*)

R. "Prince." (*Ronnie Princeton — engineer of Molly's various contraptions*)

J.F.P. (*Joe Frank Parker — Choreographer*)

Nance. (*Nancy DeWitt — Costume Designer*)

(When the UK edition of *Cause Célèbrety* was released in November, the list had expanded to include Belle Brandice, Ronnie "Tech" F. [*The Tech Guy, Tour Manager 2008–2009*], R. "Gina" N. [*Regina Nix*], and David Walker: The Librarian.)

The members of the General Council helped create the subway-map body paint design that decorated her in the "New

Vogue Riche" music video, her now-iconic metallic bodysuit from her 2009 MTV Video Music Awards performance, and the LED "mini city" from the "Apocalypse Dance" video.

In an interview with NeonLimelight.com, Molly described the formation of her General Council: "I brought together a costume designer and a choreographer and a makeup artist and instead of making just a team or just a family, we made a team and a family that *lives in a city together*" [*italics mine*].

For Molly Metropolis, songwriting wasn't a simple process of writing lyrics and selecting beats, it was creating a large-scale work of art. While she tweaked her hooks, she sketched costume ideas for the song's music video, discussed choreography ideas with Parker, and designed cover art for the single. She treated writing a song like making a movie and as such, she needed a full crew.

Molly Metro traveled almost constantly during 2008, even when she wasn't touring; she lived in Chicago, but spent half of her time in Los Angeles for music industry–related business. Her friends and the members of the General Council thought Molly visited Chicago to see her dancer friends Ali and Peaches, who had once been members of a very early version the General Council, but whose contracts Molly had terminated in early 2008. Instead, Molly spent her time assembling The Ghost Network with Nicolas Berliner.

Once she and Berliner had completed The Ghost Network, Molly stayed in Chicago to work with her General Council and write, produce, and record songs for *Cause Apocalyptic*. Although none of the songs on the album had been officially released before, at least three of the tracks that ultimately made it onto *Cause Apocalyptic* stemmed from previously leaked early Molly Metropolis demos. Those three tracks reworked for her new album include "Lost," "Beneath the Pavement," and "Bang Bang."

In Chicago, Molly fell into a creative routine. She woke up mid-morning and after a long workout with her personal trainer, she went to her studio space to meet with the members of the General

Council. Everyone assembled around lunchtime. Sometimes Molly was social, eating, talking, and drinking wine with her friends and collaborators. Sometimes she shut herself up in one of her private recording rooms, blocked off the windows, and wrote her lyrics in isolation. She shared the themes she was developing, as well as some snippets of lyrics and melody, which the other members of the General Council used to begin designing stage sets and developing marketing strategies. Parker started choreographing the "Apocalypse Dance" music video before Molly had even finished the song. The choreography involved a lot of leaps and sudden drops to the floor.

In the early evenings, the General Council had "family dinner." Molly required that every member of the G.C. attend at least two family dinners a week, and she preferred when everyone attended all of them. The dinners were catered; the food was paid for by SDFC. Most nights, all the Council members met around the large wooden dinner table. While they ate fish, salad, and quinoa (Molly had gained a few pounds and was on a strict diet and a directive from the label to slim), they discussed the aesthetic focus of the new album and the tour that would support it. Everyone was invited to offer suggestions, but Molly's final word was law.

While Molly was developing *Cause Apocalyptic*, she also communicated extensively with noted fashion designer Johan Van Duncan and his assistant, Angela Sebastian-Hay to discuss costuming for her music videos and live shows. Van Duncan reportedly sent Molly early sketches of the sculpted platform stilettos and the "distressed" metallic-green-rhinestone and mirror-glass encrusted body suit she wore in the "Apocalypse Dance" video. Molly visited Van Duncan's studio, tried on outfits, and often socialized with the designer. After returning from visits with Van Duncan—who committed suicide on February 10, 2010, just over a month after Molly disappeared— Molly reported to her dancers that Van Duncan's mood was "stunningly creative, but equally stunningly dark."

In September 2008, SDFC flew Molly and the whole General

Council to Los Angeles to record the album under the watchful eye of her Executive Producer, Darren J. Horner. At six feet four inches and three hundred pounds, Horner was an intimidating presence with an unflinching work ethic. Crack his shell, though, and he has a big smile and easy laugh. He made his name nurturing Mariah Carey and Christina Aguilera's careers. Along the way, he developed a reputation for working well with difficult personalities. SDFC tapped him to produce Molly Metropolis's second record because they thought he had the wherewithal to take her over-the-top aesthetic and highbrow aspirations and shape them into a consumable pop product, without betraying the essential "Molly-ness" her Pop Eaters knew and loved.

To prepare himself for Molly, Horner ingested a steady stream of '80s synth-pop like Duran Duran and the Pet Shop Boys, as well as contemporary examples of synthwave or "Outrun Techno" like Twin Shadow's album *Confess*. He also prepared himself for a battle. Horner had heard rumors that Molly Metropolis was headstrong and argumentative, so he expected to have to reel her in. Molly defied Horner's expectations; she was a collaborative worker and as docile as a pussycat.

Impressed with Molly's professionalism and satisfied by her obedience, Horner never guessed he was being played. Molly's friends at SDFC had warned her that Horner was a "big personality" and Molly decided the best way to work with him was to make him think he was making every decision. She manipulated him subtly throughout the entire recording process, fighting quietly for her aesthetic voice to shine through the studio production. At the same time, Horner was an experienced and adept enough producer to understand when the studios had caught lightning in a bottle. He knew Molly's success primarily had to do with her distinctive point of view. Of course, under the costumes and rhetoric, Molly wrote straightforward pop songs. In 2008, Molly was a hard sell because her songs were considered "dance," not Top 40, and SDFC's marketing team stumbled a bit while pushing a non-white artist, who wasn't already a star, outside of the "urban" demographic. But by the time she and Horner were recording her second album, she'd remade the Top 40 in her image.*

After slowly cobbling together her first album with SDFC producers and ex-boyfriend Davin Karl, with whom she had a terrible, prolonged breakup, Molly wanted the production process for *Cause Apocalyptic* to go smoothly. It did, but the post-production process didn't follow suit.

Laurence Rappaport, the president of A&R at SDFC and Molly's personal handler within the company, wanted to release the eight songs as a second disc of bonus tracks, tacked onto a re-release of *Cause Célèbrety*, scheduled to drop on November 18. Molly thought the price of a two-disc set would be too expensive for some of her fans; she also insisted that the new tracks were a thematic and emotional step forward for her. Putting them under the name *Cause Célèbrety* wouldn't make sense, artistically, because the music wasn't about "Celebrity" anymore, it was about dancing 'til the end of the world. Rappaport thought the album would sell better with the name *Cause Célèbrety*. He cared about her "artistic vision," but he cared more about engineering a hit record. He thought the music business, and his own career, couldn't afford splashy failures. He thought Molly was still too new, and the album-buying public wasn't ready for a second album and a second set of singles. Radio DJs were still playing "Don't Stop (N'Arrête Pas)" on Saturday nights like it was a newly released track.

Rappaport had other problems with Molly. He didn't like the

---

* From 2001 to 2007, hip-hop and R&B dominated the Billboard charts and made up the vast majority of the number one singles. In 2008, Black Eyed Peas was poised to dominate the year's charts with their two huge hits "Boom Boom Pow" and "I Gotta Feeling." Their chart domination ended when Molly's third single "New Vogue Riche" toppled "I Gotta Feeling," ending a fourteen-week number one streak.

way she conducted herself in interviews. He thought she talked too much about racism and not enough about her hair. He wanted her to pose for more "candid" photos; he wanted her to ditch the wig and weaves and let her hair "be natural." Molly told him in an e-mail that she wanted to "perform her own hair." He asked her not to refer to herself as a feminist, and instead espouse feminist viewpoints without ever using the word; whenever Molly said "feminist," she passive-aggressively apologized to Rappaport for "letting her brain show." Molly thought she was smarter than Rappaport, and that angered him most of all.

Rappaport and Molly fought dramatically. They kept it out of texts and mostly out of e-mails, out of anything that could be hacked and leaked, but their phone conversations were loud and aggressive. Nix had never seen Molly truly angry with someone before Rappaport. For Molly, her fight over the release of *Cause Apocalyptic* was the fight of her life; they weren't arguing about what to do with the eight tracks, they were fighting about Molly's whole career. "It's the only real war I've ever fought in my life," she told Nix. "This is for me and about me. I feel like I'm being born, fighting my way out of the womb, and Laurence, he's not even a person, he's just the narrow canal I'm fighting my way out of. The baby always makes it out. Or else it dies."

Molly made it out by challenging Rappaport with a high-stakes bet. She bet that when SDFC released the single "Apocalypse Dance," the song would perform well enough to support an album release. If she was right, SDFC would release *Cause Apocalyptic* as a separate EP. If "Apocalypse Dance" didn't perform, they would release the two-disc version of *Cause Célèbrety*. Rappaport accepted the bet and the "Apocalypse Dance" single was released on November 17, followed by the music video on November 30.

"Apocalypse Dance," a gutsy, throaty number in a minor key, debuted at number one on the Billboard Hot 100 chart—Molly's best charting debut. "Apocalypse Dance" was also Molly

Metropolis's fifth consecutive single to hit number one. Molly won the bet, so she got her way.

At that time, SDFC decided to release the album on January 25, 2009. Horner, Molly, and Rappaport spent a few weeks polishing, fixating on minutia in the mixing process. SDFC made the album available for pre-order in December, so that it could be given as a holiday gift. *Cause Apocalyptic* was certified Gold before Christmas Day.

On the back of the "Apocalypse Dance" single and the steady sales of *Cause Apocalyptic,* Molly Metro's Apocalypse Ball tour went ahead as planned in late November. Her garish performances of her unreleased tracks also helped increase buzz about the album. On the Internet, fans established warring camps of "spoiler" and "anti-spoiler" sects. The first watched crude cell-phone videos of Molly's performances on YouTube, and downloaded bootleg live albums, while the "anti-spoiler" fans avoided hearing the songs before buying the album or attending the live show.

Then, eleven days before the album's scheduled release date, Molly Metropolis vanished.

As Molly's disappearance remained unsolved, *Cause Apocalyptic* became an even more contested issue. Would SDFC release the album on its scheduled date or would they wait for Molly Metro to return? Molly's fans took to their Twitters, Tumblrs, and Facebook pages to demand the album that most of the media was already referring to as "Molly's last." Music journalists and bloggers spread a rumor that the album would be coming out on time, but the track list would be "retooled." Fans then demanded that SDFC release "Molly's version" of the album.

Despite the frantic tone and pace of speculation, SDFC refused to release a statement more concrete than: "We have the utmost respect for Molly Metropolis and her work. We are attempting to execute her vision of the album." In fact, SDFC was attempting to execute a version of the album that, thematically at least, resonated with Molly's status of missing-in-action. The bloggers were right; they revised the track list. Originally, Molly and Horner arranged the eight new songs in the following order:

1. Apocalypse Dance
2. Party Babylon
3. Beneath the Pavement
4. La Deluge
5. I'll Find You
6. Bang Bang
7. Dance 'Til We Drop
8. Lost

For the final version, Rappaport added an additional track, "Maps (Find Me)," which had been recorded in Molly's salad days but was never included on an album, and reworked the order of the songs to emphasize the album's dark lyrical content. The album's final track list was:

1. Apocalypse Dance
2. Lost
3. Maps (Find Me)
4. I'll Find You
5. Dance 'Til We Drop
6. La Deluge
7. Beneath the Pavement
8. Party Babylon
9. Bang Bang

The critical reception for *Cause Apocalyptic* mimicked the reception of Sylvia Plath's famous book *Ariel and other Poems*, published two years after her death by suicide, with the order of the poems reworked by her husband, the poet Ted Hughes. At first, critics psychoanalyzed Plath, pulling evidence of her suicidal thoughts from every poem; later, they criticized Hughes, saying he reworked the order of the poems to make Plath's death seem premeditated. Talia F. Gold wrote, in her *Slate* review of *Cause Apocalyptic*, "The album sounds like a synth-soaked cry for help. Even if we skip over the dark lyrics from the album's first single, 'Apocalypse,' that just leads us to 'Lost,' which opens with Molly sing-speaking 'You said "Get Lost" / So lost I got / Now we all get lost.' " Apparently, Gold didn't care to share the final line of that quatrain: "In my music." (Though, in her defense, the opening lines of first verse seem to predict Molly's disappearance, their uncanny nature multiplied when the existence of early demos of the song show Metro must've written it in late 2009, just weeks before she vanished: "Among the missing, I am missing you / My heart is twisting, I'm still into you.") A few days later, *Slate* published another piece, this one by Deb Stone, headlined: "Did SDFC Make Metro Go Dark?"

Every major review of the album touched on the lyrics' dark tone. The album sounds like a death rattle; journalists didn't even have to stretch to find evidence to support stories about Molly's "depression" or "dark moods"—but that didn't stop some people from reaching. Roger Popdidian of *Rolling Stone*, for example, interpreted the poppy, benign "Party Babylon" as the inner mono- logue of a depressed girl hiding from the comfort of her loved ones in the anonymity of a loud club.*

While the rest of the world was dissecting the album, Taer used the new wave of Molly Metropolis–related Internet dialogue to re- charge her batteries and revitalize her morale for her search. On a cold day in late January 2009, Taer loaded *Cause Apocalyptic* onto her

---

* Roger Popdidian, "Album Review: Molly Metropolis—*Cause Apocalyptic*," in *Rolling Stone* 1097, No. 2 (2010): 68.

iPod, and walked through the city with Molly in her ears and her nose buried in Berliner's sketchpad of drawn maps.*

Along with the lines he drew to represent each of the streets he had walked on, Berliner used a series of symbols on his maps: blue X's, red arrows, and black dots. Taer went to the streets that she knew Berliner had walked on. She compared the buildings and businesses on those streets with the marks on the map. She focused on a small red arrow pointing to a blue X, which appeared just south of the triangle of streets. She also examined a second red arrow, pointing to the intersection of two streets on the triangle.

Taer pondered the symbols all day and, getting nowhere, she headed for home. She looked up from Berliner's map and found she had walked to the entrance of the L stop at the intersection of North Street and North Clybourn.

She had thought a blue X might mean a certain kind of building, but as she boarded the train she had a new thought: maybe the blue X's were L stops, and red arrows indicated any place Berliner went into, whether it be a business, residence, L stop, et cetera. If she was right, the blue X with the red arrow pointing to it, the combination of symbols she'd been trying to decipher all day, could indicate Berliner had taken the L from the same North Street and North Clybourn station Taer had just used herself. The second red arrow, then, meant he went into another, unidentified building at the intersection of two streets.

Taer hurriedly scribbled the idea down in her journal, with some commentary: "This could be a non idea. The red arrows might not mean 'places he went to,' the blue X's might not mean L stops. And even if they do, the red arrow pointing to the intersection could just indicate a coffee shop he went into or something. But maybe this is actually something."

---

* *Parts of the story of Taer's search on this day came to Cyrus secondhand, from Nix. Other parts came from Taer's notebook and recordings. —CD*

Taer waited until the next day to ask Nix for help. After work, she buttered her up; Taer cooked for her, cleaned the apartment, did all the laundry, and rented her favorite Disney movie (the version of *Robin Hood* with cartoon foxes). She made sure Nix was half drunk on red wine and full of pasta before she brought up her search for Molly and her new idea about the symbols on Berliner's map. To Taer's surprise, Nix didn't fight. She drank more wine, and examined the map while Taer turned on her voice recorder and explained her theory about the arrows and X's. Nix flipped through Berliner's sketchpad, examining earlier maps they barely looked at, then she returned to the last map. "You think the red arrows are the places he went?" Nix asked.*

"Yeah, I think so. It could be."

"So you think he took the L to Clybourn to go to a building that the second red arrow is pointing to."

"Yeah! Yes. I mean, it could be nothing. He could've been getting coffee there."

"If that blue X is the L, that means the other red arrow is on Armitage. Can you pull up Google Maps?"

"Yes! Yeah. Okay. Let me grab my laptop."

"This could be really, really good," Nix said.

"I know. I'm trying not to get my hopes up,"

"You just figured it out walking around?"

"Yeah," Taer said.

Taer grabbed their laptops while Nix moved the dinner plates to the sink, and then looked up the area in question, trying to find the two streets that created a triangle with North Clybourn Avenue. Just north of the L, Clybourn intersected with Armitage, and Sheffield.

"Oh yeah, this is it." Taer said quickly.

"How are you so sure?" Nix said.

---

* At the time, Nix wasn't aware that Taer was recording their conversation and saving the mp3s. She was surprised when I played her the audio recording.

"Look at this map. Look at this little road."

While most of the streets that intersected with North Clybourn formed perfect triangles, the place where Clybourn would've met Armitage was interrupted by another, fourth street, North Racine Avenue. If Berliner had walked down Clybourn, Armitage and Sheffield, but not Racine, he would have to draw a triangle with two sides that didn't meet, just like the lopsided almost-triangle in Berliner's hand-drawn map.

At the end of Armitage, where it intersected with Racine, Berliner had drawn the second red arrow. Taer looked at the Street View on Google Maps to see what was there. At the intersection of Armitage and Racine, right where the arrow pointed, was a pair of office buildings. They were nearly identical: low, by Chicago's sky-scraping standards, gray, and nondescript. Their plain facades gave no hint about their interiors. In a word, they were boring—a capital crime in worlds populated with pop stars. One was the building that I had found, which listed Antoinette Monson as an owner.

Chapter ⑧

The next morning, a Saturday, Taer and Nix geared up for the cold. Taer wore tights under her jeans and Nix wore her blue U of C sweatshirt under her coat. Nix carried Berliner's gun in the kangaroo pocket of her sweatshirt. They put on their boots, scarves, hats, and gloves; Nix had black leather gloves she'd taken from her mother's house and Taer had one black glove and one gray because she could never keep pairs together.* They went out into the snow and took two buses (the 82 and the 73) to the intersection of West Armitage and North Racine.

They stood in front of the two gray office buildings they'd seen on computer screen, Taer a little reverent and Nix a little bored. Nix pulled one of her gloves off and flipped through Berliner's sketchpad of maps as her fingers stiffened in the freezing air. She pointed out to Taer all the maps from previous dates that featured a triangle with a red arrow pointing at the intersec-

---

* *Details from this Saturday were pulled from Cyrus's interviews with Nix, and a close examination of Taer's belongings—none of her socks or gloves were in matching pairs. —CD*

tion they were standing on. If they were right about the meaning of the symbols, then Berliner visited one of these buildings often. Taer thought they might find the *pied-à-terre* Davis had described.

Nix flipped to the beginning of the sketchpad and found the first map with the triangle of North Clybourn, North Armitage, and West Racine on it. At the top of the page, Berliner had written a string of numbers: 1142015914520205. Nix handed Taer the sketchpad so she could put her glove back on. Nix stomped both of her feet against the pavement to warm up her legs, which were so cold that her muscles strained as she moved. Taer looked at the sketchpad and tried to guess what the numbers were; not a birthday, not an address, not a license plate number.

After a minute or two of standing outside the buildings, cold and getting colder, Nix told Taer she was going to search the building on the right and instructed Taer to search the building on the left. Annoyed, Taer shoved Berliner's sketchpad into her coat pocket and—according to Nix—she said, "The cold makes you such a bitch."* They separated and made their way through the low drifts of snow that covered the paths to the entrances of the buildings. Taer reached her building first and found it oddly welcoming. The door, which was usually locked on weekends and required a key code to enter, was propped open with a small piece of wood. Inside, the icy wind blew tufts of snow onto the black-and-white tiled floors of the foyer. The lights and heat were on. Taer easily found a small bank of three elevators behind an unmanned security desk. She pressed a call button, the doors opened immediately, and she rode the elevator to the top floor.

The elevator opened into a long narrow hallway decorated with

---

* While Taer's behavior exemplifies some of the symptoms of Seasonal Affective Disorder, she was never formally diagnosed.

the same tiled floors, plus floor-to-ceiling windows with a view of the Armitage-Racine intersection. The hallway led to two suites of offices, one on either end of the building. Taer tried the doors to both of the offices; they were locked. Taer paused in front of the huge windows and spotted Nix, who was still outside, trying to find a way into her building. Taer watched Nix with renewed warmth and sympathy. She appreciated the tenacity with which Nix tried to pry open the building's windows. She noticed the perfect coordination of Nix's gloves and hat. She admired Nix's faux fur coat, even though she usually thought the coat was pretentious.

Taer felt any sense of urgency fade away. She didn't want the exploration of the buildings to feel like a competitive game between them. She didn't want to hold herself back from Nix anymore; she didn't want to fight; she didn't want Nix to sleep on the couch. Alone at the top of an office building, Taer decided to dedicate herself to Nix, to love her, and to wait for her to find a way into her building before Taer started looking around hers.

Taking the building's silence as evidence she was alone, Taer took off her mismatched gloves, sat down in front of the window, and started writing in her journal. She began by recounting the progress of her investigation: "I don't know if the openness of this building is the sign I have the right one, or if the locked-up-ness of Gina's building is a better sign. Maybe there's a janitor in here who propped open the door and will have a lot of fun kicking me out when he finds me. The building is so silent, though. I can't believe I'm seriously about to write this, but I wish the floors were carpeted so I didn't make so much noise walking around." As she wrote, Taer veered off into erotic daydreaming, in which Nix lay naked, except for her fur coat, in an igloo made of warm snow. In the fantasy, Taer had her own fur coat, which was held closed by a series of small buttons. Nix crawled across the igloo's ice floor, kneeled at Taer's feet, and started undoing the buttons.

She glanced out the window and saw Nix pressing all of the call buttons on the panel outside of the door. A few seconds later, Nix lunged for the door, pulled it open, and went inside. Taer thought someone working on a weekend, or even Berliner, had probably buzzed Nix in. Either way, she wasn't worried. Nix still had the gun.

With Nix safely inside, Taer searched the building, looking for traces of Berliner. All the offices on the eighth and ninth floors were bolted.

As Taer continued down the stairs to the seventh, sixth, fifth floors, her frustration mounted. The naturally anxious part of her personality took hold and she struggled to maintain a quiet, systematic exploration of the building.

Like a terrified rat in an impossible maze, she scurried from floor to floor, sometimes lingering for several minutes, yanking on the locked doors of the offices and searching the walls for hidden doors. Sometimes she only stayed on a floor for a moment before hurrying to the next. After half an hour of racing around, Taer paused to catch her breath and meditate on her failure. She walked glumly down the stairs, dragging her hand along the dirty railing until it was smudged with black grime.

Taer didn't realize it until she had reached street level, but the staircase she was walking down was built strangely. From the second to the tenth floors, the stairwell functioned normally, with concrete stairs connecting each level and plaster doors leading to each level's foyer. However, at the street level, the stairwell didn't have a door. The concrete wall continued, unbroken. There was no way to enter the building's lobby through the stairwell. Also, the staircase didn't stop descending when it hit the first floor. Although the elevator didn't have a "B" button, the stairs descended into a basement level. Taer hadn't considered a basement, even though most buildings in Chicago have one; Chicago is tornado country, and basements are where people hide from them.

As soon as Taer reached the bottom of the staircase, she knew she had found something. The door to exit the stairwell was abnormal; instead of wood and plaster, it was made of heavy steel and required a code for entry. Against the wall, there was a small keypad. She considered her obstacle for a few moments, then pulled out Berliner's sketchpad and opened it to the page with the strange series of numbers. She punched "1142015914520205" into the keypad and, with a lurch, the door unlocked itself.

Taer stepped into a long, dim hallway. She paused, taking a moment to prop the door open with her coat, frightened she'd be trapped inside. Then she took a few tentative steps forward, cursing as a floorboard creaked under her foot. The strange basement hallway had wooden floors.

The hallway was lined with white wooden doors, all of them reminiscent of the front door of a suburban house. Between each door hung a map, sixteen in all. At the very end of the hallway, opposite the code-locked steel door, was a final wooden door, the same as the others but painted red. Taer inched toward the red door. She looked at the maps, each of them illuminated with their own small lamp, the only source of light in the hallway. Although Taer saw the similarities in the maps, she didn't know that the type of map had a name; they were called Edge of the World maps. Popular from the mid-1500s to the mid-1600s, famous mapmakers drew Edge of the World maps as decorative alternatives to navigational cartographic maps. Their popularity arose with the excitement surrounding the news of the discovery of New Worlds. They were made to entertain while they educated, although the maps taught moral rather than scientific lessons.*

On the left side of Edge of the World maps, the artist/

---

* *I retained Cyrus's digression into the Edge of the World maps here, hoping it ramps up rather than cuts tension.* —CD

cartographer drew all the known continents, rendered with as accurate detail as possible. While it could be lovely, the left side of the map was perfunctory. Artists who didn't want to take the time to draw the continents could buy stencils or just copy another person's map. On the right side of the map, where all the action is, the water suddenly plummets over the edge of a flat earth, a giant waterfall into nothingness, the edge of the world. The real artistry of the maps was in the middle, near the edge of the falls. Guarding the edge of the world, each cartographer depicted a sea monster, or whatever creature was en vogue when the map was drawn: gluttonous whales, preening sirens, giant snakes, and krakens drawn as large as Africa. Occasionally, the cartographers would create their own monsters and give them names, like Ziphius or Steipereidur.*

Sometimes, the drawings showed the sea creatures crushing ships that dared to sail too close to the edge. In one of the maps that lined the hallway below the Racine building, a kraken held ten men in a single tentacle, crushing the life out of them. One particularly inventive mapmaker, Gérard Fournival, the "prodigal son of cartography," drew two sailors cooking their dinner on the back of long-toothed whale so large they mistook it for an island. Fournival only colored the surface of the sea, so the map's viewers could see the whale's submerged tail covered in spikes. The whale's similarly submerged head twisted as it looked over its monstrous shoulder with unveiled fury. The caption under that drawing, translated from Italian, reads: "In the moments before they realized their terrible mistake."† Ten of the maps Taer saw in the hallway were originals from the sixteenth and seventeenth centuries. The seven at the end

---

* Ziphius was probably invented by the naturalist and cartographer Conrad Gesner (sometimes spelled Konrad Gessner). Steipereidur was invented by the scientist and artist Abraham Ortelius.

† *Ancient Maps and Drawings, Volume 3: The Age of Exploration*, ed. Gerard Gumpert (New York: Macmillan, 1972), 269.

of the hallway, near the red door, were colored screen prints signed ANTOINETTE MONSON.

Taer crept as softly as she could down the hallway, past the Edge of the World Maps, with her back against the wall to protect herself, like she had seen in movies. She tried each of the white doors on the left side of the hallway; each one of them was locked. She didn't want to move away from the wall to check the ones on the right. At the end of the hallway, she grabbed the brass knob on the red door and pushed it open. Luckily, she didn't immediately step through the doorway, because the door didn't open into another room. Instead, it opened into empty space, into nothing. The Edge of the World maps weren't just decoration; they were a warning.

Taer cautiously peered through the doorway. The floor was a level below her. In the sunken room, a young man sat at a desk covered in papers and a large Mac desktop monitor. Nicolas Berliner was glaring at her.

Taer hadn't often encountered violence outside of a movie screen or television set. She wasn't well acquainted with action. As Taer teetered on the edge of the trap door, the break-in at her apartment and the gun she got out of it should've been at the forefront of her mind. Instead, she stared dumbly at Berliner, until, fuzzily captured by the audio recorder in Taer's pocket, he shouted at her:

"Caitlin Taer?"

With that, she was unstuck.

"Where's Molly Metropolis?" Taer shouted into the huge room. Her voice echoed. "Is Molly down here?"

Berliner laughed. "There's a staircase to your left, through the door. Come down here."

"How do I know you don't have a gun?"

"I lost my gun."

"Yeah, I know. At my apartment. How do I know you don't have another one?"

"This isn't a gangster movie. Get down here."

Curiosity overrode caution. Taer decided to risk descending to the bottom of the big room. She found the door to her left, which opened to a staircase that descended into the office.

"You're Nicolas Berliner, right?" Taer said, taking in the giant two-story room, enthralled with the high ceiling and at the huge painting of The Ghost Network on the wall.

"You're Caitlin Taer."

"Cait."

"I'm Nick. What do you mean, 'at my apartment'?"

"What?" Taer said.

"You said I lost my gun at your apartment, but as far as I know I've never been to your apartment."

"I'm not going to make you pay for, like, my plates or anything. We don't have to fuck around about this. You left your sketch-pad, too."

"No, listen, I've never been to your apartment," Berliner said, "Someone took my gun from me. Someone took my gun and my sketchpad weeks ago."

"Sure. You just want me to give up her notebook, or something. You can't have it."

"Caitlin—"

"No one calls me Caitlin."

"Cait. I didn't break into your apartment. Where's Gina?"

"I'm not here with anyone."

"I talked to Irene, I know you're with Gina. Where is she?" Berliner asked.

"She's at home. Can you just shut up and tell me what happened to Molly?"

"That's what I'm trying to figure out, too."

"Yeah, right!"

Their argument continued, until Berliner coaxed Taer over to his computer and showed Taer an e-mail from Molly that had arrived in his inbox a few days after she disappeared:

My dearest friend,

I hate to leave you alone in the middle of a battle. I'm writing in the hope that maybe the last thing you'll remember about me is this e-mail, and not the fact that I abandoned you in the dead of winter (both figuratively and literally).

I'll leave you with this:

I promise that leaving now was, in fact, an act of war against the people and things we've been fighting (including: Ali and Peaches, the secrecy of the members of the N.S., our own personal failings and foibles). And I've left the means for you to pursue a similar act of war—if you choose. I hope you'll strike as I've struck. Do you understand what I'm writing to you?

Berliner lamented, "Molly always liked a good rhetorical question."

Berliner had hired several private detectives and securities experts to trace the e-mail, whose names and numbers he had conveniently forgotten by the time he acquiesced to an interview with me. The experts found that Molly had sent the e-mail from her phone; she had typed it the day she disappeared, and scheduled it to send at a later date.

"Holy shit," Cait said several times as she was reading the letter. "I have to text Nix to come over here. She's next door."

"I thought you said she was at home," Berliner said, with an alarmed tone.

"She's searching the building next door, we didn't know which one you were in."

"Shit. Okay. Did you notice if anyone was following you?"

"No! Who would be following me?" Taer said.

"Can we go get Gina?"

"Why? Who was following me?"

"The people who took my gun."*

Taer checked her phone, but didn't have service in the basement, so she couldn't call Nix. She scurried back up the stairs with Berliner, back through the long hallway with the Edge of the World maps and screen prints, through the steel door, up the building's main staircase to the second floor, down the elevator to the lobby, and back out into the cold. Taer tried to zip her coat at the same time as she jogged between the two buildings, and Berliner shouted at her to hurry.

The door to the second building was again locked. Taer pulled out her cell phone, and called Nix, who answered with a hint of annoyance in her greeting.

"Stop bitching at me and listen," Taer said. "Come out of the building. I'm outside. I'm with Nick."

Nix appeared a few minutes later and Berliner greeted her.

"You motherfucker," Nix said. "You broke into our apartment."

"My apartment," Taer said.

Berliner said, "I swear to god, that wasn't me."

"Who the fuck else is there?" Nix asked.

Berliner ushered them back to the other building, to tell them about their real enemy, a pair of young women named Ali and Peaches—who were watching them from the coffee shop across the street.

---

* It is telling that Berliner and Taer's first exchange reads like a conversation between people who already know each other. Each had occupied a space in the other's brain for weeks before they actually met. They very quickly developed a shorthand.

151

PART 2

"Right now I'm a songwriter, and what I do is I perform, and write verses and choruses. But I might not always do that," Molly said. "I might cross over, not like into another genre, but into another aspect of culture entirely. I don't like boundaries. Everybody is a complicated character. It's like that poem from—what's his bucket?—Walt Whitman. 'Song of Myself.' Like, 'I am large, I contain multitudes.'"

—"LIVING IN MOLLY'S METROPOLIS," *The New York Times Magazine*

Chapter ⑨

On June 18, 2002, just after 4 a.m., every member of the New Situationists received an emergency text message. The group often used text messaging for mass or personal communications. They all had burner cell phones, the same type that drug dealers used, which didn't require that they disclose any personal information when signing up for service. Twice a month, they destroyed their old phones and bought new ones. Every member of the group used a generic nickname, like Jane or Joe or Nick, as their "phone name," and they developed a series of simple code words to cloak the meanings of their messages. A text that began with "911," for example, was personal or low priority. The message on June 18 began with the word "hey" which meant there was some kind of emergency that required immediate attention. The rest of the June 18 text was written in a biliteral cipher: a code where each letter of the intended message was replaced by a group of five A's and B's; for example, 'm' could be represented by ABAAA and 'o' could be represented by BBBAA, so 'Mom' would be spelled 'ABAAA-BBBAA-ABAAA.' David Wilson had adopted the simple code as a way for the New Situationists to communicate covertly but easily.

Although the group had scattered after planting their bombs, they were all awake when the message came in and they quickly decoded it: "M-H was arrested. Come to the headquarters now." Before Kraus's arrest report had even been filed, the New Situationists had sheltered themselves in their headquarters, the secret basement level of an office building at 2356 North Racine Avenue, at the corner of Armitage.*

The New Situationist headquarters was modeled on a building designed by Constant, but never built. Constant called the building *La Maison Astuce* or The Trick House. When he was young, Constant hoped to build *La Maison Astuce* as a personal residence to retire to, but by the time he reached the end of his life he was more concerned with painting than building. In 1992, he published the blueprints for anyone to use.

La Maison Astuce has seventeen rooms that branch off one central hallway. The first sixteen rooms, identical squares, are only accessible from the top floor. Inside each room is a little world onto itself, not unlike individual apartments in an apartment building, though with a markedly different ambiance. Each "room" has two levels, the top floor with a foyer, living room, public bathroom, and office. Connected by a staircase, the bottom floor has a bedroom, kitchenette, private library, and private office. These sixteen rooms are, as Constant put it, "like their own little worlds."†

The seventeenth room, at the back of the house, is the trick that gives the Trick House its name. Although it is the same size as the other sixteen rooms, it's not split into two levels. Instead, the ceilings are two stories high. The door at the end of the second floor hallway

---

★ *I'm not 100 percent certain where Cyrus gathered the information on these events. Kraus gave him some secondhand information, Berliner told him a few relevant stories—and when I asked Berliner to read these pages, he said they were basically right. But I can't confirm his original source. —CD*

† Constant, "Exploration of La Maison Astuce," translated by Libcom volunteers, *Internationale Situationniste*, no. 3 (December 1959): 12.

opens into empty air; from inside the seventeenth room, the door blends seamlessly into the high wall. Any visitor that doesn't know the trick to the room could, according to Constant, "fall to their death."* The seventeenth room is safely accessed from the second floor hallway's obscured eighteenth door, which has no doorknob. To open the door, you must push "in the spot where the doorknob would be"†; the door then opens to a spiral staircase.

The New Situationists also added a "back door" to the office, which wasn't on Constant's original plan. This secondary or emergency exit led to the underground garage of the building next door, through an entrance labeled EMPLOYEES ONLY, though no employee of the second building had a key. Although Constant didn't design the back door, he condoned its creation. In an explanation of the space published in *Potlatch*, a proto-Situationist publication, he wrote, "A hidden exit, or several, placed somewhere in the building could provide additional opportunities for spatial play. Design at will, according to the landscape."‡

When the New Situationists built The Trick House, they imagined that members could occupy the sixteen apartments, but most New Situationists never got around to moving in. Before the bombings, only Kraus, David Wilson, and the president of the New Situationists lived in the headquarters. Everyone else rented separate apartments. Berliner visited the headquarters often, but he was never given a room of his own to use; instead, he stayed with Kraus. There they could be alone to talk pop philosophy and have sex. According to Kraus, she let him sleep naked in her bedroom while she attended strategy meetings "above his clearance level" in the president's office.

After the bombings, all of the New Situationists hid themselves

---

* Although falling one story could sometimes result in death, more often than not the person who fell would just be injured.

† "Exploration of La Maison Astuce," 13.

‡ Ibid.

on the lower floor of their quarters. Only Berliner and Wilson came and went. Perhaps all sixteen rooms were full; perhaps some people had to share rooms. Because I don't know how many members the New Situationists actually had, and because Berliner and Kraus refuse to talk about that period of time in any detail, I don't know what hiding out was actually like. It could've been lonely, isolated, and spacious, or cramped and frustrating. I do know that all of their supplies came in from a security guard who worked in the office building. Berliner warned me not to look for that person, laboriously switching between gender pronouns as he always did when protecting the identity of someone associated with the New Situationists: "If you look, you won't find him. If you do find her, he won't have any useful information." I did search for the security guard but, as Berliner had predicted, I didn't find anything of use.

Buried in their own architectural creation, the New Situationists were forced to take stock of themselves and their organization. They were disillusioned. At first they held an official meeting every day during their sequester and argued constantly about the future of the movement. Eventually they stopped meeting and stopped talking to each other at all. No one tried to save the New Situationists except Berliner, who gave a passionate speech about courage and idealism. When another member stopped him in the middle of his rant to call him an ignorant and senseless child, Berliner punched him in the face. The conflict between Berliner and the other members ended only when he was incarcerated. By virtue of their forced cohabitation, the New Situationists limped along into the New Year, as their isolation stretched into its tenth month.

By the time Kraus's trial started in March, the police were spending less time investigating of the members of the New Situationists, for good reason. In 2003, six hundred and one people were murdered in Chicago, and about half of the homicides were related to gang or drug violence. The CPD had their hands full and a bombing suspect on trial; the newspaper headlines had shifted back to

President Bush's war in Iraq. The New Situationists and Kraus were buried on the second page of the Metro section. Though the Federal Investigation continued, and indeed remains an open case to this day, the New Situationists felt safer, and the group slowly disbanded.

After his stint in juvenile detention, Berliner didn't return to the New Situationist headquarters. He had probably been the most emotionally affected by the collapse of the group; he had treated their goals like religion and Kraus like a priest. Heartbroken, he moved back into his mother's house and sat in the courtroom every day to watch the proceedings of Kraus's trial. He wore a pair of gray suit pants and a rotating set of pale blue button-down shirts. At the end of each day in court, the bailiff led Kraus through the small band of courtroom reporters allowed to attend the trail. They didn't shout at her like on television, but the photographers took hundreds of pictures. Berliner followed in the wake of the reporters. He watched as Kraus stepped into the windowless van that transported her back to the Dwight Correctional Center, and then he walked all the way from the courthouse in the Loop to his mother's brownstone in Lincoln Park. He ruined his shiny black loafers with weeks of that kind of walking. He stayed in every evening; he never socialized or watched TV. Instead, he read fiction: the collected stories of Borges, *Drown* by Junot Díaz, several novels by Italo Calvino, *The Corrections* by Jonathan Franzen.

The trial ended on April 30; a week later, Kraus received her sentence. Berliner sat in the back of the courtroom during the sentencing and Kraus turned around to look at him three times. Kraus had refused to see Berliner when he tried to visit her in jail, so during the sentencing he wouldn't sit close enough to Kraus to touch her. When the judge read her sentence, Kraus didn't react, but Berliner burst into tears and ran out of the courtroom when the reporters took his picture.

"She's not the kind of girl that wanted some kind of protection from me or from any boyfriend—and, anyway, our dynamic wasn't like that. She hated having me in the courtroom in general," Berliner said during our third interview.

"When I visited her in prison, later, she was always saying to me, 'you shouldn't have had to see my trial'—that was the kind of relationship we had. So, [sitting in the back of the courtroom] was a teenage defiant thing like, 'Fuck you, you won't see me? I'll sit in the back. If we're going to end, let's end it dramatically. You'll miss me.' Of course, it wasn't like that. I cried. I went to visit her the next week and made sure she was still my girlfriend. She was, she still is, no matter who I'm with she will always be, but in the courtroom everything feels dramatic. Everything in my life at that point had a very heightened sense of drama, and that was the apex. I started watching *Law and Order* with my mother, and I always wished they would keep up with the characters after the trials, just so I could have a guide for how to act. My mother told me to pray, but of course I didn't have anything to pray to."

During the trial, Berliner lost touch with the other New Situationists. He didn't know most of their names and didn't try to find out, but he would've liked to talk with some of them a few weeks before Kraus's sentencing, when CNN began airing a series of investigative reports called "Who Are The New Situationists?" According to Berliner, the report got a lot of things wrong, but also got a few things right. He wasn't specific about what details fit into what category, although CNN's conclusion that the New Situationists had been hiding out somewhere in Chicago was clearly correct. More likely than not, the New Situationists returned to simple, everyday lives, started going to Starbucks again, bought business-casual attire, found jobs as assistants in offices, and moved slowly up the ladder. According to Berliner, one of the former New Situationists is now a popular food blogger; he says he saw her face for the first time in a picture in the Food section of the *Tribune*.*

"Sometimes I wonder if I'll run into one of them at a bar sometime," Berliner told me, "I wouldn't even recognize them. That's the strangest part. The group is still part of what I am but the only person that meant something to me was Marie. That's weird to think about."

After Kraus went to prison, Berliner fell in with a group of Chicago photographers and avant-garde artists, all of whom had recently graduated from Columbia College in Chicago (an arts college unaffiliated with Columbia University in New York), all of whom were at least four years older than Berliner, and all of whom used him for his cultural capital while he used them for low-effort companionship. When I asked Berliner to give me their names, he couldn't remember more than one. He recalled them as an amorphous blob, as a group of people who worked terrible jobs in restaurants and coffee shops while trying to take their art seriously, and he could only distinctly remember one out of the clump, a lesbian portrait photographer named Claire Haskal, with whom he still occasionally gets drunk.

Haskal, who helpfully provided me with prints of several portraits of Berliner at eighteen and nineteen years old, recalls him as a nearly "catatonic" social presence. "He'd come out to openings and just stand with a group of us, never saying a word. People thought it was an affectation, or that he was intimidated because he was so young. That's what I thought, I thought he was intimidated, so I tried to stick close to him, like he was a skittish dog. All the art fags wanted him as a pet. I did, too.

"But he wasn't intimidated, he was in mourning for his whole

---

* *Berliner didn't explain to Cyrus how he knew this food blogger was in the N.S., while simultaneously not knowing any of the names or faces of any of the members. He must've lied somewhere, even if only about the food blogging. —CD*

life. I found that out later, when he snapped out of it and we really became friends. Most people would've stayed in bed, but he dragged himself out to these parties. He wanted to be around the living, I guess."

Haskal encouraged Berliner to write about maps and architecture, and use his semi-infamous name to get published. Berliner wrote one essay; it was about the city as it was used by Christopher Nolan in the movie *Batman Begins* and it was called "Modern Urbanism's *Tabula Rasa*: Destroying and Rebuilding Gotham."

In the 2005 reboot of the Batman movie franchise, director Christopher Nolan and his producers decided to film the movie in Chicago (rather than New York), letting the Second City stand in for the fictional Gotham City. Until *Batman Begins* started filming, New York had been Gotham for so long that the cities were interchangeable; comics artists that depicted the city drew New York-esque skylines, and New York was nicknamed Gotham. Nolan's decision to move Gotham from New York to Chicago destroyed and re-created an entire city.

Architects that subscribe to modern urbanism aesthetics and ideals would approve of Nolan's recast of Gotham. Modern urbanists tend to "create tabula rasa for the building of cities without memory."* Cities without memory have no history. In moving Gotham to Chicago, Nolan was attempting to create a Gotham untainted by New York City.†

---

* From the preface of *Architectural Uncanny: Essays in the Modern Unhomely* by Anthony Vidler. In the tradition of Situationist *détournement*, Berliner didn't note his inclusion of the quote, neither with quotation marks nor citation.

† Nicolas Berliner, "Modern Urbanism's *Tabula Rasa*: Destroying and Rebuilding Gotham," Esquire.com, www.esquire.com/features/modern-urbanisms-tabula-rasa /ESQ0605-JUN_ARTS.

Despite the article's faults, *Esquire* magazine published the piece on its website.*

The Columbia crowd didn't make an artist out of Berliner, but he helped make an artist out of Haskal. He helped style her best work: animated gif portraits of all of her friends in party settings, looking beautiful and excited in early frames of the gif, but quickly transitioning to the grotesque with only slight tweaks in the framing of their faces. Haskal credits Berliner with helping her during "a very adolescent time in my development as an artist." As with all of Berliner's close friends, she remains fiercely loyal to him.

Berliner also let his grandmother, Helen Raulson, find him a job as a clerk in a shop that sold historical maps. The owner, Abraham Shapiro, was an old friend of Raulson's and, unbeknownst to Berliner, her former clandestine lover. According to Shapiro, nothing was more sexually transgressive and therefore stimulating to Raulson than a tall, muscular Jewish man. Shapiro acted like he was doing Raulson a favor, but he was actually happy to give the front of the shop to Berliner and spend all his time in the back room, buying, cataloguing, and pricing maps. Shapiro had never married and once told Berliner that he was a lifelong bachelor because he was "a hit with the Shiksas but never managed to get a proper Jewish girl in the sack."†

Most of the time, Berliner stood alone at a glass counter, drafting the blueprints for his perfect apartment or reading non-fiction books about mapmaking and the Age of Exploration. He discovered that if he was knowledgeable about the maps, he didn't have to be

---

* *Esquire*'s web editor, Audrey Sampson, wrote a two-hundred-word bio for Berliner, labeling him "The Last Situationist." The bio ran before the article. There was still some cache associated with the New Situationists' neo-Situationism, and undoubtedly *Esquire* published the article because of the byline, not the contents.

† *Berliner quoted Ari to Cyrus during one of their solo interviews. —CD*

nice to the customers. His favorite maps, the Edge of the World maps, sold well.*

Berliner worked in the shop for a year and a half, trying to forget the problems in his past. He learned the names of the map collectors. He occasionally dated a girl for a few weeks or a few months. He visited Kraus in prison. For a long time, nothing happened to him and he started to believe that all the excitement in his life had already passed; that, like a star athlete, the drama of his life took place entirely in his youth. But then, on a quiet Saturday morning in June, Molly Metropolis walked into his shop.

Molly was only sixteen during *The City of Chicago vs. Marie-Hélène Kraus,* and though she had appreciated the sensationalism of the trial, she hadn't focused on the specific details of the case until her first year at U of C, when she took a freshman seminar called "Modern Law and Fiction." She studied Kraus's case during her second week as a college student and it made a dramatic impression on her. Her obsession with the case led her to the Situationists, to Antoine/Antoinette Monson, to Berliner. She fixated on it for the rest of the semester and wrote about it for her final paper. After she decided to leave U of C to pursue a career as a singer, she sold all of her textbooks and trashed all of her notes, except for the ones about Kraus's case. During the thirteen months between dropping out and being signed by Harmony Records, her first record label, Molly continued to research the New Situationists. When Harmony dropped her without putting out an album, she decided to take her New Situationist research to the next level. She mined her old school contacts, canvassing poli-sci and architecture majors about

---

* He rarely sold his least favorite: sixteenth- and seventeenth-century maps that depicted California as an island off the coast of the mainland of what was to become North America. One of the most infamous cartographic errors ever, a Spanish romance novelist from the 1500s, Garci Rodríguez de Montalvo, popularized the idea in a series of books depicting California as an Eden-like garden, an island populated entirely by beautiful women.

the New Situationists. She read in a *Chicago Tribune* article that the "last member of the New Situationists" was living in Chicago, working at a store selling old maps.

Once Molly found Berliner, she didn't waste any time. Molly walked into the cartography shop wearing a pair of huge sunglasses and a black T-shirt with a very, very deep V-neck that showed off chunks of her rhinestone-encrusted bra. Though she wasn't yet famous, she already looked like a mega-watt pop star on a morning stroll. Without a glance at the maps on the wall, she sauntered over to Berliner's counter. Berliner knew exactly what she wanted. Since the trial, he had warded off journalists, historians, and the fanboys and fangirls of the New Situationist movement. Berliner wanted to show Molly the door but, true to form, she refused to walk through it.

In our interviews, Berliner was often hostile, coldly detached, frustrated, monosyllabic, nicotine-deprived, or unwilling to answer questions without providing a reason for his unwillingness. In short, he was the opposite of everything an interviewer hopes their subject will be. So, when I asked him about the early months of his collaboration with Molly Metropolis, I expected we would play our usual game of frustration and reluctance. I was wrong. He put away a cigarette without smoking it and said, "We're finally going to talk about Metro? I was beginning to think you didn't give two shits about the person who is responsible for everything."*

The first story Berliner told me about Molly was delightfully characteristic: "The first thing she said to me, I mean as she was shaking my hand, was that her name was Molly Metropolis and she

---

* *Of course, Molly wasn't responsible for everything. Guy Debord is, or Constant. Though it's true that all three of them benefited from the fortuitous combination of right person, right time, and right place that creates history out of events and legend out of man (or icon out of women). Molly didn't start anything, she was just the biggest ship to get caught in the storm. —CD*

was going to be a pop star. 'But that doesn't matter right now,' she said. 'What matters is you.' I knew immediately she was referring to the [New Situationists]. At that time, there were only two things people talked to me about, and I could tell immediately that she didn't want to buy a map. Of course, in a way, I was wrong about that. She had me make her dozens of maps."

When Berliner met her, Molly hadn't completely evolved into the public figure she eventually became, but she was a primordial version of that figure. She dressed in metallic clothing and directed the people around her like they were members of her staff. She also refused to take no for an answer; two days after Berliner told Molly he didn't want to work with her, she came back to the cartography shop and propositioned him again. Work with her, and she would give Berliner the money to build his apartment. Berliner cautiously asked her how she knew about his apartment and she told him that she had followed him to the Chicago Public Archives where his sometimes-girlfriend, Nina Johnson, worked and had discussed it with her. Molly later confessed to Berliner that this was a lie; she had actually visited Kraus several times in prison, winning Kraus's trust, and learning about the apartment from her. Not wanting to betray her new friend, Molly blamed Johnson. Berliner had unfortunately broken up with the confused archivist on the weight of Molly's lie. Berliner made a point to find Johnson and apologize once he learned the truth, and managed to salvage the relationship, somewhat.*

"Molly loved secret histories. She also loved contradicting accounts of the same historical events. She liked ambiguities. She liked answerless questions. She told me that she was investigating the world that traditional maps hide from us," Berliner said. "She said she felt like she had been walking down the street blindfolded, but

---

* *This story about Berliner, Kraus, Molly, and Johnson is strange, but Berliner "thinks" it's accurate, so I didn't cut it from the text.* —CD

she didn't know she was wearing a blindfold. One day, she realized the blindfold was there and she pulled it off, but the place she saw was so unfamiliar that she couldn't recognize it without a guide. And I was supposed to be that guide.

"That's how she talked. She wasn't crazy, not in any of the ways people thought she was, and she wasn't an idiot. She had looked up all these papers David Wilson wrote as a graduate student, about philosophy and architecture, and she thought the New Situationists were hiding a secret agenda, something more secret than the subway bombings. She thought the group, the bombing, everything was incidental to—or at least, concurrent with—some greater secret goal. She didn't think I knew what it was, she thought it had been kept at 'the highest levels of the New Situationists.' I asked her how she knew I wasn't at the highest level and she said, 'I understand how the New Situationists worked. If you had been at the highest level, you never would've let anybody know your name.'"

Berliner told Molly Metropolis he would think about working with her, but before he could agree to divulge anything about the New Situationists, he needed to check with the only higher-up he still talked to. The next day, he took the train to the Dwight Correctional Center for an unscheduled visit. He brought Kraus an expensive new bra, cigarettes, nail polish, and a croissant from her favorite bakery. They exchanged a few pleasantries, but Berliner was anxious to ask her about the New Situationists. He asked her if she thought the New Situationists possibly had a "secret agenda." Without batting an eyelash, she told him that it was very possible. Kraus told Berliner about a side of the New Situationists he hadn't seen. The president had often ranted about creating a brotherhood of politicians and lobbyists who would eventually control Chicago's infrastructure. The New Situationists were ambitious and slightly delusional, Kraus told Berliner, so of course they had secret plans. The president was always very secretive; Kraus had often been excluded from meetings. "Probably," she joked, "they wanted to take over the world."* Also, Kraus pointed out, they were incredibly well funded for an anarchist movement—suspiciously well funded.

For Kraus's benefit, Berliner recounted the story of Molly Metropolis's visit, about her "pretentions about being famous," and about her proposed investigation into the New Situationists' secret agenda. Kraus told Berliner to set up a meeting between herself and Molly. She and Molly were still pretending they hadn't met. To my knowledge, neither Kraus nor Molly ever recounted what happened during their meetings, but Molly must've charmed Kraus. When Berliner returned the next day, Kraus told him to go ahead and investigate with Molly. Kraus warned Berliner not to mention Molly or the investigation to David Wilson, because he would try to stop them. She insisted Berliner couldn't use any of his old friends or contacts in the New Situationists. She also asked him to visit frequently and update her about the investigation. She wanted to see what he would find.

That night, Berliner called Molly and asked her to meet him at the corner of West Armitage and North Racine. She arrived an hour later, wearing a vintage floral jumpsuit and black stilettos with pink rhinestones. Berliner took her into the New Situationist headquarters; the rooms weren't as impressive as they had been when Kraus took Berliner down for the first time. Berliner showed her Kraus's old room. Molly ran her fingers along the walls and asked if they could stay the night. Berliner offered to find another room to sleep in, but Molly asked him to stay, if he could be a gentleman with her. She told him she had nightmares almost every night. Berliner slept on the couch.

The next morning, Molly and Berliner spent a few hours combing through the debris the New Situationist leadership had left

---

* Berliner liked the joke. During subsequent visits, he started their conversation with a line from popular cartoon *Pinky and the Brain*: "Gee, Brain, what do you want to do tonight?" Kraus would respond, "The same thing we do every night, Pinky—try to take over the world!"

behind in their haste to make the strange, secretive political group part of their past. In the giant office at the end of the hall—he still called it "The Trick" then, though later he would offhandedly call it Metro's Room—Berliner found several filing boxes full of documents.

In the spring of 2007, Molly Metropolis signed with SDFC Records and created the General Council. She added Berliner to her personal payroll—he was her first paid staff member, ever—and christened their fledgling collaboration the Urban Planning Committee, a secret offshoot of the General Council. Molly kept her work with Berliner hidden from everyone, including her family and closest friends; taking a page out of the New Situationists' book, she refused to even write down the name. At the top of her notebooks about the Urban Planning Committee she wrote, "Here is the Secret History of the U.P.C."*

Molly only mentioned Berliner publicly once, to the German music news outlet *Knall Produktion*: "The inspiration for the General Council came from Andy Warhol's Factory as well as the entourage of beautiful, glowing people that David Bowie always had around him, his friends, the people at his parties. But I got the name from my friend Nick Berliner, who is teaching me about architecture."†

That summer, Molly Metropolis gave her first major live performance since signing with SDFC and receiving the benefit of their marketing department. She played during an early timeslot at Chicago's giant summer music festival, Lollapalooza. She had no light show, no backdrop, no pyrotechnics, just a DJ, a drummer, and a

---

* None of these notebooks survive. Information on their contents came to me secondhand, from my interviews with Berliner.

† Kristian Sommer, "Molly! The New Diva!" *Knoll Producktion* 126, no. 5 (April 2008): 89.

jeweled keyboard she played herself. Molly came onstage in a metallic, silver bra and lace leggings.* She performed some songs that eventually found their way onto *Cause Célèbrety*, including an early version of her first single "Don't Stop (N'Arrête Pas)," which was produced by Astroman and included short bridge from the producer/rapper: "Work, work, work your body/Pop, pop, pop a Molly." Molly also sang a *Cause Célèbrety* album cut called "Poptimist," as well as "Maps (Find Me)," but the crowd didn't like the show. "Too synth-y," several bloggers complained.†

After her performance, Molly hung around in the artist tent for a few hours, then left, promising to meet up with her friends and the record executives at the private SDFC after-party that night. She threw on one of her deep V-neck T-shirts, took a cab to Armitage and Racine, and descended into the basement, where Berliner was waiting for her. She hugged him and said, "I've left you alone for too long, my darling. I've missed you and the things we're doing together."

Molly told Berliner the details of her performance and complained about the lethargic crowd while they each had a cigarette in the "smoking room"—one of the apartments, which Berliner had redecorated with vintage leather armchairs, oil paintings of deer and buffalo, and of course, framed maps. When Molly asked Berliner what he had been up to in the weeks since they'd last seen each other, Berliner revealed his utter lack of a social life by jumping right into business talk: he had found something. Berliner and Molly went back to the huge two-story office where Berliner stored the documents.

Berliner knew the New Situationists' record-keeping policies. They never wrote down or recorded anything about their organization on computers, instead preferring to use typewriters or hand-

---

* She wore the same bra in the music video for "Don't Stop."
† *Cyrus didn't indicate which bloggers. —CD*

written notes to create archives that couldn't be hacked and could be easily destroyed by shredding or burning. More likely than not, the two boxes of documents contained every physical record the New Situationists had ever produced, with the exception of the letter sent to the *Chicago Tribune* taking credit for the subway bombings, which is still languishing somewhere in an FBI evidence locker. According to Berliner, the records contained mostly letters between members. In the letters, the New Situationists mostly discussed the "most public" parts of the operation, such as Kraus's anti-recruitment efforts.

While skimming the documents in the first box, Berliner found a letter from David Wilson to the NS's president, which mentioned the New Situationists' "digital and physical archives." It seemed strange to Berliner that the New Situationists would keep any kind of official archive at all—they had preached to their membership that any archive could be compromised—so he started looking through the documents for any other references to digital records. Eventually, he found another letter from Wilson to the president, asking about the "progress of the map archives and the L project." Berliner spent a few hours searching for the president's response to Wilson, and he eventually found it, crumpled at the bottom of the second box of documents. The president told Wilson he had nearly completed digitizing all the necessary maps for the "L project," and that they were only waiting for a few important maps from the early 1940s, and then they would have "a complete archive of every iteration."*

Berliner hurried through document after document, looking for more mentions of the L or the map project. He found a few scattered remarks—one member was bored with researching historical proposals for additions to the L lines that had never been adopted, and wanted to be assigned another task; another apologized

---

* Quotations from Berliner's personal notes on the New Situationist documents.

171

profusely to the president as he reported that a certain map the president wanted no longer existed in Chicago's public archives— and Berliner began to understand, at least in part, what the New Situationists had done. They had collected all of the maps of the Chicago elevated train system, including both historical maps from every year the L existed, as it expanded and contracted and morphed, and maps of every addition or change to the L proposed to the Chicago Transit Authority, including those that had been rejected. Every map of the L as it had once been, every map of the L as it could've been but wasn't; a full historical record of every L station and every station that was proposed but wasn't built.

Berliner knew from the documents that the New Situationists were actively collecting maps, but he didn't know for sure if they had acquired them all or what they did with them once they had.

While she listened to Berliner explain his findings, Molly didn't ask questions, but she did stop him several times to examine a section of a letter or a document he mentioned. Once Berliner finished talking, she wordlessly wandered back into the smoking room. Berliner followed her. She sat in one of the armchairs, lit a cigarette, and asked Berliner to pour her a little glass of whiskey. He poured hers and one for himself, and sat in an armchair. After a half a minute of silence, while Molly smoked, drank, and stared at the wall lost in thought, Berliner lit his own cigarette. She stayed silent while he smoked; when he smashed his cigarette butt in the ashtray, Molly Metropolis gave Berliner his task. He would recreate the New Situationists' map archive. Then she would take every map he collected and put them all together, into one giant map. She and Berliner would be able to see what the New Situationists had been building. They would have the New Situationists' complete knowledge of the L and would see what they wanted from it.

Molly knew she and Berliner couldn't complete such a huge task on their own, especially with her music career taking up more of her time; she would have to expand the Urban Planning Committee. Molly told Berliner she wanted to invite the two other people Molly trusted most, her friends and dancers, Ali and Peaches.

Ali and Peaches exist mostly in the corners and rough edges of the early days of Molly's career. They were with her before the entertainment and fashion media tried to squish her life into an easily repeatable narrative. Early magazine and newspaper profiles on Molly, in outlets like *Interview Magazine* and Australia's *Sydney Morning Harold*, comment on the dancers' presence, but their influence on Molly, both artistically and through their friendship, is rarely commented upon.

Ali and Peaches appear in the opening of the "Don't Stop (N'Arrête Pas)" music video, as Molly's friends, helping her crash a Gatsby-esque mansion party. When Molly performed at the Echoplex in Los Angeles in May 2008, they stacked themselves on top of each other to form a human keyboard stand while Molly played her stripped-down version of "Heart Machine." They danced when she opened for Jennifer Lopez—all before any radio station ever played "Don't Stop."

The dancers' most striking appearances, though, weren't in music videos or appearances or marketing materials, but in interviews. For video and print interviews alike, Ali and Peaches accompanied her, dressed exactly the same as Molly. As Molly debuted herself to the world, they were her shadows. No one knew why. They didn't look like Molly, and they are both white, so they didn't read as body doubles or decoys to fool the paps.

At least once an interview, in response to a question, Molly would whisper something into either Ali or Peaches's ear and they would recite her answer for her. Journalists called their presence "bizarre" or "inexplicable." MTV News's Dana Andapolis wrote that Molly chose "random" questions for her dancers to respond to on her behalf, but there is in fact a method to this particular

173

madness of Molly's.[*] Whenever she was asked a particularly invasive question about her biography or romantic life, she made Ali and Peaches answer. She outsourced the most emotional responses to her best friends. She also used the low buzz around this "bizarre" practice as a way to show her sense of humor. For her first major U.S. late-night appearance on CBS's *The Late Late Show with Craig Ferguson*, when Ferguson announced her, Peaches walked out instead.

Ali, a dropout of the School of American Ballet in New York, had thick red hair, a narrow jaw, and incredibly long legs that Molly admired and envied. Peaches was taller, but all torso, with a huge smile, dirty blonde hair, and a tendency to freckle in the summer. Molly, Ali, and Peaches spent most of their working days together and became close friends. They frequently videotaped each other and a few of their exploits found their way onto YouTube. In one video, they goof around, prancing around in Wicker Park, and in another they roll around on the floor of a spa, after a massage and a steam. In the third, they discuss the nature of art and performance while waiting for a flight at an airport.[†]

In early 2007, after Molly signed with SDFC and found Ali and Peaches, but before the record company released "Don't Stop (N'Arrête Pas)" as a single, the pre–pop star Molly kept no one closer than her dancers. She bounced ideas off them and socialized with them; she used them as sounding boards, companions, and shields. In the morning, when she woke up with a new idea that excited her to her core, Molly would call Ali. In the evening, exhausted by dance training or a long day at the recording studio, arguing with her handlers, Molly would curl up on a big leather couch with Peaches and they would softly sing "Row Your Boat" in

---

[*] Dana Andapolis, "Meeting Molly," MTV.com, February 12, 2009; www.mtv.com /news/music/3082636/meeting-molly/.

[†] Which airport? Who knows. O'Hare is my best guess, but all airports look alike.

canon. They recorded their sing-along once and uploaded the video to YouTube.* Ali and Peaches were Molly's first disciples, the first to wear outfits she designed and the first to stand behind her when she declared herself a "pop performance artist." They were the first to take her seriously, and although Molly rewarded them with loyalty, she didn't give them honesty. She was hard on them.

On the night of Molly's Lollapalooza performance, after she had returned from her meeting with Berliner, Ali and Peaches joined her at the SDFC Lollapalooza after-party at The Drawing Room on the Near North Side. They wore their Metro-designed outfits— black skin-tight deep-V shirts and copper-colored leggings—and mingled with other SDFC artists and Lollapalooza performers for nearly an hour before Molly pulled them away from the party. They hailed a taxi and rode to their hotel, the Congress. Berliner was waiting in Molly's small room. The dancers crowded in, and Molly introduced them to one another.

"Peaches seemed very tall," Berliner told me, when I asked about his first impressions of the dancers. He was bored by the question.

When I asked the dancers about Berliner, Peaches said, "What a pretentious asshole."

After I spoke to Ali and Peaches about meeting Berliner,† I realized both dancers half-blamed Berliner for Molly's secrecy, like a cuckolded wife blaming the woman her husband slept with, rather than the true source of her dissatisfaction: the husband.

In the hotel room, they all sat on the bed, drinking from mini-bar bottles, while Molly and Berliner explained what they'd been up

---

* Though the video has been removed from Molly's official YouTube channel, the copy most easily accessible via a simple search has over 500,000 views. [*It has over 505,000 views, as of the time this book went to press. —CD*]

† Ali and Peaches were reluctant to discuss the events in the book, but feared that without commenting, their side of the story would not be heard. Unfortunately, due to legal restrictions on what they could discuss, I'm afraid I'm unable to include the nuances of their experience of the events, and the young women, perhaps unfairly, remain villains in this text.

to. Molly had never hinted at her secret work with Berliner, so Ali and Peaches were surprised when Molly told them about the energy she'd already put into researching Guy Debord and the New Situationists, as well as the amount of time she'd put into the Urban Planning Committee. They never knew Molly to scheme behind their backs; she constantly updated them, overwhelming them with detail on the objects and outfits she designed for her music videos and stage shows. In introducing the dancers to Berliner, Molly revealed a secret second life, and changed Ali and Peaches's perception of her forever. That night, Molly Metropolis became a person that could keep an important secret behind someone's back, a person not to be entirely trusted.

Berliner did his best to quickly explain the Situationists, the New Situationists, and his theory of the L maps to Ali and Peaches, while Molly fixed everyone drinks and hummed the Britney Spears song "(You Drive Me) Crazy." When Berliner finished talking, Molly asked Ali and Peaches if they wanted to join the Urban Planning Committee. She said, "Everything we're doing here is top secret and vitally important not only to ourselves but the entire world." (Molly often referred to the project as "vitally important to the entire world," the same way she called herself a pop star before her first record came out.) A little nonplussed, but generally inclined to follow Molly's directions, Ali and Peaches agreed to help.

"We just have to get maps?" Ali asked.

"You will never *just* do anything," Molly replied.

However, gathering maps did become their central focus for the next few months. To gather every map of every iteration and every proposed iteration of the Chicago L system took time, energy, dedication, and organizational focus. Luckily, the materials were readily available, for the most part. The Chicago Transit Authority (CTA) posted L maps from the last twenty years on their website. The Chicago Historical Society archived every L map the CTA ever published, and the Chicago Public Archives housed all of the

City Council's meeting minutes and recordings, including discussions of all proposed L expansions or reformations. The Chicago Public Library acted as a catchall, to fill in any gaps, as did Berliner's sometimes-girlfriend, Johnson, who was both a librarian and an amateur Chicago historian. Johnson, a leggy but plain architecture student, told them the Chicago Housing Council had designed their own reconfigurations of the L system and presented them directly to the Chicago Transit Authority, not the City Council. The records of those plans were only available through the Chicago Housing Council, which doesn't make their records public.

Peaches solved the problem by seducing Andrew Pierson, the male assistant to the head of the Chicago Housing Council. Pierson had a sexual fetish for women dressed as schoolgirls (utterly boring, but remarkably common), and Peaches took to the character with relish. She returned from her trysts with her hair in messy pigtails, photocopies of the Housing Council's proposals from the early 1960s to the mid 1990s stuffed in her bag, and jump drives full of digital files of proposals from the '90s to the present.

Although she liked to play, the slow and boring work of acquiring the L maps weighed on Peaches. She wasn't studious like Berliner and Molly, preferring to live in her body rather than her mind. When she hung out with Molly, she wanted to go clubbing or cuddle or work on improving Molly's dancing skills; she didn't want to talk about maps or think about secrets. When we spoke, Peaches still sounded resentful: "Once we knew about the maps thingy it was like she stopped having to try with us. She wasn't trying to be nice anymore. Some days she'd be her old self, fun and effusive, like she was. Then other days she'd be moody and snap at me just for asking a simple question. The worst part was, she wasn't like that with Nick, no matter what. Even when he was being an idiot. She was always so goddamn sweet to him." For a while, Peaches ignored her growing resentment and directed her considerable worth ethic to the task Molly had assigned her.

While Ali and Peaches focused on acquisition, Berliner examined and organized the copies of the maps they brought to him. He created a catalogue on his computer, categorizing the maps by year, city location, and type (accepted proposals, accepted proposals that were never built due to various interruptions, unaccepted proposals, and even some plans that had been drawn but never formally proposed). When Ali and Peaches left Chicago to dance for Molly, Berliner took over acquisition duties as well, often spending fifty or sixty hours a week building his detailed archives and filing maps.

The work of a librarian suited Berliner well, as did the work of a print maker, which he also took on at that time. Molly asked him to make brightly colored screen prints of various L maps to decorate her New York and Los Angeles apartments. Berliner also purchased, with funds from Molly, several original Edge of the World maps from his old map shop and made some screen prints to hang alongside the originals on the walls of the underground hideout in the Racine building, both to decorate and claim the space formerly belonging to the New Situationists as Urban Planning territory. Molly judged Berliner's screen prints by her typical stringent standards of aesthetic quality.

Their double responsibilities as dancers and researchers wore Ali and Peaches a little thin, but Molly Metropolis never tired out. She spent all of her free time, when she wasn't writing music or designing and shopping for her outfits, compiling the maps using a custom mapmaking computer program she commissioned called Molly-Maps. She hired a computer programmer to write her the mapmaking program, where she could organize various maps based on Berliner's categories of year, location, and type. The programmer thought he was making her a platform to track her touring schedule.

When Molly visited Chicago, she copied the maps into Molly-Maps on a computer that she never connected to the Internet.

Eventually, when the number of maps became too overwhelming for her to digitize on her own, Molly gave Berliner a copy of MollyMaps and bought him his own laptop. When Berliner met up with Molly on tour or when she visited him in Chicago, they synched their maps over a closed wireless connection.

As 2007 slid into 2008, Molly's relationship with Peaches fell apart. The rift developed slowly. At first, they just snapped at each more often, poking at each other with pithy, bitchy remarks when they were both tired or overwhelmed with work. For a while, they would apologize after their little snipes. Then they stopped apologizing. When Ali was there to act as a buffer, Molly and Peaches got along fine, so to avoid arguing, Molly and Peaches stopped spending time by themselves. Very quickly, they forgot how to have fun together; alone in a room, they argued or lapsed into uncomfortable silence. Molly stopped discussing her personal life with Peaches and never asked advice about her family or romantic entanglements. They still spent almost every day together, but without meaning to, they stopped being friends.

Then Peaches asked to see the map that Molly had just begun calling The Ghost Network. Molly didn't want to show Ali and Peaches until it was finished, so she refused Peaches's request. Peaches thought it was hypocritical of Molly to let Berliner see the map but refuse to show it to her, even as Peaches collected the raw materials for it. Peaches complained to Ali, who refused to participate in the conflict. To avoid her friends' squabbling, Ali spent ten hours a day working, dancing, or copying maps, and the rest of her time with her boyfriend. Though Ali removed herself, she encouraged Molly to try to patch things up with Peaches.

During the last week of May 2008, Molly and Peaches met every night to try to work through their problems and instead spent hours fighting. Neither girl would relent, so they fought for days. It seemed to Ali that they would go on like this forever, that fighting would become the new normal mode of their relationship, then Peaches crossed a line. In early June, Molly found her trying to break into the computer Molly used to run MollyMaps. Later that night, she sent a text message to Ali and Berliner: "Peaches is expelled from the Urban Planning Committee."

Berliner supported Molly's decision, but Ali tried to reconcile the situation. She spoke to Peaches and Molly, trying to put a Band-Aid on a bullet hole. After a few days of needling from Ali, Molly wrote her an e-mail during a layover on a quick trip to Australia to promote *Cause Célèbrety*:

Ali dear, this is my last word on the subject. I don't want to cut you off or keep you from expressing yourself, but I'm not going to relent and nothing you can say, or that Peaches can say for that matter, would change my mind. I've been betrayed on a personal level, a professional level, and an artistic level—betrayed so completely that even talking about it is difficult and painful for me. If it wasn't you that I was writing to, someone I trust completely and who I feel confident that I can bare my soul to without putting myself in emotional danger, I wouldn't be able to speak about this at all. I can't talk to Nick about it, for example. I wanted to make sure you knew that. Peaches seemed to take my closeness with Nick as some kind of threat against her, and I wanted to make it absolutely clear to you that my relationship with Nick is separate from my relationship with you, and has no baring [*sic*] on how I feel about our friendship.

Peaches made it very clear to me, both in her words and her actions, that she no longer believes in our work—both in the Urban Planning Committee and our pop music. She felt trapped by my relative power. For example, she knows that even though she is no longer a part of my work, her nondisclosure agreements are so binding that if she talks publicly or even privately about any of my secrets, I will have the power to ruin her life in a serious way. I'm angry enough right now that I would probably do it. I trust she won't talk about the Urban Planning Committee, in any case. I think that, unfortunately, she would sound insane if she tried to do so. I didn't mean for it to be like that.

I know you've done some reading about the Situationists—so you know that to rigorously maintain the focus and driving force of the group, Guy [Debord] had to expel several members, including a few of his painter friends. I've exchanged a few e-mails with an academic named McKenzie Wark (under a pseudonym of course) who has just written a book about the Situationists, and has been asked to write the introduction to a collection of Guy's correspondence. I convinced him to send me a few of the translated letters he's working with and I read Guy's own words on expelling members from the Situationists.

It comes down to this: it was incredibly painful for Guy to break with his friends and oust them, but if he hadn't done so, the Situationists would've crumbled. I won't let my own efforts crumble. I've worked too hard and come to [sic] far. If Peaches didn't mean to hurt the Urban Planning Committee and my pop career, I would be able to work with her—but she acted against me deliberately. I can't deal with that. I won't ever see her again. I don't care if you maintain a friendship with her, but you can't speak to her about the Urban Planning Committee. If you do, I'll expel you too. I'm sorry to sound so strict with you. I love you. Any forcefulness behind my words is because I'm hurt and frightened of losing you as well.

The first thing I want to do when I get back to Chicago is talk deeply and seriously with you. I miss you. I will see you when I return.

Ali and Molly did speak "deeply and seriously" and Ali reassured Molly, who put the incident with Peaches out of her mind.* Molly stopped worrying, and Ali continued her friendship with Peaches.

Meanwhile, Berliner and Molly had been working like mad on The Ghost Network, piling map on top of map at a frantic pace, as "Don't Stop (N'Arrête Pas)" started to get more and more airtime on Top 40 radio. To keep up their breakneck speed, Berliner often traveled from Chicago to wherever Molly was promoting her album and singles. Berliner enjoyed visiting Molly's other world, her vibrant life as a steadily rising pop star, so they were together for the climax of the work on The Ghost Network, on the set of the "New Vogue Riche" music video.

On August 31, 2008, more than a year after Molly and Berliner had begun building The Ghost Network, Molly's dancers, entourage, and a film crew descended on a mansion in the affluent Los Angeles suburb of Westlake Village to shoot the music video for "New Vogue Riche," Molly's first EDM-influenced single. Molly conceptualized the video, which follows a girl who discovers a portal to her own city hidden inside the second floor of a fancy mansion. It is a sequel to her first music video, for "Don't Stop (N'Arrête Pas)."

As she hadn't yet proven she could record a hit, the label spent almost nothing on the "Don't Stop (N'Arrête Pas)" video production. To direct, they had hired Danielle Skendarian (not yet as in demand as she is today, and therefore cheaper), rented a mansion, and told Joe Frank Parker to choreograph a "normal pop video dance."† Parker obliged and developed a routine that combined

---

* Molly was angry enough to give Peaches a goodbye "fuck you," though—she let it slip to a few tabloid journalists that she had fired Peaches because she refused to dance at a show during the Pride Parade in New York.

† This is according to Parker himself, whom I thank for his patience, help with fact-checking, and all the hours spent on the phone discussing the finer points of music

sharp jazz movement with provocative hip-hop dance aesthetics, plus a few movements that would become dance signatures for Molly: a slinky walk with little flicks of her legs, her hands blocking her face, her whole upper body still; rolling into what, in yoga, would be called a "shoulder stand" and haphazardly peddling her legs; and overall jerking, rather than fluid, movements.

SDFC had foisted upon Molly a concept for the "Don't Stop (N'Arrête Pas)" video. It begins with Molly and her friends (Peaches and Ali) driving to a mansion on a hill, lit with teal and purple lights. During the chorus, they crash the party, and dance around as the guests dressed in Gatsby-esque costumes look on, perplexed. In a dazzling, back-lit close up, Molly lip-syncs her hook: "Don't stop stop / stop never stop / Keep dancing, dancing / dancing 'til we drop." She finds Astroman, the song's producer, among the guests and gyrates against him, mouthing his lyrics: "Work, work, work your body / Pop, pop, pop a Molly." The video ends with a long dance sequence on the mansion's grand staircase. In the final shot, Molly laughs and runs up the stairs, an outtake edited into the video for its considerable charm. In later interviews, when SDFC was giving Molly more money and creative power, she called the "Don't Stop (N'Arrête Pas)" video the intro to "New Vogue Riche."

Molly designed the "New Vogue Riche" video herself. On the concept, she took creative input from Momo Waxler, her creative director, and her choreographer, Parker. Though SDFC and Rappaport, Molly's handler from the label, had to approve of the concept before they would fund the video, they did so without giving Molly any notes and approved her choice of Skendarian to direct again.[*]

Unlike the "Don't Stop (N'Arrête Pas)" video, "New Vogue

---

video choreography.

[*] Skendarian made her name partially on Molly's videos and went on to win a Grammy for her work on Miley Cyrus's video for "Love Money Party."

Riche" smacks of Molly's own aesthetic, and despite the record company's minimal involvement, it serves as a sharp marker of her new power within the music industry and her label in particular. "New Vogue Riche" begins where "Don't Stop (N'Arrête Pas)" left off, with Molly running up the giant staircase. At the top of the stairs, Molly's costume transforms into a bodysuit outfitted with panels of LED lights.

Ali follows Molly up the stairs, and they find abandoned rooms, the furniture covered with white sheets. During the first verse, while Molly sings about wanting to be Madonna when she was a little girl, Molly rips the sheets off couches and statues. She throws the white fabric, billowing, to Ali, who uses them as props in Parker's ballet-inflected choreography.

After the first chorus ("When I get money [New!] / I throw a party [Vogue!] / For everybody [Riche!] / New. Vogue. Riche. Dance."), Molly uncovers a miniature skyscraper, the size of a child's playhouse. As Molly removes the tarp, the skyscraper's little windows glow purple. Molly wraps herself around the skyscraper, humping and licking it, and generally acting like a sexed-up King Kong.* After a verse, a door on the side of the skyscraper springs open.

Dropping to her hands and knees, Molly Metropolis crawls into the skyscraper, with Ali at her heels. Molly then finds herself in a seemingly empty city, her costume transformed again, this time into a jet-black leotard with metallic sleeves. The map travels off the leotard and, in body paint, across Molly's arms, legs, neck and face. Molly gazes at the sky, where the words *Molly's Metropolis* dangle,

---

* Kelly Rice of *Slate* dismissed this sequence as "off-putting" and "needlessly vulgar," in a piece about the sexual antics of pop stars: "From Molly to Miley—Are There Any Lines They Won't Cross?" Published September 2, 2013. The piece was reductive and "slut-shaming" in its tone. I disagree with Rogers's assessment of Molly's performance in the "New Vogue Riche" video. I thought all the skyscraper humping wasn't supposed to be sexy; it was supposed to be *funny*.

a purple neon light attached to nothing in particular. In the giant neon words, all the O's are rendered as small triangles, conforming to the visual ascetics associated with the '80s-style Outrun Electro genre Molly *détourns* for many of her tracks.

A few quick cuts later, Molly's dancers come tumbling out of doorways and join Molly and Ali in the street. Molly dances energetically with the group through a few iterations of the chorus. The video ends with Molly beginning to explore her city.

The "New Vogue Riche" music video received the best critical response of any of her videos and remains a fan favorite. I'm inclined to agree with the popular sentiment. The video is playful and fun, the choreography is top-notch, and the visuals are striking thanks to Benoît Debie's candy-colored, glow-y cinematography.

Molly's video for "Apocalypse Dance" was the third chapter of this saga, and ended in a cliffhanger. Because Molly disappeared, the cliffhanger was never resolved.

Molly invited Berliner to Los Angeles to sync their maps and to visit the set of "New Vogue Riche"; he pretended to be an old friend from high school whom she had met at summer camp. While on set, he met and hit it off with one of Molly's dancers, Irene Davis. The two immediately began dating.

Molly and her team shot the video over three days, from August 31 to September 2, 2008, during a particularly exciting time for Molly Metropolis and her General Council; "Don't Stop (N'Arrête Pas)" was quickly climbing the charts and *Cause Célèbrety* had debuted earlier in the month to larger than expected sales figures. The dancers, Parker, and even the film crew, who had no long-term vested interest in Molly's career, felt the energy and excitement on set. In between takes, the production assistants played LCD Soundsystem and M.I.A., and the dancers developed little dance moves for "Paper Planes." For the first time since Molly was dropped from her first label, she felt happy and secure in her career. In the minutes before the shoot began, she wept with happiness in front of the whole crew, then apologized to the makeup assistants for making them reapply her mascara. Molly was so emotionally overwhelmed, she didn't realize her hold on Ali had begun to unravel.

Without Peaches around to help, the weight of Molly's intensity fell on Ali alone. She treated Ali passionately, but roughly. She had always done so. For example, in an early interview with MTV VJ Nani Cook, when Cook worked up the nerve to awkwardly question Molly about her "friends," Molly answered, benignly, that they were her "followers and dancers." Then she grabbed Ali's jaw and shook her face. Ali didn't otherwise move or react, but unedited footage of the interview shows Peaches gasping as it happened.*
Cook quickly moved on to other topics. Ali thought about that moment often in the weeks leading up to the "New Vogue Riche" shoot, when Molly's ferocity reached a fever pitch. Without Peaches there to help normalize the way Molly treated her, Ali realized that moment defined her relationship with Molly. Ali didn't like that she had done nothing while Molly moved her. She felt like she was always standing perfectly still while Molly Metropolis shook her face.

For the "New Vogue Riche" video, Molly asked Parker to leave part of the bridge—a repetition of the couplet "all you nouveau / do the new vogue" layered over pulsating '80s-style synths—unchoreographed, so she could freestyle with Ali. With the cameras rolling, Molly told Ali to sit with her knees up and Molly draped herself over Ali's legs. Molly pressed the front of her body against Ali's legs, arching into her, and tightly wrapped her hands around Ali's thighs, while Ali performed a modified version of Madonna's famous arm choreography from the "Vogue" music video.

---

* Thanks to Ryan at MTV for access to the uncut interview.

Then Molly mimed a gun, pointed it at Ali's head, and pretended to fire. Ali recoiled, then gracefully fluttered down, until she was lying on her back. Molly slithered over her body, then sprung up to standing and performed the Vogue-like arm choreography herself—she'd mimed killing Ali and stealing her dance moves.

The theatrical violence shook Ali. Although she knew Molly Metropolis wasn't actually trying to hurt her, she had a sinking fear that her relationship with Molly was toxic. Molly had already started telling Ali her ideas for her next batch of songs; she called it her "album for the end of the world" and Ali, in turn, started to see Molly as a world-ender. She found herself in the precarious position of being a monster's henchman.

Skendarian shot Molly and Ali's violent dance on the first day of "New Vogue Riche" filming. After Skendarian wrapped shooting, a vulnerable Ali sought out Molly's company. She suggested a late night spa treatment at the hotel, or maybe glasses of Scotch in the suite, but Molly told Ali she needed to spend her evening working alone with Berliner. With conspiratorial glee, Molly told Ali that she had a surprise for him: she had digitized the last of the L maps and The Ghost Network was complete. Ali took strong note of Molly's wording, "working alone with Berliner," and "a surprise for Berliner"—as if Ali's involvement in The Ghost Network project meant nothing. For Ali, that was the last straw. She thought Molly considered her nothing more than a weight-bearing column, someone to lean on, but not someone who could contribute. She planned her defection.*

Berliner and Molly drank champagne and toasted the completion of The Ghost Network, calling it the first step in the discovery of the New Situationists' agenda. Meanwhile, Ali called Peaches.

---

* This timeline is according to both Ali and Peaches, whom I interviewed separately, and who seem to function as a two-part unit even when they aren't in the same room.

Ali aired her grievances with Metro; Peaches reiterated some of her own. Each girl allowed the other's negative energy to intensify her own frustration. By the end of the conversation, Peaches begged Ali to quit and move back to New York. Ali had a better idea.

"Peaches and I did a lot of work without a lot of real thanks," Ali told me in our first interview, unapologetic and still angry, just like Peaches, despite the two years that had gone by since Molly disappeared. "Metro was appreciative, sometimes, but she didn't let us in and neither of us was satisfied with doing the work without getting to participate in what came next. I could've just left, but that would've been turning my back on all the time I'd spent collecting information. I believed, and I don't think I was wrong, that Peaches and I earned the gold at the end of the rainbow just as much as she and Nick did. None of us knew what we were looking for, so it didn't seem like she deserved it more than us. She didn't."

After the "New Vogue Riche" video shoot ended, while Berliner lingered in Los Angeles with Molly Metropolis's crew to spend more time with Davis, Peaches secretly flew to Chicago and stole as many of the maps as she could; some eluded her, because Berliner had already moved them to his *pied-à-terre*, which Ali and Peaches didn't know about, but most of them were stored in a small loft Molly rented for Ali and Peaches to use as a work/live space when they stayed in Chicago. (Luckily, Berliner had a backup. He had developed an intense paranoia after the New Situationists fell apart and had already made physical copies of the maps, which he stashed in a secret storage locker in Toledo, Ohio.) Ali applied for a license to carry a gun in New York.

Half a week later, while Berliner was midair, flying back to Chicago, Ali texted Peaches to tell her that she had quit the General Council. Berliner visited his apartment later that night and found it ransacked. He called Molly, who informed him she had received an ominous series of text messages from Ali and Peaches:

Metro—We thought it might be déclassé to break up with you via text, but to be perfectly honest, the thought of hearing your voice or seeing your face one more time was too much for us to bear.

September 6, 2008, 10:26 p.m.

Goodbye, we've started a counterinsurgency. We've decided to take what you want to have. Give our regards to Nick.

September 6, 2008, 10:27 p.m.

Watch your back.

September 6, 2008, 10:27 p.m.

*Sincerely, The Society of the Children of the Atomic Bomb.**

September 6, 2008, 10:30 p.m.

---

* Ali and Peaches didn't choose the name of their "counterinsurgency," The Society of the Children of the Atomic Bomb, at random. Ali, a master at finding the best parts of people and shining a light on them, mined Peaches's childhood for the name.

Peaches's grandfather, Frank Orr, and Robert Halstead, Orr's closest friend, served together in World War II as naval officers on a ship called the *Massachusetts*. In the waning years of the war, their ship was scheduled to take part in an attack on Japan's shores. President Harry S. Truman axed that planned attack in favor of dropping a newly minted atomic bomb on Hiroshima, and then Nagasaki. Lieutenants Orr and Halsted most likely would've been killed trying to take Japan if America hadn't dropped the bomb. They were haunted by their possible alternate history as casualties of war. Jokingly, they called themselves, and other soldiers like them, The Children of the Atomic Bomb.

In 1945, the men returned, alive and uninjured, to their homes in the rural Illinois corn-farming county of Kankakee. There, they started a political action committee to push for fiscal conservatism and greater government subsidies for rural farmers. According to a pamphlet they published together in 1952, they called their group the Society of the Children of the Atomic Bomb, "because without it, our lives would've been lost, and our children, and our children's children, never would've been born."

Orr and Halsted dreamed of becoming a powerful lobbying group for Midwestern farmers, but they had absolutely no political impact, even in Kankakee. The Society quietly folded in 1954.

Forty-four years later, Ali plucked the name out of history, adopting it mostly because she liked the rhythm of the phrase.

189

To fund their fledgling "counterinsurgency," Ali called Anthony Zavos, the son of a friend of her father's: a thirty-year-old real estate lawyer and trust fund baby. Zavos was young, rich, and short—only five foot five. He often dated dancers and high-end fashion models who towered over him; if he was destined to be short, he would rather flaunt his height than hide it. He lived in Manhattan and dressed in slim, European-cut suits and men's leather ankle boots. Zavos also couldn't stand to be alone, so he'd spend most nights jumping from party to party, friend to friend, squeezing in a few hours of sleep between 3 a.m. and dawn, then heading to the office of his father's investment consulting firm where he was quickly rising through the ranks.

Zavos had money and an insatiable thirst for excitement; Ali was also one of his favorite late-night hangout buddies. She told Zavos her story about Molly Metropolis and the Urban Planning Committee, and about her plans to take what Molly wanted. Zavos thought going head-to-head with a pop star seemed fun and agreed to fund her operation. He opened a bank account with a generous line of credit.

Peaches suggested they find a spy to keep track of Molly's movements. She had someone in mind: a twenty-two-year-old SDFC intern named Tony Casares, who could feed Ali and Peaches information about Molly's schedule and upcoming projects. Ali approved and, while Peaches spent her evenings recruiting Casares, Ali doubled down on the spy operation. She wanted to turn someone who had more day-to-day contact with Molly, someone who could report on Metro's temperament and obsessions. Recruiting a dancer was Ali's best bet; she'd been close with all of them. Ali cycled through a few options before settling on Irene Davis.

Born in Michigan, Davis grew up in New York City, where she had lived in a Tribeca loft with her parents and her three brothers. Although she barely remembered Michigan, Davis preferred to think of herself as a Midwestern soul displaced on the East Coast.

During junior high school, she was a lonely introvert, friendless except for her charismatic older brother, Aaron. She started dancing in high school, when her father enrolled her in modern dance classes. She made a few dancer friends, but she hated most of her classmates at Magen David Yeshivah High School and preferred to spend her time with Aaron. After Aaron was expelled for carrying on sexually with another male student, Davis got herself expelled as well, showing up drunk to class and smoking in the girl's bathroom. With her new public high school's less demanding course load, Davis focused more on dancing.

Every afternoon after school, she danced for two hours: ballet on Mondays and Wednesdays, jazz on Tuesdays, hip-hop on Thursdays. On Fridays, she stayed out all night drinking with her brother and his various boyfriends, only one of whom made a lasting impression: Paulo Forlizzi, twenty-two, tall, skinny, handsome and, most importantly, a rising choreographer with a good reputation. Most of Davis's dance teachers had felt the need to inform her that she could never be a professional dancer because her body didn't fit the mold; Forlizzi told her to "fuck what she heard." He spent his own time working on technique with her. He said she was never going to be a ballerina, but if she worked hard enough, she could have a good career in modern or hip-hop dance, as a performance artist or backup dancer. Even after Forlizzi and Aaron ended their romantic relationship, Forlizzi continued to coach Davis. A month before she graduated high school, he called in a favor and got her an audition with Molly Metropolis.

Davis nailed it, and her body didn't matter. Molly was looking for someone with personality and zing in her dancing, not someone bland that looked like they could perfectly execute choreography. She was building her General Council and she wanted it to be sparkly, creepy, dynamic; she preferred Davis's sexy scowl, her curves, and her effortless grace to the legions of tall, skinny ballerinas with perfect extension.

Davis met Ali and Peaches on the low-budget, slap-dash set of the "Don't Stop (N'Arrête Pas)" music video. Molly Metro encouraged her dancers to goof around and riff with each other and Davis spent the better part of a day freestyling to the "Don't Stop (N'Arrête Pas)" chorus with Ali and Peaches, though Davis barely appears in the final cut of the video. During her brief screen time, in the few instrumental-only beats before the bridge, she performs a dizzying leg hold pirouette before the video cuts to footage of Molly humping the statue.

Ali and Davis stayed friends after that video shoot, though Ali had reasons other than friendship to recruit Davis to her New Society of Children of the Atomic Bomb. Firstly, Ali had heard about Davis's budding relationship with Berliner, so she knew turning Davis would give her access to more than one key person. Secondly, Ali knew Davis was susceptible to bribery. Davis's family, once comfortable financially, now struggled to pay hefty medical bills following first Davis's mother's then her grandfather's prolonged battles with cancer. Ali turned Davis over the course of six weeks, pushing her toward duplicity one inch at a time before she buckled and agreed to betray both Molly and her boyfriend in exchange for a hefty payoff.*

With The Ghost Network finished, and Ali and Peaches nipping at their heels, neither Berliner nor Molly knew which direction to head in next. Molly still adamantly believed the L maps would unlock the secrets of the New Situationists, but couldn't figure out how. Berliner started thinking of The Ghost Network as a sort of stalling tactic, a way to feel like they had accomplished something

---

* I never had a chance to interview Davis, so I remain unenlightened about how spying on Berliner and betraying him weighed on her, though I do know she followed Ali and Peaches's directions without question.

192

when they had actually discovered nothing. "The Urban Planning Committee felt like a joke during those days," he admitted, "and Metro and I were arguing. Half of the time we met or talked on the phone, we fought and fought about the importance of The Ghost Network. I thought she was clinging to a sinking ship, to be frank. She was worried I was going to freak out and leave her, like Ali and Peaches did."

Berliner checked in with Kraus during his weekly prison visits. She agreed with Berliner that The Ghost Network seemed like an exercise in futility. She encouraged him to keep fighting with Molly, and to explore other avenues without her when she was out of town. Molly's rising fame troubled Kraus. She worried about the conflicts in being both a Situationist and a pop star.

In the meantime, Molly Metropolis prepared for war with the dancers. She bought the building on Armitage and Racine and re-placed the New Situationists' security door with a newer, thicker, more secure model.* She tried to get Berliner to reengage with The Ghost Network. He wouldn't, so she spent hours alone with her giant composite map.

On Molly Metropolis's final day in Chicago, Berliner was baffled by her mood. Over breakfast in her Peninsula Hotel suite, instead of arguing about The Ghost Network, she told Berliner tour stories of broken animatronic costumes and dancers' lovers' quarrels. Then she impulsively suggested visiting the Museum of Contemporary Art (MCA). Berliner asked to join her at the museum, expecting her to

---

* According to state records, Antoinette Monson owns the building, and the basement rooms are rented by U of C on behalf of the University of Westminster, London, as an off-campus extension of the Westminster Natural Sciences program, housing experiments that can only be performed in America. When I tried to confirm whether or not the University of Westminster ever rented office space in the Armitage and Racine building, I entered a never-ending feedback loop, where officials at U of C sent me to the University of Westminster for confirmation, and the University of Westminster sent me back to U of C, *ad infinitum*.

say no. As she'd grown in popularity, her SDFC handlers had become more wary about Molly appearing in public with a "known terrorist." Instead of refusing, Molly embraced Berliner and told him she was so happy he asked to come along.

She roused the rest of her friends and security entourage and drove her little convertible to the museum. She walked through the galleries wistfully, brushing her fingers across the molding on the doorframe as if savoring the texture. She signed autographs without a hint of exhaustion or annoyance. She wore a black veil, a neon purple shirt, and a pair of neon orange pumps by shoe designers DSquared2, with a white wooden heel carved into letters. Her left shoe said EAT and her right shoe said POP.

Berliner blended in with the rest of her small entourage; even with all the scrutiny the museum trip eventually received, no publication or gossip blog reported that Molly Metropolis had been gallivanting around with a member of the New Situationists just before her disappearance. According to Berliner, Molly Metropolis loved the silence and stillness of museums. She loved looking at a piece of art hung or placed against an unscuffed white wall. She loved installation pieces, because they felt truly ephemeral, unable to be captured or copied. She once told Berliner that she treated her naked body like the white walls of an art museum and her clothing like the art hung on those walls.

In that way, Molly lived in opposition to the Situationists, who abhorred the stiffness of museums' "climate-controlled art" and expelled all their artists for being artists. The art world, Debord argued, participated in a capitalist system that treated art like commodities and sold them for money; art museums were big players in the Society of the Spectacle. The artists with the most recognizable or trendy "names" would fetch the highest prices regardless of the quality or emotional significance of the art they produced. All creation of art was tainted by this system, Debord insisted. Art was complacent, as were the artists.

Debord had once wanted to infiltrate the art world, but soured on the idea of changing the system because he never had the power to do so; Molly, at the apex of her career, had the power to change popular culture. Top 40 radio didn't play singles that sounded like her synth-infused tracks before Molly released "Don't Stop (N'Arrête Pas)." Now, despite her disappearance (or perhaps partially because of it), Molly's sound remains *en vogue.** If Debord had been her judge, Molly would've been ejected from the Situationist International.

Berliner and Molly were both delirious from the power she wielded as a cultural force. Imagine spending years following the path of men and women you deeply admired, only to realize you were coming close to eclipsing them. Imagine lifting your heroes onto your shoulders; imagine how powerful and strong you would feel.

After the museum visit, Berliner remembers Molly hugging him, a goodbye hug he recognized in hindsight. She lied to Berliner, telling him she needed to go have a phone meeting with a Swedish producer named Michael M. about tracks for her new album. She left in her car, alone. Berliner was probably the last of her friends to see her before she was gone.

After Molly Metropolis disappeared, Berliner sunk into the underground rooms of the Urban Planning Committee's headquarters, as he had done after the subway bombings. He tried to figure out if Molly had left of her own volition and, if so, where she had gone. Berliner was terrified that Ali, Peaches, and their New Society had abducted her. He went as far as searching the New Society's headquarters.

All the threads intersected in the anxious days right after Molly's disappearance. Ali and Peaches immediately ransacked Molly's

---

* *Check out the soundtrack to Nicolas Winding Refn's movie* Drive, *for example.* —CD

abandoned hotel room—they knew Molly had found something, and believed the key to finding it themselves was in her notebook. They didn't find the notes, but they did leave the mess Nix and Taer found when they packed Molly's belongings several days later. At the same time, Berliner suspected Davis was involved with the New Society and wanted to test his theory, so when Nix and Taer contacted Berliner about the notebook, Berliner told Davis they had called. Berliner and Davis discussed Nix and Taer over drinks in a trendy bar called the Violet Hour. They speculated that Nix had wanted to keep it as a memento of her time with Molly. Then Berliner excused himself to use the bathroom and hid behind an adjacent accent wall. He overheard Davis call Ali to relay the whereabouts of the notebook. Betrayed, Berliner abruptly cut ties with Davis. He left the bar without saying goodbye, immediately canceled his iPhone plan and switched to a burner cell phone, and retreated to the New Situationist headquarters. He decided not to meet Taer and Nix.

While Berliner retreated and Taer and Nix waited for him at Redfish, Peaches sent Casares to break into Taer's apartment. Casares was skinny, earnest, and gullible. Besides a slightly cleft lip, he was attractive and wore a sleeve of faded tattoos well. Casares excelled at intricate, difficult tasks, like picking locks, and he was the most loyal of all Ali and Peaches's followers. Tasked with finding Molly's notebook at any cost, Casares waited for Taer, Nix, and Taer's roommate to leave the apartment, and easily broke through Taer's ancient lock.

Inside the apartment, Casares couldn't find anything pertaining to Molly, so he left. Peaches and Ali devised a new plan; they decided the easiest way to find Berliner was to let Nix and Taer do the searching for them. Then they could focus their own efforts on reconstructing The Ghost Network, without having to split focus. Ali figured they'd have to give Taer the tool the New Society had in their possession, so she gave Casares the sketchpad and gun they had taken from Berliner. Later that evening, Casares broke into

Taer's apartment again, got his head smacked, and purposely dropped the gun and the sketchpad to frame Berliner.*

When Taer and Nix visited Michigan, Davis surreptitiously texted Ali to ask what she should say to them. Ali and Peaches suspected Berliner was hiding out in the Urban Planning Committee's main headquarters. They knew if they found the right building, they would have both Berliner and The Ghost Network. The dancers told Davis to help Taer and Nix look for it, whatever way she could, hoping that Metro's former assistant could figure out Berliner's map for them. They waited for Taer and Nix to find their way through the snow.

---

* And here's where everyone got confused. Taer and Nix thought Berliner had broken in to steal Molly's notebook. Berliner thought Nix and Taer might be working with Peaches and Ali to draw him out. Peaches and Ali thought Nix had some secret information about where Molly had gone and were trying to find Berliner to reunite them with Molly. Everything got all muddled and Cyrus did his best to put all the threads together, failing in places, sometimes blinded, sometimes wrong. —CD

Chapter (10)

Every time I interviewed Berliner and Nix, we met in my apartment in Chicago, a small but elegant one bedroom with historic 1920s moldings Berliner admired. Berliner wore the same gray suit and pale blue button-down shirt every time. Nix wore tight blue jeans and loose tank tops.

When they met me at my apartment, to talk to me about Taer, Molly, Kraus, the New Situationists and the old, they refused my offer of beer or wine, but ate any snacks I offered them. Sometimes their answers were candid. Other times, they sounded rehearsed. Together, they could be quite intimidating.

After months of dodging my calls and threatening to sue me, after Berliner finally agreed to be interviewed, the first question on my list was "How did you become involved with Caitlin Taer and Regina Nix?" When he explained how he heard about them from Davis and waited to see if they would find him, a much more interesting question arose: "You and Molly never trusted anyone. Why did you trust Taer on that first evening you met?"

When I asked him this question, Berliner's attitude toward me changed. For the first time in our long, frustrating interaction, he really opened up and spoke honestly. Later, he would open up again about Molly, but when I asked about Taer I saw for the first time Berliner as the charismatic figure who could attract the attention of both compulsively secretive political groups and enigmatic, budding pop stars.

"God, I don't know why I trusted her," he said, "Very often, when you meet a person for the first time, their emotions are really turned off. Even people who are really open, I'm not just talking about closed-off people. Most of the time, people don't show you their heaviest, deepest emotions the first time you meet them. I mean, they don't want to show you that vulnerable part of them-selves and you don't want to see it. You don't want them to see yours either. There's a social contract between people who have never met before, to be some diminished version of yourself.

"Until I met Cait, that was par for the course. But with Cait, I saw the intensity of her emotions so instantly. It was like I could just look inside of her and see all her emotional junk, all her fear, all her love. And it was like she was letting me see it. And when you see that in someone, when I saw that in her, I began to feel that I knew her deeply before I really did. I felt that very quickly. That would've been dangerous, had Cait not been basically good.

"On top of that, because Irene had told me Cait was coming, and I had been waiting for her to arrive, I'd done a lot of research on her. I had this parasocial relationship with Cait before I ever met her. All of those factors came together. And I just knew I should just . . ."

Berliner trailed off without completing his thought, and let the silence stretch to an uncomfortable length. Then he continued: "Molly always said to act on instinct, and trusting Cait felt like what Molly would've wanted me to do. Molly was deeply important to me and I wanted to find her. Then I met this person, and she wanted to find Molly, too. I'd been alone. I'd been looking for Molly alone for a long time."

On that Saturday morning when Taer found Berliner, he took Nix and Taer back into the Urban Planning Committee headquarters. Taer showed Nix the trick door. Berliner offered them wine—they took it—and he told them a little bit about himself and his history with Molly. Taer reminded Berliner she was in possession of Molly Metropolis's personal notebook and would only show it to him if Berliner let her help look for Molly. He agreed.

Berliner called the taxi, and the three of them rode to the Chicago First National Bank and Trust. Taer retrieved Molly's notebook from her safety deposit box, then they returned to the Urban Planning Committee by L, checking over their shoulders as they rode.

Taer expected Berliner to recognize the notebook and to know how to unlock its secrets, but he had never seen it before.

Unlike Berliner, Ali and Peaches had seen inside Molly's notebook. Because Molly used the notebook for both her New Situationist research and her ideas for her pop career, she had shown Ali and Peaches selected pages, while carefully concealing others—and they wanted to see inside it again. One of the New Society's young members had followed Taer to and from the bank, but she didn't know about the notebook and didn't understand its value to the leaders of the New Society. When the spy reported Taer's activity to Ali, the dancers finally knew where the notebook was: behind a steel door they couldn't yet breach. They refocused their energies on finding a way through the door.

Back at the Urban Planning Committee headquarters, Berliner scoured the pages of the notebook for anything he would understand but Taer would've missed. He didn't find any secret codes, any words with double meanings that only he could understand. All he found were the same exclamations of Molly having "found something," which Taer had read before; nothing he knew about Molly added a new and revealing context to the words.

After two days of reading and re-reading Molly's notebook, Berliner concluded that if Metro had written down anything important, they didn't have the context to understand it yet. This was very optimistic of him; he said it for Taer's benefit, mostly. Privately, he thought Metro had probably never put anything on paper that could point them to something in The Ghost Network. Molly was too tied to the old New Situationist ways, protecting herself by never writing anything down.

Berliner put the notebook aside and spent his days with The Ghost Network, re-examining the hundreds of historical documents and maps he and Molly had used to build the mega-map. He also returned to the Situationist texts—which he hadn't read in years, not since he first met Kraus. In his return to the Situationist books, letters, and journals, Berliner focused on two prominent Situationist concepts: psychogeography and *dérive*, or the "drift."

Dérive was walking without destination, moving through urban space without a specific purpose, changing course based on feeling rather than on traffic signals, breaking the boundaries implicit in the inflexible confines of roadways, sidewalks, and other route designators. On their *dérives*, Debord and the Situationists searched for new routes through the familiar neighborhoods of their city, seeking to make the familiar seem unfamiliar.

They left graffiti on the streets, claiming them as their own space through Situationist markings. Asger Jorn painted, "If we don't die here, will we carry on further?" on the Rue du Sauvage, just across the river from one of the Situationists' favorite buildings, a nearby morgue. Ivan Chtcheglov linked sex to the city, painting, "I came in the cobblestones," with white paint on some cobblestone streets.

The Situationists had fun during their *dérive,* and fun was one of their goals, but enjoyment wasn't the only thing they were after. In defying how city planners wanted them to move through the cities, the Situationists also considered the *dérive* a serious tool for remaking the city and a cornerstone of the way of life in their potential Situationist city, New Babylon.

Debord described how the *dérive* could be used to both destroy the modern city and build New Babylon, by discovering boundaries defined by the psychological feel of the city, rather than by arbitrary lines on a map. Debord wrote: "From a *dérive* point of view, cities have psychogeographical contours, with constant currents, fixed points and vortexes that strongly discourage entry into or exit from certain zones."* The Situationists drifted in order to discover the "contours" that create boundaries, and they called the ethereal, intellectual tool they use while drifting to find those contours *psychogeography*.†

While Berliner studied New Babylon and The Ghost Network, Taer stayed with Molly's notebook, trying to follow Molly's logical paths and retrace her research steps from the days just before Molly disappeared. Though they were consuming different texts, Taer and Berliner's research was linked, as demonstrated by a passage in Molly's notebook that Taer often returned to, quoted from the opening of Debord's *Theory of Dérive*. Debord was interested in a sociological study performed by Chombart de Lauwe in 1952, where de Lauwe strove to show that the average Parisian doesn't live in a neighborhood so much as a small swath of the city determined by her own habits and preferences. Debord liked the description of a student living in the 16th *arrondissement* of Paris, whose movements de Lauwe tracked for a full year. Molly was also fascinated by

---

* *The Situationist City*, 77.

† To explore further, psychogeography is the Situationists' attempt to marry subjective and objective experiences of the city, the myriad ways that people interact with the cities they live in. From *The Situationist City*: "On one hand, [psychogeography] recognized that the self can't be divorced from the urban environment, on the other hand, it had to pertain to more than just the psyche of the individual if it was to be useful in the collective rethinking of the city."

this student, copying the details into her notebook: "Her itinerary forms a small triangle with no significant deviations, the three apexes of which are the School of Political Sciences, her residence and that of her piano teacher."*

Taer copied this paragraph into her own journal and also asked Berliner to make a quick black-and-white screen print of the paragraph to hang above the bathtub in her room at the Urban Planning Committee headquarters. On the screen print, the quote was attributed to Debord, but in the bottom left-hand corner, Berliner included a version of the signature Molly gave him, SCREEN PRINT BY ANTOINE MONSON.

Taer's fondness for the passage developed into something like a personal gospel. Although Debord was the author, the paragraph consists almost entirely of quotations from another man. Taer liked quotations, moments pulled from longer expression or ideas.

"The tone of a moment can be spoiled by its context," Taer wrote. "A single moment creates a mood."

Taer also latched on to the character of the female student—both a strangely vivid and maddeningly vague figure. Sometime in the late 1940s or 1950s, there was a girl, probably between the ages of eighteen and twenty-three, walking through Paris in a narrow triangle. From those bare bones, Taer created a person. Taer imagined she looked and dressed like the actress Carey Mulligan in the movie *An Education*, even though *An Education* takes place in the '60s. Taer started calling the unnamed student Jenny, after Mulligan's character. Taer wrote:

How shocking is the image of the piano teacher at the end after everything else? Suddenly, we know something about Jenny. She took piano lessons, often enough that the lessons

---

* *Situationist International Anthology*, trans. Ken Knabb (Berkeley: Bureau of Public Secrets, 2007).

formed one of the three apexes on her triangle. She was probably very good at piano. She was probably very passionate about her piano playing. She went to her piano teacher's house more often than she went to the grocery store to buy food! She rarely went to the grocery store, her triangle tells us. Not to mention, the piano lessons imply a person in her life, a piano teacher. Another person.

After thinking about the piano teacher for a little while, I started looking back at the rest of the paragraph. She was a poli-sci student. Did she want to be a diplomat? In the early 1950s? Could she have even done that: run for office, be in politics? Or maybe she was the kind of girl that was looking for a husband that would become a Member of Parliament (MP) or something, did she want to live through him? She was living in the 16th *arrondissement* which probably means something about her, like the way living in Logan Square means you're a different person than someone who lives in Wicker Park. Also, the way Jenny thought about her neighborhood, she built up some idea of the 16th *arrondissement* in her mind, and that helped create the neighborhood. It seems like a never-ending cycle of living and thinking about living and drifting into a precise triangle. It's a kind of drifting, I think, because Jenny didn't consider her life to be contained inside of one triangle until one man came along and showed her where she really was.

How did he diagram her movements? Was he a professor at her School of Political Sciences? Did he ask for paid volunteers? Was Jenny the only one, or did he diagram the movements of many students over the course of one year? How could he do this? Did he just follow her around all day? Did he ask her to document her own movements? Maybe he did and she didn't report things—she went to the same student bar a lot and didn't mention it because she often picked up men there and brought them back to her residence-apex. She would leave that out, wouldn't she? It would be considered slutty. She'd want to present herself as this Student of Political Sciences and Student of Piano. She'd want to keep her dirty deeds to herself. Perhaps she was picking up women, not men. Ponytailed girls in blazers, also poli-sci students, named Joan, or Jeanne en français. Perhaps she masturbated at night to thoughts of someone recording her movements from the bar and home again, night after night with Jeanne. She imagined de Lauwe reading about her movements and she gasped, shocked and turned on at once, and that's what made her cum, revealing herself to this older man and his stupid study.

Taer's own life morphed into Jenny's; the three apexes of her own triangle were Rainbo, where she still worked, the headquarters of the Urban Planning Committee, and the closest coffee shop. She went to the grocery store less, living off organic peeled baby carrots, clementines, red wine, and bacon.

Taer and Nix moved out of Taer's apartment and into one of the unused rooms in the headquarters on Racine. With Berliner, they fell into a comfortable routine. Their days began when Berliner arrived at the Urban Planning Committee headquarters with three Americanos and three chocolate croissants in hand. Berliner and Taer opened their laptops and spent a few minutes checking the Internet for any news about Molly.

In the late morning, Berliner turned his attention to the vast quantities of information he, Ali, Peaches, and Molly had collected during the Urban Planning Committee's most productive months. Taer spent her time with Molly's notebook, or the assembled Ghost Network. Molly had actually thought of The Ghost Network as a three-part system. The first part was the collection of maps and blueprints Molly and Berliner had used to build the map. The second was the huge wall mural Berliner had painted at Molly's behest. Berliner painted the two-story wall of Molly's office using hundreds of shades of paint, one for each L train line, against a pearly, eggshell white. This copy of The Ghost Network was beautiful, but not practical.

The third version of The Ghost Network was digital. Molly's programmer had designed the visual base of MollyMaps as a detailed road map of Chicago and the surrounding area, pilfered from Google Maps. Over the base, Molly added the train lines and stations by typing in the address of a station, or never-built station, and connecting the address to another address, where the next station would be, had been, or was. The digital version of The Ghost Network also contained a well-designed search function. The user could search for any train line or train station by name or location. MollyMaps also recorded every revision to the map in a searchable archive.

Taer used MollyMaps' search function to cross-check an L map or blueprint or L expansion proposal plan with The Ghost Network, but her favorite way to interact with The Ghost Network was to zoom in on the first station of a train line and examine the details of the area around each train station. Because MollyMaps' core map had been stolen from Google, Taer could see the restaurants or parks or office buildings that had been built on land once considered a place for transport. When Taer picked a train line to examine in such detail, she rarely did so for a concrete reason. She chose her train lines impressionistically, because a color caught her eye or a particular curve in the line seemed interesting to trace. She moved between lines based on feeling; she was conducting her own virtual *dérive* through the fake train city that Molly had built.

While Taer and Berliner spent their days researching, Nix read about the Situationists, trying to come up with theories about what the New Situationists might've been hiding. She searched for

206

various Situationist keywords in MollyMaps. She compared a collage called "The Naked City"—which Debord and Constant made using map fragments—to the painting of The Ghost Network on the wall, looking for repeated patterns.

At 5:30 p.m., Berliner insisted the working day was over. He worried the three of them would go insane if he didn't impose some kind of forced down time. They ate dinner together every night. They frequented the nearby Italian and Mexican restaurants or picked up Chinese or Thai carryout. When they ate Chinese, they drank beer. At the Italian restaurant, they split two bottles of wine between the three of them, always red. They all ordered spicy dishes or passed a bottle of hot sauce around the table.

At dinner, they caught up on each other's personal histories. Berliner told them about his exorcism; Taer tried to explain the way her drive to be a successful writer had shaped all of her emotional experiences since she was sixteen. Nix talked about being best friends in high school with another latent lesbian, watching *Mulholland Drive* and fast-forwarding through the sex scenes.

A few nights a week, Taer worked at Rainbo. On those nights, Berliner walked Nix back to the Urban Planning Committee's headquarters and stayed with her until Taer returned. They watched movies: *Videodrome*, the Wachowskis' lesbian heist movie *Bound*, and Kathryn Bigelow's vampire movie *Near Dark*. They drank more. Sometimes, Berliner told her stories about Kraus. Nix wanted to hear everything about the strict regulations Berliner had to follow when he visited Kraus at the Dwight Correctional Center.

When Taer didn't have to work, Berliner sometimes walked home alone, Taser in his pocket just in case. He was living in his Molly-built *pied-à-terre* at the time, occasionally entertaining his archive girlfriend, Johnson. Sometimes Berliner and Taer spent a few hours hanging out alone in a nearby beer bar, Local Option, Nix at home in the Urban Planning Committee headquarters, drinking and reading alone. Perched at the bar in front of a row of taps, sipping on tulip glasses full of highly alcoholic craft beers, Taer and Berliner debated the utility of psychogeography and *détournement*.

During our interviews, Berliner likened his friendships with Taer and Nix to an adolescent summer camp friendship. "Each hour in summer camp is the social equivalent of, basically, a week," Berliner explained to me. "Romantic relationships that are eight hours old are practically marriages. Intense bonds form, clique loyalties are basically immobile once they coalesce. Then they're over, just as fast."

Berliner also told Taer his stories about Kraus, but Taer didn't ask for more detail the way Nix did, preferring to debate at length whether Constant's New Babylon could ever be built, and if it was built, if it could thrive. Berliner and Taer agreed it could somehow be built, but Berliner thought New Babylon would implode and Taer thought it could work. When Berliner asked Taer about her own relationship, she never said much, though more than once Taer told Berliner she was in love with Nix. Except for Taer's one-on-one drinking sessions with Berliner and her nights at Rainbo, the young women spent all their time together, comfortable now in extreme geographical and physical closeness. They no longer knew what it was like to spend more than a few hours apart.

"We were 'nesting,' other dykes would call it," Nix later told me. "It was shockingly wonderful to have this constant companion. Neither one of us had ever had a girlfriend like this before, someone we basically wanted to fuse with. To attach ourselves to so completely. Everything was very surreal, and we had this idea that maybe when things got 'back to normal' we would get torn away from each other. Which seemed overdramatic at the time but was, of course, what happened. So we were smart. We were smart to think our whole world was going to end."

Some nights, they watched old episodes of *Buffy the Vampire Slayer* on Berliner's Netflix account. Some nights, they played elaborate games of tag.* Some nights, when the wine had soaked her brain and Nix blurred in front of her tired eyes, Taer almost forgot about the absent pop star and their desperate search for what had happened. Some nights Taer and Nix did nothing but talk for hours. Some nights they lay in bed, not talking to each other, their heads jammed together on the same pillow.

While they worked during the day, Nix, Berliner, and Taer listened to music. Taer put on her favorite bad-mood albums: Elliott Smith's *Either/Or* and a single by The Zombies, "Girl Help Me." Nix and Berliner liked these albums as well. They played them dozens of times while Nix read biographies of Debord, Taer clicked her way through the digital copy of The Ghost Network, and Berliner re-read another L map. They sang along with "Girl Help Me," and the *Either/Or* track "Between the Bars" in unison.

Perhaps because of the mood these albums created, Taer developed a vague but constant sense of ill ease. She started working at night, once Berliner had left and Nix had fallen asleep. She obsessively re-read portions of Molly's notebook, as if trying to crack a code, or uncover a heretofore hidden reference to The Ghost Network or the New Situationists. Occasionally, Molly wrote about the specific maps incorporated into The Ghost Network, but those passages were observations, not conclusions, and littered with her thoughts and emotional responses to the information she was gathering—interesting on first read, but useless to her once she'd read the passages dozens of times. Molly also interrupted her discussions of the maps to make oblique references to her "Eye of Horus," or "Third Eye," or "Pyramid Eye," which had something to do with the reasons she sometimes held one hand over one eye during publicity photo shoots. Taer couldn't find any connection between

---

* *Which doubled as foreplay.* —CD

209

these disparate parts of Molly's notes, nor could she find a connection between The Ghost Network and Molly's departure. She started to lose hope.

But on a warm April evening, almost seven weeks after Nix and Taer had found Berliner in the Urban Planning Committee headquarters, Taer found something.

Chapter (11)

On April 16, 2010, Taer was drinking red wine alone in Molly Metropolis's two-story office, trying to focus on a proposed addition to the Purple Line circa 1950, meant to more fully accommodate the expanding western suburbs. (The proposal wasn't considered cost-efficient and the Transit Committee rejected it.) Taer couldn't concentrate; she found herself standing in front of Molly's full-length mirror, experimenting with drugstore eye shadow. With a glass of red wine in her left hand and a makeup brush in her right, she listened to *Cause Célèbrety* and watched a "smoky-eye tutorial" on YouTube. She then wrote a Tumblr post, complete with selfies, describing her lack of proficiency with eyeliner and comparing the helpfulness of a variety of tutorials.

Half an hour later, her eyes were very smoky and she was significantly more drunk. As she later described to Berliner and Nix, Taer stumbled back to Molly's desk and, humming along to "Famous Case," Taer opened the MollyMaps program. She clicked around aimlessly for a while, not researching so much as stumbling through the program, drunkenly ambling from corner to corner of the crowded virtual map.* She turned on the voice recorder on her iPhone and rambled for a bit about wanting to meet Molly, how happy she was to be with Nix, who her Carey Mulligan–inspired character Jenny had been, what she had wanted in life, and what, exactly, Molly meant when she was going on about the "Pyramid Eye."

"There is a website that says pop stars are Illuminati puppets," Taer said, "which is of course ridiculous until you start thinking about how I'm sitting alone in a secret headquarters basement place, which is so weird, and maybe she was just in the Illuminati and all the rest is bullshit to trap me and trap Jenny in a triangle forever, just walking around in the same terrible triangle her whole life. How sad is that? We're all trapped all the time aren't we, except Molly who got out of here. But I bet even Molly had a triangle! I wish I could—"

Taer stopped talking and for nearly ten minutes, her phone's voice recorder only picked up some faint clicks from the mouse on her computer.

Then she spoke again, one final rejoinder: "Oh holy fuck."

Maps have never been accurate. The best they can achieve is a high navigability. In the Exploratory Age, during the first big brouhaha over mapmaking, early cartographers with imperfect knowledge of foreign geographies used flawed equipment to draw maps with as many errors as accuracies. Cultural biases, such as those displayed in the Edge of the World maps, created absolutely abysmal conditions for rigorous accuracy. While Christopher Columbus attempted to circumnavigate the globe in search of gold and spice, most of the "rude class" still believed sea monsters filled the boundary waters between the safe continents and the black void of the unknown.

---

* *Wine and* dérive—*how Situationist of her!* —CD

Modern day maps are still full of inaccuracies. They do a terrible job documenting borders, and are a hopeless match for the rural dirt roads that run between corn and sod farms in Ohio. Lazy mapmakers who use blueprints provided by city planners, rather than conducting their own cartographic surveys, accidentally include "paper streets" on their maps: streets that city planners or subdivision developers include on their blueprints but, for a variety of reasons, never get built.

Beyond even these unintentional discrepancies, some maps have inaccuracies deliberately added, those maps offered up as consumer products like London's ubiquitous street guide, *A–Zed*. They are called "trap streets," and they are purposefully fictitious; map publishing companies add them to protect their copyright. If another company sells a map that includes their false trap street, the first company knows their copyright has been violated and can sue. Trap streets are used as a weapon in corporate warfare, but in certain circumstances, trap streets can be used to fight a different kind of battle. Molly Metropolis certainly understood the importance of trap streets, and as she constructed her map of real train lines and paper ones, she included traps of her own.

Molly's trap street was a train line that didn't exist on any of the historic maps. By the time Taer was looking through The Ghost Network, it had been reduced to one errant, and tiny, dot. On the digital version of The Ghost Network, each train line was marked in a different color, and every dot that represented a station on the line was the same color as the line. Clicking drunkenly through The Ghost Network, in her digital *dérive*, Taer got lucky and stumbled upon a dot not connected to any train line.

At first, she thought she'd accidentally deleted the connection between the dot and the next nearby station. Then Taer noticed that the color of the dot, a pale and almost metallic pink, didn't match any other dots and lines nearby, nor any other dot she could see. The dot had been placed on the map at the intersection of Armitage and

Racine, at the location of the very building Taer was then sitting inside. Taer scoured the map for any other trace of the distinctive pink. She didn't see it, but she wasn't discouraged.

She flipped to a particularly oblique passage in Molly's notebook:

I found that the [New Situationists] left enough marks to follow, toeing the Party Line but didn't leave their Pyramid Eye to make an easy path. I can't tell if they were performing or acting, or if there is a difference between performing or acting, but I will find out and if I find anything, I'll leave my Third Eye behind to make a map on top of a map on top of a map like I've always done. To be fair to them (Debord and my sweet Nick, who answers to a higher power [currently incarcerated]), I won't leave an A–Zed sort of a guide, will I? Everyone will have to find something in the lattice. Who am I to deny my dearest ones the fun of their own mystery to solve?

Taer copied the passage into her own journal, circled the word "marks" in the first line, and next to it, she wrote: "pink one at A&R." Taer also wrote several question marks next to the phrase "Party Line," and wrote: "Why capitalize this?" Next to the words "Third Eye," Taer wrote: "Third Eye equals a Pyramid Eye equals a triangle, like Jenny's triangle. We have to find Molly's triangle." She thought the errant pink dot was one apex of a secret triangle, not present on any of the historical maps, which Molly had embedded into The Ghost Network.

For the next several hours, Taer searched the map for the second point in Molly's triangle, and finally found another pink dot outside of Chicago proper, at the Chicago Executive Airport in Wheeling, Illinois.

The wine caught up with Taer then. She took off her bra and fell asleep on Molly's couch. She slept until nine the next morning when Berliner nudged her awake and playfully flung her bra at her head. Rather than share her discovery with Berliner immediately, Taer decided to investigate the pink dots herself. Berliner and Nix still don't understand why.

"She's motivated by emotions rather than thought," Nix said.

"She *was*," Berliner corrected, and Nix flinched.

"You don't think she wanted to find something without you?" I asked Nix.

"Maybe. I don't know. It's frustrating to try to guess about it now. I thought maybe she had written something to explain why she would go searching without us, after everything, but there was nothing in her journals."

"Maybe she was trying to protect you," Berliner said to Nix.

"Oh yeah," Nix said sarcastically, raising her hand with two fingers missing, "she did a really good job protecting me. I'm literally scarred for life."

Berliner didn't respond.

Nix said, "Can we stop fucking around and just tell him Taer's story about her Special Secret Investigation of the Secret Pink Dot now?"

"Please do," I responded, before Berliner could say anything.

That day, Taer told Berliner and Nix she was picking up an extra shift at Rainbo. At about 3 p.m., Taer left the Urban Planning Committee headquarters and rode the Metra Union Pacific Northwest Line to the location of the second pink dot.*

Taer searched the outermost boarder of the grounds of the Chicago Executive Airport for a full hour. She couldn't wander the grounds because a security guard chased her off when she tried, but luckily, she didn't need to go deep into the airfield to find what she was looking for. Just south of the small terminal, near a stretch of

---

* *Nix and Berliner recounted the events that follow to Cyrus during one of their dual interviews. Cyrus combined their account with Taer's journal entry. —CD*

runway running alongside South Milwaukee Avenue, Taer found a small brick building painted almost the same color pink as the dots on the digital version of The Ghost Network. The pink paint, though chipped, stood out against the bleak airport landscape of gray and faded green. Taer stood on the hood of someone's car, smashed through one of the windows with a branch, cut through a flimsy wire screen with the sharp side of one of her keys, and heaved herself over the window ledge.

Immediately, Taer looked for a staircase to the basement and found another steel door with a little keypad lock. She entered the same combination she used to enter the Urban Planning Committee headquarters and the door opened. She descended into darkness.

Taking pictures with her phone as she went, Taer descended on stairs made of rotting wood. She kept one hand on the brick wall to steady herself, and in the other held her cell phone, with her flashlight app activated. Just before she reached the bottom of the staircase, the stairs changed to concrete and tile. Her hand, moving blindly along the wall, bumped into a light switch. She flicked it, and with a loud hum, the lights turned on. Taer was in a train station in disrepair, decorated with signage from the 1950s, plaques that said in fat, black letters "NO SMOKING. NO SPITTING" and "WATCH OUT: DO NOT LEAN OVER THE PLATFORM." She kicked up clouds of dust and she walked across the floor of cracked tile, arranged in a formless white and green mosaic. Coughing from the dust, lighting her way and taking pictures, Taer found a single incongruous item: a plaque made of plastic, lightly backlit by an LED lamp, designed to look like one of the '50s plaques, but which clearly had been affixed to the wall of the station more recently. It said "PLAQUES TOURNANTES TROIS" in the same black lettering.

Taer only spent a minute or two exploring the station before a dim beam of light suddenly broke the darkness, emanating from the tunnel beyond. She froze, then scrambled out of the pathway of the light. She waited. The light intensified quickly, and she heard the screech and chug of an approaching train. Had Taer stayed, all her mysteries would've been solved, but she was terrified. She ran.

On the long ride from the airport back to the Urban Planning Committee headquarters, during which she anxiously transferred between Metra trains and L trains and buses in case someone was following her, Taer tried to call Nix and Berliner several times. Neither of them answered their phones. Taer's mind reeled with the memory of the unknown train's bright light, and she spent about an hour in a coffee shop near the headquarters, writing furiously in her journal. Her notes from this writing session were penned so sloppily as to be almost unreadable. As if she was trying to get her hand to move as fast as her racing mind, she neglected to finish sentences and ignored the lines on the paper. As she wrote page after page, she returned several times to a single thought, first expressed as: "I bet Molly got on that train." By the end of the hour, she had dropped all speculation: "Molly got on that train."

Taer walked to the headquarters still dazed, where she was surprised to find Berliner in his kitchen, icing a fresh wound on the back of his head. While he and Nix were walking through an alley shortcut between the Urban Planning Committee headquarters and the nearest liquor store, someone jumped them from behind and knocked Berliner unconscious. When he came to, Nix was gone.

Taer panicked. She called Nix's cell phone about fifty times; Nix never answered. Eventually, the phone stopped ringing and went straight to Nix's voice mail. Crying in fear and frustration, Taer wanted to call the police and report Nix missing, but Berliner stopped her. He had a different way to help Nix, which involved revealing a secret he'd been keeping from Taer since she had found him.

Because Berliner knew how important Molly's pop star career was to her and her ideals, when Molly didn't show up for the sound check on January 9, Berliner immediately assumed she had been taken against her will. He believed nothing would've made Molly Metropolis give up her position of power.

Berliner suspected Ali and Peaches had kidnapped her. He stole his grandmother's gun and quickly found the New Society in a downtown apartment that Zavos owned, on the seventh floor of the Anne De Zoet building in a posh area of Chicago called River North. While Nix frantically searched through boutique clothing stores and Molly's dancers rehearsed during sound check without her, Berliner stormed the headquarters of the Society of Children of the Atomic Bomb.

Actually, "storming" isn't the right word to describe Berliner's actions. It's not as though he burst through the doors of the apartment complex with a double-barreled shotgun in his arms and a S.W.A.T. team at his back. The doorman, Ray Mitchell, opened the door for him and called up to number seven to see if Ali was in. She told Ray to send Berliner up. Berliner allowed the doorman to put his coat, with his gun and his map sketchpad in the pocket, in the apartment complex's coat check, where he assumed his items would be safe. He was worried that if he brought them up to the apartment, Ali, Peaches, and their compatriots would overpower him and take them.

Peaches greeted Berliner at the door, checked him for weapons or papers and, finding nothing, invited him inside. Berliner noticed the wooden flooring and the chic, minimalist furnishings and décor. He sat in the living room on a brown leather sofa, a seat which afforded him a great view of the downtown skyline. One of the younger members of the New Society brought them glasses of white wine, then lingered in the corner during Peaches and Berliner's conversation. Berliner never saw a New Society member older than Ali; they gave the collective impression of malleable young cult members.

Berliner declined to drink the wine and refused to stay on the couch. He believed Molly was tied up in a closet somewhere. Peaches allowed him to go through every nook and cranny of the apartment. He spent a full hour searching, even looking for secret panic rooms (and later he acquired blueprints from the city, the building's management, and the building's security company to make sure he hadn't missed anything). No Molly to be found.

Instead, resting on a nightstand in the fourth bedroom, he saw the circular purple quartz necklace Davis always wore. This discovery rattled Berliner; he didn't want to believe that a woman he'd trusted had betrayed him so thoroughly. He decided not to mention his discovery to the New Society and test Davis's loyalty at another time—a test that, as previously described, ultimately led to Taer's involvement in his investigation of Molly's disappearance.

When Berliner was satisfied Molly wasn't stuffed in a closet somewhere, Peaches asked him to leave. In the lobby, Berliner reclaimed his own jacket in a huff. He was so upset that he didn't realize until he was out in the snow that both his gun and his sketchpad of maps had been taken out of his pockets. Ray Mitchell, as Berliner should've assumed, was on Ali's payroll. Berliner was unable to reclaim his stolen items.

Once he brought Taer up to speed, they decided to go back to Michigan and talk to Davis. Berliner hoped he could force Davis to reveal where the New Society had taken Nix. Taer stopped weeping and accessed a quiet, aggressive rage. She dressed in her thickest pair of jeans and a T-shirt with the sleeves cut off, and pulled her hair into a tight bun on the top of her head. During those hours after Nix's abduction, Berliner said Taer was numb and inconsolable.

"She was really freaking out, but silent, which was unlike her,"

Berliner said. "All that intensity she had—she just channeled it into making Gina's kidnapping into this solvable problem. She'd seem fine, totally in control, then just burst into tears in a second. And yell at me if I tried to comfort her. She was so, so aggressive."

Berliner and Taer traveled by train to Davis's parents' house. Davis's father George answered the door. He led them to the living room, where the uncomfortable couches and lack of side tables exemplified the house's overall uninviting quality. Davis was reading, slumped in an armchair. George quickly left for the evening, believing his daughter's ex-boyfriend had come for a visit with his new girlfriend. George wanted to give his daughter space and avoid overhearing any awkward details.

In Davis, Taer expected to find a conniving operator, a young woman who had only pretended to be sad to deceive her and Nix, like the villain in a fairy tale. Instead, Davis was the same sad girl, mourning her mother and conflicted about her role in the war between the Urban Planning Committee and the New Society. When she saw Berliner, Davis broke down in tears and never quite recovered. Berliner took some whiskey from the kitchen and poured three glasses. After being in Davis's parents' house for ten minutes, he decided he hated it.

"I don't believe in ghosts," Berliner said, "but I do think a home can be imbued with a ghost-like presence from the people who've been left behind. Irene's mom's house definitely had that problem. It was the mostly ghostly house I've ever been in. I think Cait expected real horror movie shit to go down while we stayed there.

"It's the worst feeling. Architectural uncanny. The house wasn't, like, deep in the woods or on Fear Street* or something, but it had that feeling like when you're all alone late at night walking down a street and all the windows in the buildings are dark. You feel weird

---

* A reference to a series of horror novels for young adults written by R. L. Stine.

déjà vu and then you realize why—you've seen this before, but it hasn't happened to you. You've seen it on television. You've seen it in a movie. You are walking through, like, a pastiche of bad horror movies. You start fumbling with your keys because you expect to be fumbling with your keys and when you can't find the right key on the key ring, you fully expect the ghost of Jack the Ripper or something to stick his hook-hand in your back. And then you find your key, and it's behind the keychain card from Jewel-Osco* and everything's fine once you have the lights on."

Davis gave Berliner the details of her betrayal, speaking directly to him as if Taer wasn't in the room—Davis had lied to him, spied on him, but most importantly, she had sent Taer and Nix in his direction so the New Society could follow Taer and Nix to the Urban Planning Committee headquarters.

Davis cried again and begged for forgiveness. Berliner asked where they would take Nix. To repent for spying and working against him, Davis told Berliner that the New Society had a property in Michigan, a lake house officially owned by Peaches's maternal grandmother Roberta Parish. Schizophrenic and suffering from emphysema after a lifetime of smoking, Parish lived in a high-end senior care center in Ann Arbor. Peaches and the New Society had free reign of her lakefront property. Davis gave Taer and Berliner the address, and assured them that if Ali and Peaches had taken Nix anywhere, it was there. By that time, it was nearly 3 a.m. Taer wanted to leave immediately, but Berliner thought it would be better to sleep for a few hours and persuaded her to wait until the sun came up.

Taer passed out in the guest bedroom and Davis took Berliner to the screened-in porch, where she ripped holes in the fraying screens until Berliner became sexually overwhelmed, pinned her to the

---

* Jewel-Osco is a Chicago-area grocery store chain.

concrete floor, and pulled off her pants. They had sex several times that evening.*

"I really did like her, a lot. She had this openness, where she would accept anything about someone she loved, but still remain true to her own desires," Berliner said during one of our solo interviews. When he spoke about Davis, he was quiet with heavy regret. "I blamed Irene for getting Gina kidnapped and for hurting Cait. I wasn't nice to her, that last time I saw her. I wish I'd been nice to her."

The next morning, Davis's father drove Taer and Berliner to the Hertz so they could rent a car, then he stopped at the farmers' market. George spent a leisurely hour and a half choosing greens, melons, and tomatoes. When he returned to his mother's house, he found his daughter hanging by her neck in her bedroom, blue in the face, and dead for at least half an hour.

---

* During my conversations with Nix and Berliner, I was able to pry from them some details of their various sexual encounters, which they hadn't given to Cyrus. Maybe they were more comfortable talking to me about sex; maybe it's because they, for some reason, decided to drink with me even though they wouldn't drink with Cyrus. —CD

Chapter (12)

Nix woke up on a bare mattress, her legs covered with a purple duvet. Her head pounded and her vision was slightly blurry. As she struggled to sit up, someone handed her a plastic cup full of water. Disoriented, she thought she could smell pasta sauce, the kind from the jar Taer used to heat in the microwave to make spaghetti for Nix after she'd gone for a long run.

Nix vomited on the stained carpet below her makeshift bed. After she emptied her stomach, Peaches appeared and wiped her face with a warm washcloth while Ali cleaned the mess. Ali and Peaches spent the rest of the night making sure Nix didn't fall asleep and slip into a coma. Ali had hit Nix over the head much harder than she had intended and Nix had a concussion. There was a ringing in her ears for the better part of twenty-four hours. Nix now jokingly refers to the concussion as her "sports injury."

Ali and Peaches held Nix hostage in their crumbling, mostly unlived-in South Loop apartment. They kept her in the second bedroom, a bare cell of a room with concrete walls and windows obscured by blackout curtains. They cuffed and chained Nix's ankles together with restraints they had purchased at a sex toy shop on North Lincoln Avenue called The Pleasure Chest.

The next day, Ali and Peaches took the cuffs off her legs, tied Nix's wrists together, and walked her out of the apartment, down to an underground parking garage, and into the backseat of a black Escalade. They buckled her in and tucked a blanket around her shoulders to hide the restraints. They covered her eyes with an eye pillow. To the casual observer, she looked like she was napping in the backseat of the car. Nix asked them if they had done the same to Molly Metropolis, and they laughed at her. Then Ali started the car and pulled out of the parking garage. Nix couldn't see Ali drive down the mostly empty lanes of I-90 East, cross into Indiana, and transfer onto I-94 East on a crescent moon–shaped route around the curved bottom of Lake Michigan. Her destination was a place that Nix, and most Chicagoans looking for an alternative to the crowded city beaches, knew well: Michiana.

Michiana is an awkwardly shaped lakeside region, with a cultural center in South Bend, Indiana and territory across the borderland areas of both northern Indiana and southwestern Michigan. The boundaries of Michiana are composed of about sixty square miles of lakeside area, but the region's true heart, its thematic core, is the invisible border between Michigan and Indiana, which visitors and summer people cross and re-cross with a kind of geographical blindness. Above all else, Michiana is characterized by a lack of boundaries and a feeling of neither here nor there. It is fitting, then, that over half of the residences in Michiana are vacation houses or second homes.

Full-time inhabitants know exactly where Michigan stops being Michigan or Indiana stops being Indiana. Parents know where the school district of one state ends and another begins. Summer visitors know the farmers' markets are better on the Michigan side but the hamburgers are better in Indiana. Adolescent boys know where fireworks are legal to buy and use and where they aren't.

The New Society chose their location headquarters cleverly. Not only did the Michiana House give them a place to retreat to, away from Chicago's urban battleground, but the lakeside backstreets are also some of the most topographically complicated matrices of roads to be found in the tri-state area. In comparison to Chicago's grid of streets, the Michiana residential avenues are something out of *Alice in Wonderland*. Some curve like snakes, some zigzag. Dozens of cul-de-sacs, dead end streets, and crescents twist through the landscape. Occasionally, one of the crescents meets the same street twice and creates two crossroads with the same name—for example, there are two different intersections of Hillside Trail and Birchmont Trail. These lakeside streets form an asphalt labyrinth, and the New Society had a house in the middle of the maze.

Driving the Escalade, Ali navigated the labyrinthine streets expertly. She turned down a small trail-like street, half a block east of the beach. The asphalt was dusted with a fine layer of icy sand that crunched under the SUV's tires. She approached a house that nearly straddled the border between Michigan and Indiana and pulled into the driveway. The dancers each grabbed one of Nix's arms and carefully walked her up the house's small, cracked staircase.*

Like many lakefront homes, the value of the property was in the location, not the building itself. The flooring was warped. To Nix, it smelled like unwashed laundry, mildew, mold, and dirty dishes. The house was cluttered with knick-knacks, some kitschy and cheap, others expensive and delicate.

They removed Nix's blindfold and led her through the first floor; Nix saw the dining room and living room, both crowded with over-stuffed bookshelves. Ten or fifteen women and men in their early twenties sat at the dining room table or on the couches in the living room. Some worked on laptops, some of them examined the maps on the table, some of them crowded around a big iMac. Some of

---

* *At some point, Cyrus visited this house.* —CD

them greeted Ali and Peaches with little waves. They had left their half-empty coffee mugs and teacups everywhere. Platters of fruit, vegetables, cheese, salami, and pastries balanced on top of stacks of books. They stared blankly at Nix when she asked them for help, and covered their papers with their arms so she couldn't see what they were working on.

Stacks of newspapers, magazines, and pamphlets lined the walls. Between the piles and above them, the fading wallpaper was speckled with water stains. The thick carpet curled up in the corners of the room. The huge table was missing a leg; concrete blocks kept the thing upright and shouldered the weight of the table's contents: a massive collection of maps and blueprints, as well as the iMac's twenty-seven-inch screen and two external hard drives. The living room was equally stuffed with books, newspapers, and maps.

Ali and Peaches hurried Nix to the staircase and led her up to the second floor. The wooden flooring was so warped from years of humid summers and damp winters that it actually sloped under Nix's feet. She tripped over the top stair and, with her hands still tied behind her back, couldn't catch herself. She banged her chin on the warped wood and began to bleed, then cry from the shock of the pain. "Embarrassing," Nix recalled to me. "But I was very scared."

As Ali and Peaches marched Nix deeper into the dark house, Nix began to feel as afraid of the house itself as of the people in it. "The floors were creaking and, I swear to god, a light bulb was flickering, like something was haunting it," Nix said. "Not like, the ghost of a murdered child or something, but like there was this ephemeral rotting horrible thing in there. And I wanted to leave, I wanted to leave so badly. I've never wanted something as much as I wanted that. It is a strange, almost psychic feeling when you realize something life-changing and terrible is happening to you while it's happening."

Ali and Peaches walked Nix to the end of the hallway, through a bedroom with someone asleep, though faintly stirring, in the bed. They led her into the adjoining bathroom, which had no windows and only the one door. Crowding the doorway so that she couldn't slip past, they untied her hands and locked her inside.

Nix spent three and a half hours alone in the bathroom. For the first half hour, she tried to escape by breaking through the door, succeeding only in bruising her left arm, shoulder, and foot; breaking off two fingernails; and badly scraping the palms of her hands. Teeming with energy and adrenaline, she ran in place for the next twenty minutes trying to come up with an escape plan. She couldn't think of anything. Then, for a little while, she gave up.

The next two and a half hours felt unimaginably long. She recalled Taer's preferred method for curbing anxiety, a hot bath and a glass (or two) of wine. Nix couldn't drink the wine, but she could take a bath. She stripped down, filled the bathtub with hot water, and got in. She soaked until the water went cold. Exacting the only kind of revenge she could on her captors, she emptied and refilled the bathtub until she had used all the hot water in the entire house.*

As the hot water lulled Nix's exhausted body into a state of semi-consciousness, she knew she was making herself even more vulnerable, but she fell asleep in the pool of cooling water. That was how Ali and Peaches found her. Nix woke up when she heard the door open.

Once Nix was dressed, Ali questioned her. Unfortunately for Ali, she had made a critical mistake. Ali had assumed that Nix was the one encouraging Taer to look for Molly, that Nix was in charge of their search. Ali had also assumed Molly had told Nix her secrets

---

* During a conversation we had about her and Taer's sex life, Nix also mentioned to me that she masturbated while she was in this bathtub. I asked her if she had ever thought about Taer while "jerking off" (my words) and she told me the bathtub had reminded her of Taer. Nix said, "I obviously didn't want Taer to have been kidnapped too, but I wanted her there with me. I thought about her and, yeah, I masturbated. Which I know sounds strange, but she and I, we had this thing about bathtubs and faucets and we were always having sex in the tub. It started out by us kinda making fun of Nick's thing, and then, I don't know. It escalated. So, I did jerk off about her that once. And then more lately, you know, since the Lake Michigan thing." —CD

227

and given Nix essential information about Berliner and The Ghost Network. Peaches distrusted Molly so much she thought Molly had told Nix things that Molly had refused to tell her. But the dancers were wrong. Nix knew nothing that Ali and Peaches didn't know. She couldn't remember the combination to the lock on the Urban Planning Committee's steel door.

Ali asked Nix to confess Molly's endgame. If she didn't, Ali warned, something violent would happen to her. Nix told Ali she didn't know what Ali was talking about. Ali asked Nix to tell her where she had hidden Molly Metropolis's notebook. Nix refused to answer. So, Peaches pulled a Swiss Army knife out of her pocket and cut Nix's left pinkie and ring finger at the root, nearly severing the digits from her hand.

"For a second, I didn't feel anything. Then it hurt so much I couldn't stop screaming," Nix said. "I could feel my heartbeat in my hand and with every pulse more blood came out. I was so scared, and Peaches, she was laughing at me."

Casares had been an EMT before interning at SDFC and joining the New Society. He crudely anaesthetized Nix and sewed her fingers back together. He bandaged the cut on her chin. He gave her a Vicodin and made her a bed with pillows and couch cushions in the bathtub. Nix fell asleep or passed out. Casares spent several hours in the bathroom, sitting on the toilet, reading *The Clash of Kings*, making sure Nix didn't start bleeding again, while Peaches slept in the bed in the next room.

In the early morning, around 5 a.m., Peaches walked into the bathroom, waking Nix in the process. She took Casares into the bedroom. Nix heard the two of them have sex. They didn't make an effort to keep quiet and at one point, Peaches moved them from the bed to the wall the bedroom and bathroom shared. She made sure Nix could hear the sound of each and every thrust.

•

I saw Nix happy once during our interviews, while she was describing her escape.

"Can you tell me what happened that afternoon?" I asked.

Nix giggled. "I'm such a bad ass."

Ali and Peaches left Nix alone during her second day of captivity at the Michiana house. She listened through the wall to the change of guards and peeked through the door when they opened it to give her food and clean clothes. She determined that she had a rotating set of guards, only one at any given time, armed with a small pistol that they passed to each other when their shift ended, like relay runners passing a baton. She saw one reading when Casares opened the door to give her lunch. She heard one take a phone call from his mother in the middle of the afternoon.

The next day, recalling how effective Taer had been with the dictionary during the break-in, Nix armed herself with the heavy porcelain lid from the back of the toilet. She waited until Casares brought her lunch, a little after noon. When he opened the door, she swung the toilet lid at his face, knocking him out cold and breaking his jaw and three of his teeth. The force of the blow reverberated through the toilet lid back into Nix's arms, which went slightly numb with shock. Her hurt fingers throbbed. She let go of the lid with her left hand, but didn't drop her weapon.

The guard, a nineteen-year-old girl named Andrea Stone, fumbled with the safety on the gun. Nix ran out of the bathroom and swung the lid at Stone as well, hitting her on the side of the head, though using only one arm, she couldn't hit Stone with full force—lucky for her. Nix might've caused brain damage if she had hit Stone as hard as she could. Stone fell to the ground, bleeding and stunned. Nix dropped the toilet lid, grabbed the gun, and ran to the stairs, making a beeline for the front door. Peaches was waiting for her in the foyer.

Peaches stood in front of the door, her arms spread out like a human shield. From the top of the staircase, Nix pointed the gun at

Peaches and told her to move. When Peaches refused, Nix aimed for the stomach and fired; she missed, but hit Peaches in the shoulder. The bullet went all the way through her muscle and the wood door, finally stopping somewhere in the asphalt street. Peaches collapsed, while the young members of the New Society screamed and crowded around her, blocking the front door. Nix pointed her gun at everyone to keep them away and ran to the back of the house, through the kitchen, looking for another door. She burst out of the house.

Nix ran. She didn't have shoes or a coat but she ran anyway, as far and as fast as she could, into the maze of streets surrounding the New Society's Michiana house. She threw the gun into a bush. It took her an hour to find her way out of the lakeside area, but none of the New Society members pursued her. She was lucky she was kidnapped in April; if there had been snow on the ground, her feet would have frozen before she could find her way to the main road.

Nix went into the first business she saw, a diner, and told the waitress she had escaped from an abusive boyfriend and needed to call her sister in Chicago. She couldn't remember Taer's cell phone number off the top of her head and had to look it up in her e-mail account using the waitress's iPhone.

Half an hour later, Berliner and Taer arrived at the Michiana diner, where Nix was drinking coffee, eating pie, and listening to the waitress's own harrowing tales of bad men. Taer almost couldn't look at Nix, with the ominous bandages on her chin and around her fingers, the fresh bruises on her elbows from banging into the side of the tub while she slept, the bruises forming on the inside of her fingers where she'd gripped the toilet lid.* As the Civil War histo-

---

* The waitress forced Nix to pose for cell phone photos to give to the police. Nix used them for her 2010 Christmas card.

rian Fredrick Doyle wrote, "Young soldiers don't truly believe in the cruelty of war until they see their first casualty."* In a burst of public emotion, Taer sobbed. She cried so deeply she choked, while Nix hugged her.

Taer pulled herself together. She awkwardly pulled off her puffy coat and handed it to Nix. Nix was moved by both the crying and the gesture. She took the coat from Taer. Even though it didn't fit her properly, Nix put it on.

Berliner drove Nix to the nearest hospital, a small emergency-care facility called Franciscan ExpressCare. An attending physician redid Casares's sutures and prescribed more Vicodin. On the long drive back to Chicago, Taer sat with Nix in the backseat. She put Nix's head in her lap and ran her fingers through her hair, lightly massaging her scalp and gently working out all the tangles and knots. They didn't speak. Nix wouldn't discuss her own experience of the kidnapping while she was still fleeing from it.

Back at the New Situationist headquarters, Taer ran Nix a bath. She helped her undress, then sat next to the tub with her fingertips in the water while Nix soaked and cried a little. After the bath water went cold, they went to bed together and slept.

Nix refused to get out of bed the next day. She curled up in a ball, under a heavy comforter. Though she wouldn't let Taer get into the cocoon with her, Taer could see she was shuddering from the way the comforter shook. Nix refused to consume anything except water and more Vicodin for her aching fingers. Taking Vicodin on an empty stomach made her nauseated. Berliner visited the bedroom of the apartment Taer and Nix had claimed and spoke softly to Nix about the strength of the steel door.

---

* Fredrick Doyle, *Sugar, Cotton, and Boys Fighting Boys* (New York: Random House, 2001), 12.

"But they know where we are," Nix said.

Berliner assured her that Ali, Peaches, and their New Society couldn't get through the door. Nix didn't speak to him again that day.

Taer stayed with Nix all morning and afternoon, writing in her journal, reading about the Situationists, and begging Nix to eat the Kraft Easy Mac she had found in Berliner's room.

Nix didn't move or respond until early evening; she was suddenly starving. Taer made her the microwavable macaroni and cheese, which tasted like plastic. Nix threw it all up, perhaps because of the Vicodin, or anxiety, or her body rejecting the chemical mess that flavored the Easy Mac. Taer held her hair as she vomited, then wrapped her arms around Nix's shoulders while she sat on the bathroom floor, shaking.

Meanwhile, Berliner took the rental car with Michigan plates out for one last spin. He stopped at a Walgreen's and cobbled together a gift basket of Virginia Slims, M&Ms, and seven different shades of red nail polish. Then he drove to the Dwight Correctional Center. On the way, he received a call from Davis's father, informing him of her suicide. By the time Berliner reached the wide plastic table where he met Kraus during visitation hours, he was already shaking and crying. He buried his head in the crook of one arm and sobbed into the table, with his other arm stretched toward Kraus. The guards permitted her to hold his hand, so she comforted him that way.

In the prison's visiting room, outfitted with various cameras and recording devices, Kraus and Berliner couldn't speak freely about Nix's kidnapping. They could talk for hours about maps and sex apartments and pop stars, but use phrases like "almost cut off her fingers," and the prison guards would start to take notice. Berliner spoke as freely as he could; he could talk openly about Davis's death at least, which he did as Kraus stroked the back of his hand.

Berliner was afraid he wouldn't be able to fight back, he was afraid he wouldn't find what Molly Metropolis had found, and he was afraid that he, Nix, and Taer wouldn't be able to protect themselves from the New Society. Kraus wouldn't let him be afraid. She held his hand and whispered ferociously to him until Berliner no longer had the urge to cry.

Taer didn't tell Berliner and Nix about the secret train for another day and a half. She waited until she decided Nix was recovered enough—still nervous and jumpy, but able to leave the Urban Planning Committee if she carried the gun with her. Preparing for a dramatic scene, Taer brought Berliner and Nix takeout from their favorite Italian restaurant, turned on her iPhone voice recorder to continue to track the story, and attempted to combine apology and explanation while their mouths were full.

Nix and Berliner were both livid that Taer hadn't told them sooner. Most people have a particular arguing style, developed through years of familial conflict or friend-group infighting. Taer, Nix, and Berliner all argued differently. Berliner learned from his mother to be quiet during a fight; Dana Berliner didn't appreciate raised voices. Nix, a veteran of popular girl hierarchies, hated conflict; she made jokes to amuse herself and defuse the tension. Taer, who had three stubborn brothers, immediately became defensive.

"Why didn't you tell me about it this morning?" Berliner asked.

"I'm not telling you anything until you calm down and listen to me."

"I'm perfectly calm."

"Yeah, sure," Nix said.

"I don't have to tell you every little thing I do," Taer said.

"I thought we were working on this together," Berliner said.

"I think I've sacrificed enough to warrant full disclosure at this point," Nix said.

"You could've trusted us, maybe," Berliner said.

"How did I know you wouldn't have figured something out from what I found, and not told me about it? How do I know I can trust you when it really comes down to it?" Taer said to Berliner.

"Well, two nights ago, you said to me, 'I've been living in your lair for two months now, and you've been the best friend to Nix and me. I totally trust you.' So there's that."

"I meant I trusted you not to make a move on me in the night or something."

"That place really is like a lair," Nix said.

"Stop fucking with me," Berliner said. "This is exactly what Metro did. Leaving cryptic messages and just fucking off."

"I'm not doing that," Taer said.

"It feels like you're doing the exact same thing."

"I wanted to find what she found. You met her, you knew her."

"I could've hid this whole thing from you, but I didn't want to do it by myself," Berliner said. "Is that what you want?"

"No," Taer said.

"To go at it alone?"

"No, I said," Taer said. "Okay, okay? Let me tell you! I found some stations on the map, these little pink dots, they were just floating there, all by themselves—"

"This is exactly why you should've told me right away," Berliner interrupted, "We didn't get a chance to check everything, they might be errors—"

"Well, they're not errors, and this is exactly why I didn't want to tell you right away, because you're not listening—" Taer said.

"I'm listening!"

"No, you are interrupting me when I'm trying to tell you what happened."

"Guys," Nix said, firmly.

"Okay, so, I think that when Molly wrote in her notebook about the Pyramid Eye, or the Third Eye, or even all that stuff with

234

Chombart de Lauwe mapping that triangle for that girl, do you remember that?" Taer asked.

"Yeah," Berliner said.

"When she was writing that, I think she was trying to make us think about triangles, in relation to The Ghost Network. I think she hid a triangle on there somehow, and I think I found two points on the triangle. She marked them as stations on the digital map. One of the marks is on this address, the Urban Planning Committee headquarters, so I think Molly thought of this as a metaphorical station—unless there is a train station under here, I don't know, I don't think so, though. Anyway, I found a second dot in the same color, and I went there."

Taer then told Berliner and Nix the story of finding the station and running from the approaching train. As Nix and Taer discussed the train, Berliner opened MollyMaps, pursuing an idea that had been nagging at him since Taer mentioned she had found some station dots unconnected to any train lines. Berliner checked the revision history of the digital version of The Ghost Network and saw that on January 9, sometime after Molly had left the Museum of Contemporary Art, she had added a map to The Ghost Network and then deleted it. Berliner restored the deleted map. It appeared on The Ghost Network as a narrow, pale pink triangle. One apex landed at the Urban Planning Committee headquarters; the second apex was the Chicago Executive Airport, where Taer had run from the mysterious train; the third apex was at a location neither Berliner nor Taer recognized, but it intersected with a station on a train line that had never been approved by the city.

The non-approved train line would've been 154.8 miles long, stretching from the most affluent southern suburbs of Milwaukee all the way down to the country clubs in Chicago's southern suburban region. The line would've sideswept the overcrowded Loop lines meant for businessmen and other commuters. Most of the line's

235

stations would've hugged the waters of Lake Michigan. Once it left the water, it veered into the Theater District.

The Chicago Transit Authority proposed the train line in 1957, in a project co-sponsored by the State Tourism Board. The CTA and Tourism Board designed the line not only to increase tourism to the city's beaches but also to attract the "right kind" of tourists by stopping only in the wealthiest suburbs.* A *Chicago Tribune* reporter, writing about the tourism proposal in its entirety, dubbed the train line "The Party Line," both referring to the leisure-based purpose of the line and mocking the city's newly elected mayor, Richard J. Daley for 'toeing the party line' of his political party.[†] The Party Line was supposed to be a cost-efficient line because it reused some bomb shelter/underground stations that had gone out of service in the 1940s, but when Daley and the CTA discovered that each of those underground stations would need about a million dollars in renovations before they would be up to code, the Party Line died. The plans for the line were filed with the rest of the city's transit records. Decades later they were mined from the Public Archives by Peaches. Molly Metropolis added the Party Line to The Ghost Network on August 3, 2009.

Berliner relayed the history of the Party Line to Nix and Taer. They decided to go to the third point in Molly's triangle the next day, in the early afternoon. They didn't even have to take the L;

---

* Incidentally, the man who actually designed the train line, William Alexander Carnevale, Jr., grew up in the South Chicago industrial neighborhood now called Burnside. Locals refer to the neighborhood as "The Triangle" because it is fenced in by three railroad tracks: the Illinois Central Line on the west, the Rock Island Line on the south, and the New York Central Line at the east. Carnevale's father was a blue-collar factory worker in the Burnside Steel Mill. W. A. Carnevale, Sr., continued to live in the neighborhood even when the factories closed and white flight reached a fever pitch. W.A. Jr. eventually died in the neighborhood where he was born on December 25, 1981. He was visiting his ailing father and, on his way back to his Wicker Park apartment, caught a stray bullet during a sudden burst of gang violence. He bled to death on the street, calling for help that didn't come.

† Sal Barbar, "The City of Impossible Trains," *Chicago Tribune*, March 3, 1957; 68.

the Party Line station was within walking distance of the New Situationist headquarters on North Wells Street, halfway between West North Avenue and West Schiller Street, at the site of the Old Town Aquarium, a boutique tropical fish store. The land had been privately owned by a real estate company called Rind-Grandin Global since the mid-1960s. Jim and Ian Schakowsky, brothers and world-class deep-sea divers, had first rented the property in 1972 and had been running Old Town Aquarium for nearly four decades. Although they didn't advertise this service, the Schakowsky brothers' elite clients could hire them to procure any aquatic lifeform "physically smaller than Jim," the taller of the two. A regular customer, who spoke to me on the promise of anonymity, has a secret collection of endangered sea life acquired for him by the Schakowskys.

In the shop, Berliner and Taer pretended to browse while Nix actually did. She watched a tank full of jellyfish, a species colloquially called "moon jellies." She gazed at their ghostly, translucent bodies until the clerk, a middle-aged woman named Nancy Franklin, noticed her intensity and sidled over to give Nix her sales pitch. With the clerk conveniently distracted, Taer and Berliner searched the small shop for a way into the unused train station below. They didn't find anything. Nix asked Berliner if they had the money to buy a large tank and jellyfish to swim in it. They didn't, but Berliner agreed to buy her a bowl of small bioluminescent fish. While filling out the delivery slip with his *pied-à-terre*'s address, Berliner casually mentioned he might know the Schakowsky brothers from either "a political group" or the Urban Planning Committee, testing the waters. Franklin promised to pass on his greeting to the owners.

Nix was elated with her purchase. She curled her arm around Taer's as they walked down the street. Taer appreciated the attention but she was frustrated by not finding anything and batted Nix away. They decided to split up; Berliner would go to meet Nina Johnson at the Chicago Archives to try to find a blueprint or a city survey of the building that housed the Old Town Aquarium, while Nix and Taer returned to the Urban Planning Committee headquarters. Taer would look for anything they had missed on The Ghost Network. Nix would tend to her fish.

At the Chicago Archives, Berliner met Johnson. She fetched him the blueprints of the Old Town Aquarium's building as well as the last architectural survey the city conducted of the unused train station below, when Daley still hoped to build the Party Line. In their examination of the blueprints, Berliner found plans for a hidden staircase, leading into a basement area.

Johnson locked the door of the Archives, took off her dress, and unscrewed the bolts that held one of the benches to the floor. She and Berliner copulated while the bench rocked and scraped across the maple wooden flooring.

Taer and Nix's return to the Racine building was equally exciting. As they descended into the Urban Planning Committee headquarters, they noticed that the security door had been tampered with. Someone had tried to take the heavy steel door off at its hinges. The New Society was the most likely culprit, and Nix panicked. She insisted that they move out. Taer agreed, and called Berliner to hurry home to help. The plan was to transfer everything to Berliner's *pied-à-terre*.

When Berliner arrived, they began packing for their quick move. Taer wrapped the external hard drives that stored The Ghost Network's data in her heaviest sweaters. She and Nix were transferring them into a backpack when a bomb went off in the Racine building.

Chapter (13)

The explosion knocked Taer, Berliner, and Nix across the room, into the wall, as paint chips and wood splinters rained on their heads and the rooms of the Urban Planning Committee shook. Luckily, the small amount of plastic explosive the New Society had planted wasn't designed to bring down the building, just destroy the steel door, so Taer, Berliner, and Nix suffered only small cuts and bruises. Within a few seconds, the shaking stopped, and they picked themselves up.

Berliner knew they had to leave the Urban Planning Committee to the New Society, to give up the space he'd devoted a decade of his life, but he wouldn't let them take the small physical archives of the New Situationists and the UPC.

"I was shouting at Gina and Cait, probably really incoherently, trying to make them understand we needed to take everything or ruin it, so Ali and Peaches couldn't have it," Berliner later told me.

"You weren't incoherent," Nix said.

Berliner pulled several half-empty cans of white paint out of a cabinet and, standing on Molly's desk, sloshed paint over The Ghost Network on the wall. Taer threw the desktop computer to the floor and beat it into bits with a chair. Nix stuffed the remaining external hard drives and Molly's notebook into her messenger bag. Berliner poured paint on the maps. When they heard footsteps and voices in the hallway, they fled through the secret door in the northwest corner of the office. As they raced up the stairs, Taer, Nix, and Berliner heard a scream and a crash—someone had fallen through the trap door.

"I hope it was that bitch," Nix said, meaning Peaches. They hurried away from the building.

It wasn't "that bitch" who had fallen; it was Ali. She shattered the bones in her left elbow and left leg; she also cracked three ribs. Two other members of the New Society carried her out of the building and called an ambulance. (They told the EMTs she had climbed to the roof of the alcove in front of the building and fallen off.) The New Society had reached the heart of the Urban Planning Committee headquarters, but their small hunting party of ten had already been diminished by three.

When they saw the wreckage of the computer and the mess on the wall, the members of the New Society frantically tried to mop up the paint with their scarves and sweaters, while Peaches, her arm in a sling, smashed pieces of computer under her snow boots. She got paint all over her clothes and good hand as she tried to find some unsullied documents under a mound of paint-soaked maps. She didn't find anything. Frustrated, she sent two of her team to find Taer, Berliner, and Nix, and told the rest of them to stop looking for something and run. Peaches set fire to a pile of maps soaked in paint and the Racine building burned.

Taer, Berliner, and Nix moved as fast as they could down Armitage. They didn't run into anyone, but they couldn't hide on the sidewalks brightly illuminated by streetlamps. They didn't know if anyone from the New Society would follow them, but just in case, they took a long, inefficient route to their destination. They walked, looking over their shoulders, to the L station at Armitage and North Sheffield Avenue. They took the Brown Line one stop south, to the Sedgwick station, exiting the car just as the doors closed. They doubled back, taking the Brown Line north to Fullerton, where they switched to the Red Line and rode to the Grand Station. They left the L behind and walked to Berliner's *pied-à-terre*.

Berliner offered Taer and Nix the semi-hidden second bedroom, but instead the three of them piled into the main bed and spooned together, trying to feel protected and safe. Berliner slept, Nix slept, but they said Taer's anxious fervor kept her awake all night. The adrenaline that had surged through her body in the moments after the explosion didn't dissipate. At 8:30 the next morning, Nix would've preferred to stay asleep, but Taer shook her and Berliner awake. She had already made a Dunkin Donuts run. The Old Town Aquarium opened at 9 a.m. and she wanted to get going.

Nancy Franklin was, again, manning the store and the jellyfish, but this time she greeted Berliner warmly, as if she knew him. According to Berliner, she said something like: "Jim and Ian said you are friends with Antoinette Monson. You should've mentioned that the other day and I would've let you do whatever you wanted." Franklin led them to the emergency exit, disabled the alarm, and pointed the way to a narrow passage which led to the staircase Berliner had seen on the blueprints of the building. Taer descended into the darkness without a second thought.

The staircase wasn't very deep but it took them a long time to reach the bottom because it was narrow, unlit, and unstable. At the base of the staircase, Berliner felt around for the breaker box— subway regulations during the year the station was built called for breakers at the foot of every service staircase. Berliner opened his cell phone and shone his light against the wall. He found the breaker and flicked the switches. All of the light fixtures on the ceiling,

241

ornate 1920s-style chandeliers strung with heavy crystals, lit up.* The station stretched out in front of them. In some ways, a subway station is the perfect secret space in Chicago. Even though the L trains run underground for huge distances, everyone in Chicago still thinks of public transit as something hovering above the city rather than creeping below.

Continuing her obsessive self-documentation, Taer turned on her iPhone voice recorder.

"It's pretty," Nix said, her voice echoing against the tiled walls. "I mean, like, it looks fancy, like Union Station."

Berliner sneezed. "I'm allergic to dust."

Taer said, "This place is so rad!"

A few minutes later, bored and underwhelmed after the first train station she visited produced a train so quickly, Taer had changed her tune, grumbling: "What do we do now?"

The three of them explored the train station from end to end, but besides a few benches and a surprising lack of mold or grime, they didn't find anything. They sat on the benches and waited. Nix laid her head in Taer's lap and made weak jokes: "They really need to get more funding so that they can add more trains. This wait is ridiculous. I'll be late for work." Berliner ate some trail mix Nix had in her purse and answered some of Taer's questions about his mother. They played the app version of the board game Life on Taer's iPhone. Two and a half hours went by. Then, as Taer complained about not being able to nap on a hard tile floor, the crystals on the chandelier started to shake.

"Jurassic Park," Taer said, referring to the scene where the water ripples from the vibration of the footsteps of an approaching T-Rex. A few seconds later, the voice recorder picked up the unmistakable rattling clank of an approaching train.

---

* Cyrus didn't visit this station while he was writing this book; more information on the station to come. —CD

The train was two cars long, and old, and green. It had probably been in the underground station since the '50s, but someone had taken care to repaint it. The sides were a forest green, the window frames a yellowish off-white. On the front was a big beacon-like light, and two stoplight fixtures on either side of a door. Where there would've been a sign that displayed the name of the next stop, there was instead a sign with a black triangle painted on it.

On Taer's recording, mixed in with the clatter of the train and the screech of its brakes, I could hear Berliner speaking quickly, though his words were indiscernible to me. Berliner told me he was giving Taer and Nix a quick history of the train car—vintage 1950s, painted like they would've been painted—as well as identifying for them the man who was driving the train.

It was David Wilson, the other publicly known, non-incarcerated member of the New Situationists. He stopped the train and stepped onto the platform.

"Hey!" Taer said.

Wilson ignored her and spoke to Berliner instead. "I suppose Marie-Hélène told you something ridiculous."

"She didn't tell me anything, she told me she didn't know anything," Berliner said. "This is Cait and this is Gina."

"Okay."

"Did she know something?" Berliner asked.

"Marie's the kind of person who wouldn't tell me if she'd found something out," David said. "I assumed—"

"I was the one who found it," Taer interjected. "It wasn't him."

At the same time, Berliner said: "It was kind of a group effort."

"Okay," Wilson said. "Good for you."

"So what now?" Taer asked.

"I guess you might as well get on the train," Wilson said.

Wilson went to the engine room to start the train car again, while Taer, Nix, and Berliner climbed inside the first car. The seats,

243

some facing forward and some facing back, were covered in decaying red fabric. The white paint on the walls was chipped and the stuffing was coming out of the plush seats. Nix sat, squeezing the fabric of the seat cushions in her fist, feeling the dust on them. She felt uneasy but didn't speak up. Berliner picked at the peeling paint with his fingernails, collecting a handful of millimeter-long paint chips, then pocketing them. Taer, exhilarated, grabbed the metal handrails and walked up and down the center aisle of the car, examining everything she could. When the train started she could barely contain a shout.

"We followed Molly Metropolis's map," Taer said, when Wilson walked back into the train car. "Where is she? What is this train? Where are we going?"

"Are we not going back there?" Nix asked. "Because let me off."

"Seriously?" Taer said.

"I'm not going somewhere random with this dude," Nix said. "Fuck that."

Wilson laughed, a dry wheeze. He said, "I'm sorry to tell you this, Caitlin, but this train is nothing."

"It's not nothing," Taer said. "It's a train."

"It's a toy," he said. "You found the life-size version of a child's train set."

"What do you mean?" Berliner asked.

"But," Taer said, painfully hopeful, "there's a train here that's not on a regular map. That you can only find on Molly Metropolis's crazy map."

"Our crazy map," Berliner said.

Wilson laughed again.

"How did you know we were down here?" Berliner asked.

"There are security cameras. And I come down here a lot," Wilson admitted sheepishly.

Berliner laughed, perhaps cruelly, but Wilson wasn't shamed. "You came into the group too late, Nick. And you were still young.

244

Your life wasn't affected the way our lives were. The rest of my life is going to be about the New Situationists, and I was just some kid who smoked too much pot and read too much about Guy Debord. I didn't understand what being part of the group was going to mean for the rest of my life."

"This doesn't make sense," Taer said, ignoring Berliner and Wilson's side conversation. "This train has to be something, because Molly's map—she pointed us right here."

"She pointed me to the train," Berliner said.

"She came down here too, in January, big day for me," Wilson joked. "I've had a lot of action recently."

"So you told her what you told us," Taer pressed. "And then what?"

"And then I showed her what the train is. The New Situationists restored it as a kind of pet project. There are three stations, restored like the one I picked you up in. The entrances are hidden. Sometimes the higher ups would have little cocktail parties here, or they'd use it as a private way to get around the city, but mostly they just liked that they had a secret train no one else knew about. And like I said, it's a toy. So, I told Molly all this. I took her to the other two stations, where I'm taking you, and showed her. And then we went back to the Aquarium station—that's the best one. I dropped her off. She was upset. She was crying and wearing something ridiculous. She left and that was it. I heard she disappeared."

Chapter 14

"It is known that initially the situationists wanted at the very least to build cities."
—Guy Debord, quoted from *The Situationist City* by Simon Sadler

The Situationists wanted to change the world. They failed.

Molly Metropolis's situations—her songs, her videos, her albums, all of her insane clothing—did what the Situationists could never achieve. She completed their work; she changed the world; at least, she changed popular culture, a driving force of the world. She shaped pop culture in her image. She achieved global reach, global name recognition. She prepared to continue their work, ready to sacrifice her career in order to do so. What did they give her in return? A toy. No wonder she decided to leave.

When I first began researching Molly Metropolis's and Taer's disappearances, I immediately contacted Berliner and Nix to request interviews. They declined, as did the members of their and Molly's immediate families. After several e-mails, Nix took pity on me and responded with something more than "No, thank you." She wrote, "I can tell you everything you need to know to write about Caitlin and Molly right now: there is no secret. You are looking for something that doesn't exist." Instead of heeding her warning, I plodded on, occasionally e-mailing her and Berliner with a renewed interview request and reports of my steady progress—often overstating the magnitude of my discoveries.

Most people overstate, I told myself at the time. I also told myself that by exaggerating the depth of my progress on discovering either where Molly had gone or what had happened to her, I could somehow will those discoveries into being.

For fifteen months, I researched and wrote, focusing mostly on the historical portions of the narrative. I developed a fondness for Debord's first wife, Michele Bernstein, and her coquettish novels about the bohemian society lives of the Situationists. Debord had asked her to write them as a source of income, but she liked having her name on something, even if that thing was the period's equivalent to *Gossip Girl*. I'm proud to report that I retained enough of my French to read the novels in their original language—a lucky thing, as her second novel, *La Nuit*, still hasn't been translated into English.

Taer's family gave me her journals and computer files without question, and just as I was coming to terms with relying on them completely for the contemporary portions of the book, Nix and Berliner jointly replied to one of my monthly e-mails, agreeing to speak with me. At the time, I believed I had scored a great victory. I know now that Berliner and Nix agreed to be interviewed to try to kill my book.

I spoke with them a combined total of twelve times: seven conversations with Berliner, four with Nix, and one with them together. The final interview was the dual one; in my last meeting with Berliner, I had pissed him off by asking too many questions about his relationship with Kraus, after he repeatedly told me he was "finished with that topic." Nix had to convince him to talk to me again and finish telling their stories. At that final, joint meeting, Nix described the anticlimactic train ride:

"So, after David gave his speech, he took us on a ride around the whole train track and showed us the other two stations. It took about—what would you say, Nick?—forty-five minutes? An hour? But we couldn't have been going more than twenty miles per hour the whole time. I mean, the tracks and the train were really old. I'm not good at judging dates of design and architecture and stuff."

"The train's infrastructure was just worn out. Really unsafe, actually. It kind of groaned along," Berliner said.

"That's true. It was, like, rickety, I don't know."

"That's accurate."

"Sort of rocking all the time," Nix said. "I guess the L does that too, but you trust the regular L trains to hold you up and you didn't trust this train. Anyway, we saw the other stations, then he dropped us off back where we started. We left. There was really nothing else. Cait still thought he might be lying to us, she was a little bit crazed. She kept talking about breaking back in, but I believed [Wilson]. He seemed really tired."

"So, that's it?" I asked. "That's the end?"

"I guess," Nix said.

After their hour-long train ride, Nix, Taer, and Berliner returned to the Racine building. They found it half burned and swarming with firemen. Antoinette Monson still officially owned the building, and Berliner was also still officially an employee of Monson and legally authorized to speak on her behalf. The security footage from the building was backed up offsite. The footage showed Ali, Peaches, and a crowd of their young supporters going into the building. ("We don't put cameras in the basement because there's nothing down there," Berliner explained to the investigating detectives.) A few minutes later, the video showed Casares and another boy carrying Ali out of the building. Twenty minutes after that, the rest of the group fled the fire. Berliner and the CPD detectives watched the security footage until the flames destroyed the cameras. Most of the members of the New Society were convicted of arson. They served short prison sentences.

The night after the fire, Berliner, Nix, and Taer went to Rainbo and got very drunk together. They took the L to the Loop and walked to the beach. They stole a boat.

"We were very upset," Nix said. She cried a little, recounting the evening's events. "I don't remember everything that happened. It's a little bit blurry. But we didn't mean to make it so mysterious. Cait really drowned. We just. I mean. I didn't even know to look for her in the water, I didn't think about anything except getting to shore and I saw Nick was kicking with me. He passed out at some point. It was cold.

"She died and it was a stupid death."

In the introduction to *The Situationist City*, Simon Sadler wrote, "This book searches for the situationist city . . . I rummage with a sense of guilt: situationists didn't want to be just another avant-garde, but the last avant-garde, overturning current practices of history, theory, politics, art, architecture, and everyday life."* The Situationist International wasn't the last of the avant-gardes. It isn't even the best remembered avant-garde—that distinction goes to the

---

* *The Situationist City*, 1.

249

Surrealists. The Situationists thought Surrealist thinking was old, dead, and boring. In *All the King's Horses*, Bernstein parodies a Surrealist dinner party: "His friends paraded out—in the usual order—all the ideas from thirty years ago, which was amusing. People from those times allow so much room for sick humor that even their stupidities can come off with a certain ambiguity."*

The Situationists still aren't widely known by name, but psychogeography has become fashionable again. Everyone likes to decorate with old maps; they fetishize the idea of transcending their borders. The Situationists have been assimilated into a commodities culture, the Spectacle, which would kill Debord if he were still alive. For the Situationists, this is a fate worse than death.

Debord didn't live long enough to see his work bastardized into violent politics and consumerist trends. He did, however, live to see the Situationists' relevance turned from active politics into passive academic interest. He even had to suffer through several reputable journals using the word *situationism*. After he wrote, "There is no such thing as situationism," for years the word wasn't used even by the Situationists' political enemies, as if his writing was a royal decree. Then, when Debord was old and his power was sapped, the academics began using it. In a sense, those few times the word "situationism" was printed were like bells tolling Debord's death.

This is the unsatisfying end to Debord's story, to the story of the New Situationists, to Molly's story, to Berliner's story, to the New Society's story, to Taer's story, and to mine. I can't satisfy you, so I wish, at least, that I could ease you more gently into an ending. I can't do that either. I have nothing left for anyone. No one will be reading this, anyway. Why revise? Why edit? Why narrate?

---

* Michèle Bernstein, *All the King's Horses*, trans. John Kelsey (Los Angeles: Semiotext(e), 2008), 22–23.

Where is Molly Metropolis?—this question is left unanswered and might never be known. I certainly won't be able to answer it. I'm content now to drift, like Caitlin Taer must've done, clinging to the scraps of a ruined boat in the dark and freezing Lake Michigan water, waiting for my turn to sink and disappear.

"We have published several texts . . . that in thirty years will still be the basis for the creative movement that will not fail to constitute itself."

—Guy Debord, in a letter to Constant Nieuwenhuys, 1959

Epilogue
by Catie Disabato

July 1, 2014

Maybe this is funny or maybe it isn't: Cyrus Kinnely Archer did, eventually, disappear. I'm not speaking metaphorically—Cyrus is as gone as Molly Metropolis or Caitlin Taer. His book ended when he reached the end of the story that Taer told him with everything she left behind, but his book also ended before the story ended.

Cyrus was born in Mequon, Wisconsin, outside of Milwaukee. I've seen a few pictures of him as a young, blonde child at the water park at Wisconsin Dells: at the top of the waterslide, eating apple-sauce with his brothers at the family-style themed restaurant Paul Bunyan's Cook Shanty. He seems at home among the artifice of amusement parks and tourist traps.

When he was a teenager, his parents moved to Hoboken, and he began spending his weekends in New York City, listening to music and sneaking into gay clubs. He read everything he was supposed to read: Isherwood, Rimbaud, and Burroughs. He went to Oberlin, where all the NYC hippies and queers went to smoke pot in the snow, out from under the thumb of the East Coast Ivys with their secret clubs and homosocial boozing. He returned to Oberlin to teach after getting his PhD at Columbia University. I don't know why he decided to go back to the cold Midwest.

Cyrus dated David Woodyard, formerly of *The New Yorker* magazine, off and on for nearly twenty-five years; their relationship began when they both attended Columbia University. Cyrus began his first year as Woodyard finished his dissertation. The grad school part of their romance was public and dramatic, with a lot of screaming breakups in front of colleagues, followed by sudden reunions. It might've ruined Cyrus's academic reputation. They evened out as they hit their thirties and lived together for a decade and a half before Cyrus's book broke them up.

Their spectacular, final break up, and Woodyard's purchase of an equally spectacular Chelsea townhouse to serve as his new bachelor pad, provided the *Gawker* bitches with excellent gossip fodder for several months. At the time, I reviled the loose tongues of Woodyard's assistants and underlings, but I have to admit that I found their lack of discretion helpful while putting together Cyrus's book.

Cyrus and Woodyard didn't have to trifle with anything as tiresome as divorce papers and the legal splitting of shared assets, though I did hear that many of their final arguments were over custody of Squiggy, their dog, and that Woodyard won. Squiggy wasn't equipped to handle Ohio's winters.

Their "divorce" occurred during the spring of 2011, while I was finishing my senior honors project in Creative Writing (a series of personal essays that were supposed be the first half of a memoir about my adolescence in suburban Illinois, but which I have put in the proverbial drawer). After three years nurturing my "budding talent"—he called my writing promising and my personal voice nearly

developed ("nearly there" is a state I will remain in eternally)—
Cyrus agreed to be my honors advisor. Although his own work and
the details of his personal life distracted him, he managed to eke out
of me the best work I could manage at that age. I graduated with
honors in May, though not with high honors, which I would've
preferred.

I spent the next two years living in Chicago, writing freelance
articles for various not-so-prestigious websites without being
paid. I would've been jealous of Taer's career, had I known about
her at the time, and despite her own frustration with her writing life. I lived in a carpeted, occasionally mold-infested apartment, probably not unlike Taer's walk-up. My sister, whose
name you might've heard because she is the only American to
be accepted at the Bolshoi Ballet Academy in Russia in fifty
years, sent me videos of her and her schoolmates performing the
Small Swans' *pas de quatre* from Swan Lake—who do you think
my parents talk about when they are at dinner with their friends?
I posted my sister's videos on Tumblr. I remained frustratingly
anonymous.

Sometime in early August 2013, Cyrus stopped answering my
e-mails. I thought he was finally tired of my depressing life. Then I
found out that he had disappeared. On August 9, his sister, Fran-
cesca, filed a missing persons report with the police. On August 12,
the Chicago Police Department found Archer's car in an abandoned
train yard near Pullman, Illinois. The car had been completely in-
cinerated; there was a body inside, burned so severely that they
couldn't even take dental imprints. Archer was declared dead. His
meager assets, and all of his books, went to his sister. He bequeathed
all of his research for this book—his manuscript, Taer's recordings,
her journal, transcripts from all his interviews including the ones
with Berliner and Nix—to me.

I'm absolutely certain of the reasons why Cyrus chose me to
complete his book. I had stayed in contact with him after I left

school, while his colleagues and peers shunned him; I liked Molly Metropolis, a weird cyborgian fantasy pop star, and talked about her to Cyrus. Also, I went to the same high school as Regina Nix and Caitlin Taer. They were older than me, but I saw them around. Although Taer had attended Oberlin, and had taken Creative Writing classes, she had never studied with Cyrus and he didn't remember her. I did, and he wanted to borrow that memory.

So, to continue Cyrus's story, here is the first revelation:

The last chapter of this book (before this epilogue) is a pack of lies. Nix and Berliner lied to Cyrus and he wrote the lies down. What I'm saying is, his intentions were good, and he failed. He finished his draft of this book, then he sat down on the couch, watched a lot of reruns of *Law and Order*, took a sabbatical from Oberlin College, and, for some reason, decided he must've been lied to. He began searching for the truth, for himself.

When Nicolas Berliner and Regina Nix agreed to meet with Archer, they insisted on a number of conditions. If Cyrus refused to honor them, they refused to speak to him. Cyrus agreed to their conditions.

Cyrus wasn't allowed to ask any questions about the identity of the other New Situationists. The most important stipulation for the interview was, as Cyrus jokingly called it, the Provision Against Real Place Names. Before meeting with Cyrus, Berliner and Nix agreed on a litany of made-up street names to stand in for the real locations of, for example, the underground headquarters of the New Situationists/Urban Planning Committee and the entrance to the subway station where they caught David Wilson's train. Cyrus agreed never to investigate or print the actual location names. He actually signed a few legal documents assuring he never would, non-disclosure agreements. Berliner knew that anyone who wanted to look could find the location of the Urban Planning Committee, but there is nothing left there now. You can look if you want, but you will be disappointed.

I'm not sure how long Cyrus believed Berliner and Nix were telling him the truth about the train ride. I don't know when he realized that they were lying to him—that the train wasn't a dead end. But when he did realize, he broke his word and searched for the real location of the Urban Planning Committee underground headquarters. It wasn't difficult for him to find, he just looked through the fire department's publicly available incident records for the month during which the Urban Planning Committee burned. From Armitage and Racine, Cryus traced his way to the Old Town Aquarium, and from there he descended into the train station. Once something hidden has been found, it's much harder to re-hide.

He left me his discoveries; I lightly edited Cyrus's original man-uscript to reflect the actual locations of all the events of this book. I made a trip to the train station hidden below the Old Town Aquar-ium (that trip is chronicled below), and following my visit to the train, all of the infrastructure has since been destroyed or concealed completely. With me, the chain was broken.

To visit the train, I didn't have to study any maps or even make a long commute to find the hidden train station. Archer had left me instructions and I followed them: David Wilson would be waiting for me at 3 p.m. on Thursday, every Thursday for a year, until I showed up. I live within walking distance of the Old Town Aquarium.

On Thursday, May 16, 2014, 2:34 p.m., I descended the southwest staircase of the Old Town Aquarium and made my way to the train station platform below. Near the breaker box where I turned on the light, someone had written on the wallpaper in chalk: "If we don't die here will we carry on further?"* How the phrase showed up on the wall of the New Situationists' train station, I don't know. Maybe Nix and Berliner saw it but didn't mention it to Archer. Maybe Archer left it there for me.

The wall of the train platform was made of faded blue tiles. Little chunks of white tile, among the blue, neatly and largely spelled the French words PLAQUES TOURNANTES UN. *Plaques tournantes* is another old Situationist term, associated with the *dérive*: while wandering, the Situationists would identify areas they believed were linked together through some kind of shared ambiance, subdivisions of the city that didn't follow the same neighborhood boundaries the city government set. They called the areas *unities of ambiance* instead of neighborhoods. Some of the *unities* served as "stations" during the drift, or "junctions in the psychogeographic flow of Paris." They called the junctions or stations *plaques tournantes*, a pun in French with so many subtleties of meaning and so many connections to cultural conditions of the time that it is difficult to satisfactorily translate the phrase into English. In a certain sense, a *plaque tournantes* is a railway turnstile; the phrase can also refer to the center of something or a place of exchange.

With a few minutes to spare before the train was supposed to arrive, I walked the length of the train station a few times, fidgeting, taking pictures with my phone, and listening to the DJ Shadow track "Building Steam With a Grain of Salt," from the album *Endtroducing.....* I felt anxious. I switched from "Building Steam" to "Apocalypse Dance," and I felt better.

I peered into the dark tunnels on either side of the station until I saw the bright light that meant the train was approaching. I sat down on the bench to give the impression I had been waiting patiently the whole time. When the train stopped, I expected David

---

* *The Situationist City*, 97.

Wilson to be alone, but he wasn't. The woman beside him has been called Miranda Young, has taken the name Antoinette Monson, and was the world's biggest pop star. Molly Metropolis.

She was dressed simply, as is her *modus operandi* now. She wore a pair of high-wasted beige pants, a white T-shirt with a very low V down to her belly button, showing off a triangle of skin, and a pair of black boots with a huge wedge heel, which she said she built herself. Her fingernails were bare and she wasn't wearing much makeup. She wore sunglasses with small, round, very dark lenses, but took them off when we talked. She seemed pleased to see me. She made me feel nervous.

She introduced me to Wilson and after a word or two of greeting (he called her "Molls"), he disappeared into the control room to get the thing chugging. I didn't see him again. Molly gave me a quick tour of the train. She explained that they had made some changes to the original design. She personally had ripped the seats out of the front car to make room for a table. The second car retained its traditional seats—slightly more legroom than L trains have today. She apologized for the noise, the rattle of the train. I drank water, she drank red wine, and we both ate from a bag of walnuts.

"Thanks for the water," I said. "I'm a little starstruck."

It was hard to talk to Molly. Her voice was familiar, her face was familiar, but it felt like if I had reached out to grab her, my hand would pass right through her body like a ghost on a TV show. In other words, Molly was unreal. She spoke to me like she was speaking to Barbara Walters, which was fitting. Molly has so many interviews left ungiven.

"I'm so glad to have you here," she said. "But we have limited time. Unless you're interested in staying on the train."

"I'm not sure exactly what you mean, but that seems like a dangerous choice. After all, Caitlin stayed, didn't she?"

"Oh my goodness, of course you're worried! But don't

be worried. Cait is alive. She is perfectly alive and perfectly fine. Adjusting. Some people have a harder time adjusting, but she didn't, she's doing so well. Were you two close?"

After this little speech, I had more new questions than answers. Thankful Taer was still alive, I checked to make sure my voice recorder (which Molly agreed to me using) was working.

"I'm sorry," I said, referring to the interruption to check the recorder. "Can we go back? Cait's alive and 'adjusting'? What are you talking about?"

"You knew Cyrus better than Caitlin, didn't you, and you are probably worried about him. I don't mean to be a tease!"

"Yes. And he's alive, too, you're saying?"

"Yes, alive and fine," she over-exaggerated the word *fine*, like she was singing it in a musical.

I took a moment to assimilate this information. I cried, and she reached across the table, and held my hand.

"I'm sorry," I said again.

"No!" she said. "Cry!"

She kept holding my hand, in her surprisingly strong grip with surprisingly soft fingers, until I stopped crying. In writing down this moment, I'm reminded of Taer and Nix's first post-college encounter, when Nix cried. Did Molly do this intentionally, so my rendering of the event would echo an earlier incident she knew was in the book? I wish I'd heard the echo at the time.

"This doesn't make any sense. The burned-up body, Archer's car? Where did that come from?" I asked.

"Dead when it was put in there," Molly said.

"How did—"

"We didn't kill someone. There are a lot of dead bodies around. In hospitals, for one thing. And while it wasn't strictly ethical what we did to get the body, we didn't steal the corpse of some grieving family's grandfather. If you look hard enough, not in the papers, you might find reports of a stolen cadaver from a medical morgue

262

in Chicago. By 'unethical,' I mean we used the body for art, not science."

"Was everything in Cyrus's book a lie?" I asked.

"No. The end of the book was a lie because Gina and my Nick lied to him. It says in the book, though, that Gina cried at one point during their interviews. She did cry."

I think she said this because she could tell I was ashamed I had cried.

"I heard the tapes," I said. "I heard her cry. I don't think Cyrus described her crying well, but it's hard to do that."

"How would you describe it?"

"She was really crying, like the kind of crying when you end up all disgusting and snotty."

"Poor Gina. She didn't take Cait leaving well."

"There are all kinds of people who aren't taking it well," I said. "People who don't know she's alive. Cait's mom, for one."

Molly picked at one of her nails. "I don't want to lie to you, or argue with you. But, I'd prefer to steer the conversation in another direction."

"But this is important," I insisted. "Your parents—"

"That's enough," she snapped, her cute little snarl, captured by so many paparazzi, now directed at me. "Do you want me to stop talking?"

"We have to address this," I said.

"I never like to be rude, especially to people who are interviewing me, I really try not to be. But I'm here at my own discretion and I can drop you off anytime I choose. People make sacrifices, I made my own and it was a very important learning experience for myself. I will make more, you will make some, many other people will sacrifice, and that isn't the topic I choose to focus on, so you won't either. I won't speak to any questions about my parents."

So I dropped it, and we moved on, starting with the extent of Berliner and Taer's lies to Cyrus.

Molly told me that Cyrus's book (whose ending I've preserved in its entirety, despite the lies) is true up until the first time Taer, Nix, and Berliner boarded the train, with Wilson not happy to see them. They rode the train, and Wilson begrudgingly informed Taer, Berliner, and Nix they passed a test by finding it. Having succeeded, they had a choice: they could get off the train at *Plaques Tournantes Deux,* or continue to the final stop, where their journey would continue. The first train ride had metaphorical importance. If they chose to continue, they would have to fake their own deaths. Wilson suggested the drowning in Lake Michigan, during stormy weather and rough waters and a current that hypothetically could pull a lifeless body miles away from shore in a matter of hours. Then they would have to return to the train, travel for many more hours, and they would never be able to return.

"You're on the Edge of the World," Wilson had said. "You liked those maps, didn't you, Nick?"

Ignoring the ominous tone of Wilson's declaration, Taer had pushed him for more information. "Where would the train take us?" she demanded.

"New Babylon."

I made a surprised noise.

"Finding the train is like passing a test," Molly said. "The train has three stops. The first stop is where you get on. And you can get off at the second or third stops. If you get off at the second stop, that means you don't want to come to New Babylon, you don't want to build a new world with us. If you get off at the third stop, that means you want to keep moving."

"And getting off at station two, that's an acceptable choice?" I wanted to make a joke like *if I tell you, I'd have to kill you,* but I was still a little bit nervous around Molly. It really was exactly like talking to the ghost of someone really, really famous.

"It's what Gina chose," she said.

"And Nick Berliner."

"Well, yes, sort of," Molly said. She smiled. "For the time being. He's waiting for Marie-Hélène and then they will come to New Babylon together."

"Waiting for her to get out of prison, you mean."

"Yes, that's my darling Nick, he's very romantic about her. It's wonderful to be around two people who are so dramatically fucking in love with each other. It's been an inspiration to myself."

As Marie-Hélène Kraus has been in prison since before Molly met Berliner, I'm not sure how she spent time around both of them (did she visit Kraus in prison with Berliner?) or whether it was enough time to adequately understand the depth of their love. I didn't bring this up.

"Okay, so, New Babylon. Let's go back to that. I've heard of that, it was a city Constant Nieuwenhuys designed, but it wasn't a real city, it was never built."

" 'Realness' doesn't mean it had a zip code. It was a real city then but, no, it was never built. But he didn't design it to make an art project. It was a city, a potential city. Until now, when its potential has been realized."

"What does that even mean?"

"We are building New Babylon, and we are living there. Cait is there, and Cyrus."

"Is that where all the New Situationists went after the bombing?"

"I can't answer questions about that."

"But—"

"Stop asking."

"Had you built the city from Constant's original design?"

"New Babylon, by its very nature, is never 'finished,' always changing based on the desires and pleasure of the inhabitants but—restricted to traditional definitions—one might say that it is built. We have, for example, running water."

"You built it since you were gone, a whole city?"

"Oh no." She laughed. "You shouldn't attribute the building of this city to me just because I'm famous. I'm not the builder of New Babylon, merely one of its most prominent citizens."

"Who is the builder?"

"To explain that, let's go back for a moment to the nature of New Babylon and Constant, because if you've studied his documents—we have a lot of the originals, actually—you'll notice that he wasn't very specific in regards to the practicalities involved in building his city. Their city, the Situationist city. So we've had to be very innovative. A lot of that innovation originated before I arrived. I'm not an engineer, though I'm becoming one, which is very exciting for me. I think every citizen of New Babylon will be able to self-identify as an engineer, that will be part of our national identity."

"National identity?"

She nodded.

"Okay," I said. "In terms of intent, has that remained the same, from Constant's drawings?"

"For the most part."

"So who is the mastermind? The guy who decided, fuck it, fuck America, I'm moving to New Babylon even if I have to build it myself?"

Molly looked at me. "You're not as imaginative as Caitlin. Or perhaps, that's not fair, just less well-read. The architect of New Babylon is Guy Debord."

You might remember, as I remembered at the moment, that Guy Debord committed suicide in 1994 when he shot himself in the heart.

"Obviously he didn't," Molly said, when I pointed that out.

According to Molly, the manifestation of New Babylon began in 1984, with the murder of Gérard Lebovici, Debord's friend and fellow filmmaker. Debord was investigated as the French equivalent of a "person of interest" in Lebovici's death, though never arrested or even officially labeled a suspect. The murder reminded Debord of his own impending demise and his lack of impact on the world. When he was young, he had wanted to change everything, but he had changed nothing and while he grew old, the Society of the Spectacle only strengthened and spread. Debord felt he had failed. Rather than give up, he decided to carve out a new space for himself, a true Situationist space. He decided to build the Situationist city.

Quietly, with a few of his closest friends (all male), he began planning the construction of New Babylon. They found a location and developed strategies for how to actualize, how to "manifest," Constant's fictional city. Debord simultaneously began planning his final film *Guy Debord: son art et son temps*, that is, *Guy Debord: His Art and His Times* (which, despite the title, isn't a biopic) as a cover story, to keep his acquaintances and wife, Alice Becker-Ho, in the dark about the New Babylon project.

Over the next decade, Debord supervised the building of the city from afar. In 1994, the city was inhabitable enough to accommodate even an aging man like Debord. To remove himself from the Society of the Spectacle and become a full citizen of the Situationist city, Debord faked his own death by suicide on December 1, 1994. Molly wouldn't tell me the methods he used to fake shooting himself through the heart (perhaps he paid off the cops, coroner, etc.?) and maybe he never told. His two co-conspirators, publisher Gérard Voitey and writer Roger Stéphane, followed him on December 3 and December 4. Their deaths were called "copycat" suicides.

Debord, Voitey, and Stéphane, all old men in 1994, didn't build and inhabit the Situationist city alone.

"Lots of young French men and women, people in their twenties, psychogeographists, went missing in 1994 as well."

I must've looked startled.

Molly laughed. "I didn't mean to make that sound so nefarious!

Nothing untoward happened. I merely meant to imply . . ." She paused again, laughed again, exuding such warmth and vivacity, was so familiarly herself, so much the woman I remembered from MTV and the "Don't Stop (N'Arrête Pas)" music video, that I shuddered.

She said, "My aim was to soften the blow of explaining that Guy and many of his contemporaries, while geniuses, can't do the heavy lifting. At the time they were doing a lot of building. We are still doing a lot of building. Our building will never end."

Molly held her arm above the table and flexed her bicep.

"You see how strong my arms are getting. We have a number of manufacturers but there is still some heavy lifting to do. I'm speaking both metaphorically and literally."

"So you are designing and building, both."

"Yes!"

"Can you explain the city to me?" I asked. I realized, the moment after I asked the question, that I was interested not out of journalistic impulse, but because I wanted to picture where she and Cait were living.

"It's not hard to explain. In the early days of the Situationist International, especially then, they were basically declaring that architecture would revolutionize all lives, everyone's everyday lives. People could be released from ordinary activities—wake up, drink coffee, go to work, drink wine, fuck somebody, sleep—and become citizens of a city in a world of experiment and play. Possibly this would mean some kind of anarchy, but most likely not, order comes out of chaos, that's what happens. It happens inevitably, I think. Several millions of years ago, we were hunting bison with our hands and teeth and now there are magazines that are designed only to report on the music business—how many peoples' lives are supported by just one of those magazines, even now, when print media is falling apart? I'm not sure Guy would agree with me on this point, but he chose not to visit with you.

"So they promised this new way of living to the whole world, but when you promise something to the world, the first person you promise it to is yourself."

She put her hands on her heart, and continued speaking while holding that pose:

"And the second and third people that you promise it to are your comrades, the ones who are helping you make that promise. The Situationists failed the world but mostly they failed themselves. They wanted to keep their promises, even belatedly, to as many people as they could."

"It's a compromise," I said.

"No."

"They said—I researched this—they said they didn't want to create, what did they call it? 'Holiday Resorts.'"

"New Babylon is not a Holiday Resort."

"No this—this is a Holiday Resort that you're describing. You're selling me a timeshare in New Babylon."

"No. For one thing, you don't get to go and come back to your 'regular life.' A Holiday Resort is something you can visit on the weekend, and when the season is over, you can leave. And when the resort becomes unfashionable, you can move on to the next one. But not for us. It's either old world or New Babylon. The only reason I disappeared rather than fake my own death was because we were aware my body would be more highly scrutinized than the average citizen of New Babylon. To live there, you must renounce your citizenship of this 'Society of the Spectacle,' to quote Guy."

"Some people would say that, by becoming a famous pop star, you were actively upholding the Society of the Spectacle."

"I was trying to change what pop culture was, what it meant—"

"You did that."

"—until I discovered I didn't have to. We have large plans. We won't stay a secret place for very much longer."

"That's why you let Cyrus give me his work? And why you came to talk to me?"

"Guy and everybody didn't want me to come," she said, running her fingers through her thick mane of messy blondish hair, so long that the ends still retain some of the blue dye I recognized from her "Apocalypse Dance" music video. "But I thought it would make a good end to the book."

"Yeah," I said, "it will make a very good reveal, I think."

"Cyrus showed me his draft and I thought it lacked narrative symmetry and I realized that I was the only one who would be able to provide it. So I made a decision, even though there are people who won't believe that this is actually happening. They will dismiss you." She spoke slowly and firmly, enunciating every word—her style from a life of giving interviews.

"You'll let me take your picture?"

"Sure. That will make some people believe it. Some people will always think you faked it. I hope the right people believe you."

I must've looked deflated. She was right, of course. Before visiting the train station, I had begun to face the reality that putting my name on this book would be the end of something for me, but it was disconcerting to hear it so assuredly confirmed.

"I understand that it might be a bit frightening, but we all have to put a bullet through our hearts. Even you, in your own way. You'll be killing your *credibility*, which is a version of yourself. Your death will be as metaphoric as Caitlin Taer's."

I told her I agreed, even though she sounded a little insane to me. I also refrained from mentioning how much she liked to talk about metaphors.

"Don't worry about what they will think of you," Molly coached. "We should always try to be our best selves. And our best selves are always moving forward." Then she slipped into her pop star pout, and threw half her hair in front of one eye as she had in so many red carpet pictures. "Haters gonna hate," she said.

"'Don't worry what they think of you,'" I repeated. "So that's

270

why you're letting this book happen? To come out of the closet, so to speak."

"That will happen with or without the book. Debord has been negotiating politically for years, we will be an independent nation eventually."

"Then why did Cyrus have to fake his death? If I wanted to come, would I still have to 'die'?"

"Yes, you would have to fake your own death. And the reason you would have to is the same reason as why Cyrus had to. We require complete commitment."

"How do you pay for it?"

"Every inhabitant contributed their wealth when they arrived. We have several incredibly wealthy inhabitants—you might've heard of a family called the Pullmans? I have become close with Liz Pullman. They still receive income through various covert means, as do I."

"Why do you use the train? It seems unnecessarily complicated. And why the special map that you changed at the last minute to lead Berliner to the train? All of this drama? Some kind of fucking war with the New Society?" I asked.

"The train is a thing to find, and you have to really commit, really care about figuring out what the New Situationists were up to, in order to find it. Finding the train helps people get ready to fully commit to New Babylon.

" 'Why the train?' Of course the train! The point of New Babylon is to live in your fantasies. The train is a huge magnificent toy. The reason the New Situationists failed was because they decided to do the bombing—not because one of them got caught. Their passion for the group soured because they forgot that they were supposed to be playful and fun. New Babylon is an ever-changing city built on the idea that playfulness is just as important as efficiency. Becoming a pop star was the best fun I could've had, before New Babylon. The point is to live your fantasy!"

Without thinking about it, I reached across the table and grabbed her hand.

"Will you stand up so I can hug you?" she asked.

I stood up and we hugged. I think I shook a little bit, in her arms.

"Can fun be fun if people are getting hurt?" I whispered into her hair. "Even emotionally hurt? Especially emotionally hurt?"

"Most people are ready to suffer, as long as it's for the right reasons."

What is my role in the narrative supposed to be? I wondered this as our hug ended and the train began to break for *Plaques Tournantes Deux*. I remembered something an old boyfriend had said, during a seven-hour stretch of time when we were trapped at an airport waiting for our delayed plane to take off. "You don't need the same things as everyone else," he said. "You can have fun anywhere." We still talked every month even though we'd broken up years ago, because neither of us liked the idea that we would never hear each other's voice again.

I said, "What does *having fun* even mean?"

Molly responded, "How can I answer that for you? You have to figure it out for yourself. You can find your own path or you can try following other people's maps. Repeating someone's actions, taking their choices as your own can be a creative act. Or, if you want, you can deviate."

The train slowed under my feet and I held Molly's shoulder to stabilize myself as we rocked to a stop.

"What's going on?" I asked.

"We've looped around a few times so we could talk, but now we've pulled into the second stop. Do you want to get off?"

"Can we loop around a bit more, I have a few more questions, some important ones."

Molly signed heavily, over-emphasizing her distress. "I'm afraid

272

this is it. You can get off, or travel with us to the third station and get off there."

"But if I do that, that basically means, I'm committing to going to New Babylon."

"Yes."

"So if I don't want to go to New Babylon, I have to get off now?"

"Yes."

"That's not fair. I need to know who the New Situationists are, and, like, what Cait's job is in New Babylon. And where it is, for fuck's sake."

"Off," Molly said. "Or on?"

I couldn't stay.

I grabbed my voice recorder and Molly hustled me out of the train car.

"Please," I said, from the platform of *Plaques Tournantes Deux*. "Please tell me where it is."

"What does it matter if you're not going?" Molly said. This was the last thing she said to me, the door of the train closed and she was gone again. I've listened to the recording dozens of times and I think I can hear disappointment in her voice. I think she was angry at me for staying behind.

I walked up the wide and well-lit staircase, which terminated in a heavy door set into a brick wall. I pulled open the door and felt a gust of warm air; leaning against the wall opposite the door was Nix, smoking and waiting for me.

"Did she tell you where it is?" Nix said.

"No," I said. "She refused."

"Fuck, I thought maybe she would. I guess that was stupid."

"So, you don't know?"

"Nick doesn't know yet and no one would tell me, not even Cait," Nix said. "I don't even know why I'm here, I mean like, she's never coming back even if I find her."

"Did she leave without telling you?" I asked.

Nix laughed. "No, I'm the fucking idiot that helped her fake her own death so she could run away and never see me again."

Nix noticed I was holding a voice recorder.

"Could you please turn that fucking thing off?" She asked. "I'm so sick of everyone taping everything I say."

I obliged.

Plaques Tournantes Deux is under a neighborhood called Edgewater in a northern part of the city proper, close to the lake (as you can probably tell by the name). The door to the train station is in the alley behind an Ethiopian restaurant on North Broadway. Once I let it close, it nearly disappeared into the wall. I could only see the lines of the door because I knew they were there. There was no knob, and as far as I can tell, no way into *Plaques Tournantes Deux* besides the train from one of the other stations.

After I turned off my iPhone voice recorder, Nix and I walked to a Red Line stop (Granville) and rode to North Ave & Clybourn/Halsted. We walked to a bar Berliner likes called The Violet Hour. The bar is like a bunker, no windows and dimly lit, but with beautiful baroque decorations and booths isolated from one another by huge chairs with tall backs. Berliner met us and bought us all old-fashioneds. He and Nix explained that the work they've been doing is to try to find the location of New Babylon. Nix doesn't know what she'll do when she finds it, she doesn't want to live in the city, but she can't leave it behind. Kraus wants to know, too, so Berliner is looking.

About a month after old-fashioneds, while I was working through this book, I had a little epiphany and called Nix to explain. I told her I thought that New Babylon was on Sable Island, the narrow sliver of land once called Fagunda, the map of which had decorated Molly's hotel room wall. Sable is called "The Graveyard of the

274

Atlantic," and everyone who went to New Babylon had to fake their own death—this was the kind of symmetry all those tricky bastards had liked. Nix and Berliner seemed very excited about my idea. A few days later, I got a text from Berliner:

> *We got a boat and we're gonna go check out Sable. We'll let you know what we find.*
>
> April 9, 2014, 8:28 p.m.

I texted back:

> *I want to go.*
>
> April 9, 2014, 8:28 p.m.

Berliner didn't respond.

Nix and Berliner returned a week later with nothing; they had hired a large, commercial fishing boat to take them out to Sable, but rough seas had crippled the boat's radar navigation and they couldn't find it. Sable is a small slip of an island, hard to find in the best of circumstances, easy to crash on in low visibility. They turned back, but aren't finished. The last time I saw Nix, she looked awake. They are going to try again a few months from now, in the summer, when the weather is clear. I'm going to try to convince them to let me come along.

ACKNOWLEDGMENTS

From the content, it's clear he wrote it sometime after he discovered the truth about New Babylon.
—CATIE DISABATO

For years I struggled to assemble the book you just finished reading, but I never struggled alone. This book never would have come together without the help and support of colleagues, friends, and the men and women whose stories I wrote and whose lives were affected by Molly's. The work of dozens went into making this book something special, and I remember dearly everyone who contributed their time and effort. I wish I could thank them all by name, but I will satisfy myself by acknowledging those who stuck their neck out for me at a time when I'm not sure I would've stuck it out for myself.

I owe everything to my agent, Ellen Raineau, who had faith in this project when I was ready to give it up, and who never doubted my instincts. The editor of my previous books at Gidden Warburton, Louis Monroe, acted as a friend when he generously gave me his thoughts on early drafts of this book.

Janice Franklin in the office of the Chicago Transit Authority was generous with her time, helping me find answers to my questions about the history of Chicago public transit and helping me navigate the CTA's archives. Without her work, the historical elements of this book would be a vague muddle.

I want to thank fellow professors at Oberlin College: Kathryn Pelliff and Rhonda Smarts, whose belief in me never wavered and whose interviewing techniques provided invaluable.

Finally, I acknowledge Molly Metropolis and Caitlin Taer, the two young women who led me down this rabbit hole. Thank you for giving me Wonderland.

ABOUT THE AUTHOR

CATIE DISABATO writes for *Full Stop*. She has written essays for *This Recording, The Millions,* and *The Rumpus.* Her short fiction was recently featured on *Joyland.* After growing up in Chicago and graduating from Oberlin College, she now lives in Los Angeles and works in public relations.

READING GROUP GUIDE

1. How does the framing device of Cyrus Archer's reporting and Catie Disabato's editing alter your connection to the characters? Does it create distance, or does the journalistic aspect make the narration seem more objective? How does the structure of this storytelling reflect larger themes of exploration and fantasy?
2. The price of fame, especially on one's social circle and the ability to trust people in it, becomes a major element as Molly's relationship with her entourage begins to break down. If you could rise to Molly Metro–level fame, but knew you would lose friends and loved ones in the process, would you?
3. Catie is following Cyrus, who is following Taer and Nix, who are following Molly Metropolis. What does this mean for you, as the reader, as you follow them in another sense? Did you feel implicated by your reading, or even tempted to join them? Which characters did you follow most closely, ideologically or emotionally? Did you find your reading taking on the Situationist idea of *dérive*?
4. Does your perception of Molly change over the course of the novel? When the book went into detail about Molly's childhood and background, did this alter your impression of her otherwise larger-than-life persona? How so?

281

5. Ali decides to join forces with Peaches when she realizes the extreme control Molly has over her life: "Without Peaches there to help normalize the way Molly treated her, Ali realized that moment defined her relationship with Molly. Ali didn't like that she had done nothing while Molly moved her. She felt like she was always standing perfectly still while Molly Metropolis shook her face" (page 186). Are the dancers justified in forming the New Society to foil Molly's plans, or do they take it too far? What do you think happens to them after the New Society falls apart?

6. In your opinion, does Kraus deserve to be in jail? The murder was unintentional, but should she be held responsible?

7. What role does queerness play in this narrative? What about triangles—beyond the landmarks in the city, do you see any sets of three? Who or what are they?

8. Molly Metropolis grew up in a predominantly white space where she felt out of place. Do her feelings of never quite fitting in contribute to her strong passion for the New Situationists and her desire to join their society? Could the same be said for Berliner and Kraus? Taer and Nix?

9. In the epilogue, Catie asks Molly about her family. Molly views her decision to leave as a sacrifice: "People make sacrifices, I made my own and it was a very important learning experience for myself" (page 263). Do you agree with Molly that she has made a sacrifice? Did you see her decision to leave as self-indulgent or brave? What did you think about Taer's decision? Did you expect her obsession with Molly to lead her to this?

10. Would you stay on the train like Molly, Taer, and Cyrus did, or would you get off at the second stop?